DEBRA WHITE SMITH

Heather

HARVEST HOUSE PUBLISHERS

EUGENE, OREGON

Debra White Smith: Published in association with the literary agency of Alive Communications, Inc., 7680 Goddard Street, Ste. #200, Colorado Springs, CO 80920. www.alivecommunications.com.

Cover photo © Jim Whitmer Photography

Cover by Dugan Design Group, Bloomington, Minnesota

HEATHER
Copyright © 2007 by Debra White Smith
Published by Harvest House Publishers
Eugene, Oregon 97402
www.harvesthousepublishers.com

Library of Congress Cataloging-in-Publication Data
Smith, Debra White.
Heather / Debra White Smith.
    p. cm. — (The debutantes ; bk. 1)
ISBN-13: 978-0-7369-1929-6
ISBN-10: 0-7369-1929-5
1. Debutantes—Fiction. I. Title.
PS3569.M5178H43 2007
813'.54—dc22

2007021754

Printed in the United States of America

07 08 09 10 11 12 13 14 15 / LB-SK / 12 11 10 9 8 7 6 5 4 3 2 1

ONE

"Did you see this?" Lorna Leigh plopped the latest edition of the *Houston Star* on the marble-topped counter.

Heather allowed the warm water to run over her hands as she scanned the headline: "Houston Mayor Shot at City Hall."

"Oh my word!" she gasped and snatched up the newspaper. Water trickled to her wrists and melted the paper while she scrutinized the story. According to the report, the gunman was still at large. The police were scrambling for information. And the mayor's wife was clueless regarding motive.

Lorna stepped around her friend and turned off the water. "I had a hunch you hadn't seen it," she said.

"Are you kidding?" Heather replied and lowered the paper. "Candi wouldn't let me out of her sight today. I've been exfoliated, polished, blow-dried, painted, and poured into this dress." She yanked at her neckline and gazed at her reflection. Even though the blonde-haired, blue-eyed damsel in blue satin looked like she belonged on the cover of a glamour magazine, Heather Winslow would have preferred half the makeup, a casual sundress, and some cute sandals. She observed her friend in the wall-to-wall mirror.

"If Martians invaded Houston on Harley Davidsons today, do you think *I'd* have known about it?"

Lorna snickered and fished a tube of lipstick out of her sequin-crusted handbag. The brunette in red looked every bit as polished and annoyed as Heather felt. She, Lorna, and their other friend, Brittan, had discovered each other ten years ago at a blue-blood prep school in eighth grade. They'd bonded at the tennis court and rebelled against upper-crust conventions. Never had their friendship wavered.

By some miracle, the three of them had convinced their filthy rich parents to postpone their coming out parties until after college. Even though they'd each attended debutante cotillions, none of them had formerly hosted a party that officially ushered them into Southern society. While most of their peers lived for the event, the archaic tradition seemed inane to the three friends. But at this very minute the Winslow's castle, a Scotland replica in all its glory, was crammed with eager bachelors, young and old. Heather already had three hints at matrimony tonight, and her party was only half over.

"So...whaddaya think?" Heather asked and lifted the paper again.

Lorna lowered her lipstick and replaced the cap. She eyed the paper and dropped her lipstick into her handbag. "I think they might need some help. Don't you?" she said, her usually husky voice a bit deeper.

Heather smiled and examined the small print. "Doesn't sound like they're even close to solving the case," she mused.

"Of course, it just happened last night." Lorna turned and leaned against the marble wall near the sink.

"Yeah, but..."

"Beats hanging out at these parties any day." Lorna covered a yawn. "I can't believe some of these dudes here. It's like all they live for is going from one party to another and keeping up with who's got the biggest yacht. And I'm supposed to *marry* a guy like that? Somebody deliver me!"

"Deliver *us*!" Heather replied, and the two friends exchanged a long glance that held loads of unstated speculation. "So, what does Brittan say?" Heather folded the paper and set it on the countertop.

"She's all over it." Lorna's hungry gaze examined the headlines. "I think she's in, whether we are or not."

"She *would* be." Heather crossed her arms and thought about their friend. While Lorna's tall, athletic build assured she ruled in more sports than just tennis, Brittan's brains wouldn't stop. After their first and only undercover case, Heather had decided no criminal in America stood a chance against that half-Chinese chick who'd graduated summa cum laude.

Fresh out of Princeton three months ago, they'd found themselves bored beyond reason. All three of their families insisted a career was off limits—unless they wanted to pour themselves into the management of their respective family empires. But Mrs. Winslow far preferred that Heather pursue a worthy husband who, while equally idle, would bring more old money to the family's mounting assets. Of the three, Brittan's family seemed less driven by the antiquated husband fixation or the independent career concerns, but the pressure was still there. That left all three weary and ready for adventure.

So when the media was full of news about a cyber virus that shut down all the banks in Houston, the friends had secretively snooped until they uncovered the source—a 20-year-old college dropout who'd decided to pour his genius energy into illegal internet activity. The ladies had anonymously left their information with the *Houston Star's* managing editor, who in turn alerted the police, who "solved" the case. For Heather, Lorna, and Brittan, the thrill of their involvement was heightened by their anonymity.

The *Star* had also done a write-up on the anonymous "person" who gave them the facts. Since the three women had left a single-stemmed red rose with the envelope of clues, the media dubbed them "The Rose." All three friends celebrated their clever and sneaky accomplishment for weeks. Now the triumph had worn off. The Rose was no longer a news item. And lo and behold, here was another mystery showing great potential.

"So, are you in?" Lorna asked.

"Are you?" Heather replied, her anticipation prompting a smile that answered the question.

Lorna smiled back and leaned forward. "I've got an idea where we can start." The bathroom door thumped open and Brittan barged in. "Move it or lose it, sister," she warned. "Yo Mama is on the prowl, and she's got your name all over her." She pointed at Heather.

"Oh great," Heather grumbled. "Looks like I've hidden out as long as I can."

"What's next on your to-do list?" Brittan strode forward, gazed into the mirror, and fluffed her cropped hair. She wore light make-up, and her narrow, black glasses screamed of an intellect that guaranteed Mensa membership. Her little black dress heightened the effect.

Heather glanced in the mirror once more and sighed. "It's an interview and photos with that society reporter from your parents' paper," she grumbled. "Duke somebody or other."

"Ooooo!" Brittan cooed and waggled her brows.

"You know him?" Heather asked and swiveled toward her friend.

"Well, I've seen him around a time or two," Brittan said, and her grin increased. "He's supposed to be managing the Lifestyle section now, and he doesn't do as many interviews himself anymore." Brittan winked. "You must rank high. And just so you know, he's not hard on the eyes at all."

"Oh really?" Heather queried.

"Break a leg, girlfriend," Lorna said and slapped Heather's behind like they were two football players.

"Woo hoo!" Brittan shouted and the two hustled toward the doorway.

"I owe you both *big*," Heather growled and didn't have time for more because her mother burst into the room.

"What are you doing in here?" Marilyn Winslow snapped. "I've been looking all over the place for you. This is *your* party, and you disappeared."

"Okay, okay, Mom!" Heather sighed. "I'm coming. I just had to go to the restroom and…" She shrugged.

Marilyn eyed Lorna and Brittan as they filed toward the door. Once behind Marilyn, Lorna wiggled her fingers and held up the paper. "Later," she mouthed.

Heather barely nodded and itched to be in on her friends' inevitable conversation.

Mrs. Winslow grabbed Heather's arm and pulled her toward the exit. "We can't keep this reporter waiting," she insisted. "He doesn't have all night, you know."

"I'm coming…I'm coming." Heather trotted across the imported stone floors to keep up with her mother's strides. Marilyn was as tall as Heather was petite, and her daughter only resembled her because of her blonde hair and blue eyes. Every other feature Heather possessed—except the slight crook in her nose—was shared with her late Grandpa Morris.

The slight crook came when Heather was in a karate championship five years earlier. Her mother had been appalled that Heather had broken her nose. But Heather viewed the flaw as evidence of her determination to win.

"And it's a cryin' shame he's nothing but a society editor," Marilyn groused.

"Why?"

Marilyn paused at the end of the domed hallway, just outside the great room teeming with music and laughter and more schmoozing than should be legal. She lowered her face to Heather's.

"I might have been married to your father for 28 years, but I'm not blind," she said in a low, urgent voice. "And I know you like I know the back of my hand, deary." She bobbed her head from side to side. "I'm telling you right now—don't even *think* it!"

"What?" Heather asked innocently, but Brittan had already provided the answer to her mom's concern.

"You'll know what I mean in 30 seconds," Marilyn growled and moved forward.

Heather shook her head and marveled that her 48-year-old mother had been content with running a household and nothing more. The woman needed a corporation...or three...anything to keep her from micromanaging Heather's life. At least Lorna and Brittan had the advantage of siblings to share their parents' focus.

Marilyn swiveled and stared at Heather. "Are you coming?"

Resigning herself to the chore, Heather walked forward and maneuvered through the labyrinth of guests, waiters, and waitresses.

She strained to gaze through the crowd for a sight of this newspaper reporter whom her mother had so cryptically warned her about. He must be something for the Winslow matriarch to already be laying down the law. Heather had a checklist from her mother regarding any man she was "allowed" to associate with. The number one priority was "Large Family Fortune." Newspaper editors usually didn't qualify. With every step she took, he was sounding more and more like her kind of man.

The exquisite smell of hors d'oeuvres and rare perfume heightened the moment as Heather approached the alcove that led into the flower gardens. Finally she glimpsed the profile of a man bending over a camera, his lips pursed. His face relaxed. He lifted the camera and snapped several shots of the crowd. When he lowered the camera, Heather's eyes widened.

Her mother's warning made perfect sense. The dark-haired guy stood every bit of six feet tall. He looked like *he* should be featured in the society pages. He wore a black tuxedo jacket, an open-necked shirt, low-slung jeans, and a pair of scuffed-but-polished cowboy boots. His hair was stylishly tossed as if he'd just stepped in from a windy beach. He needed a shave, but Heather figured that was on purpose. At closer range she noticed a few adolescent acne scars across his cheeks.

So he's not perfect after all, she mused, and that made him more attractive. An air of "who cares" cloaked his chiseled features as he eyed the crowd, and that was enough to drive Heather blissfully mad. She guessed him to be just over thirty, and she instinctively glanced at his left hand.

No wedding band.

Heather smiled and followed her mother to his side. *Maybe tonight won't be a total loss after all,* she decided...and wondered when her mother would ever learn.

TWO

Duke Fieldman eyed Heather as her mother made the appropriate introductions. This chick looked a lot like she fit in with all the other filthy-rich damsels in Houston—perfectly polished and as fragile as eggshells. Duke figured she was probably as shallow and conceited as the last debutante he'd been forced to interview. At least his new position as lifestyle editor normally kept him from having to interview these twits. This time the rest of the crew had been overassigned, and Duke was left holding the bag...the debutante in this case.

This can't be over soon enough, he groaned.

When Mrs. Winslow finished her empty spiel, Heather extended her hand. Duke looked at it and then realized the woman was giving him the respect of acknowledging a new acquaintance.

That's a first. He juggled his camera before engaging in what he figured would be a limp shake.

"Nice to meet you," she said, her grip firm and strong...and lingering.

Startled, Duke looked Heather Winslow squarely in the eyes and wondered how he'd missed that they were blue—really blue. *Probably contacts,* he groused. They wouldn't be half as blue au naturel. He released her grip and counted the minutes until he could ditch the tux coat, get out of this castle wannabe, and head home to his one-eyed pit bull, a bowl of popcorn, and a serious baseball game. The Houston townhouse was a long way from the ranch he grew up on, but everything there was real. These socialite parties were nothing more than tinsel and lace and emptiness.

Blah...blah...blah. He suddenly realized Heather and her mother were waiting for something...something from him.

"Oh, uh, nice to meet you too," he lamely commented.

Mrs. Winslow's penciled-in excuses for eyebrows arched, and she shot her daughter a satisfied look that Duke wasn't even going to try to interpret.

"Well, I thought we'd sit here on the terrace for the interview and then you can take all the photos you need." The matron motioned toward the fashionably gnarled doors, and Duke figured Mommy-O was going to babysit during the interview.

He grabbed his leather duffle bag that held his camera gear and notepad. When Duke rose, he noticed Heather looked as harassed as he felt. Arms crossed, she gazed across the noisy room filled with pieces from the Renaissance era and pop music and people doing the cha-cha, or whatever it was they called it these days.

Her dress matched her eyes, and Duke found himself wishing they really were that blue. He trailed after the matron like a good little boy and then stood to one side for Heather to precede him onto the terrace. When Mrs. Winslow was about to close the door, someone called her name.

A man holding a tray and wearing black appeared and said, "We've got a problem in the kitchen, ma'am." He glanced toward Duke, leaned closer to Mrs. Winslow, and whispered something.

The matron's lips turned down. She touched her temple, mumbled under her breath, and lowered a hard glare at her daughter. "I'll be back," she warned as she turned and walked away.

Duke wondered if Heather was allowed out of her cage for special occasions only.

The terrace door soon snapped shut, and the sounds of southern crickets surrounded Heather and Duke. A bejeweled sky that would inspire poetry in somebody poetic stretched into forever. But all Duke could conjure was, *Sunset's not bad tonight*.

He dropped his bag on the nearest wrought-iron table and wondered how he'd allowed himself to be talked into this job. When he left the sticks for the big city, he'd envisioned himself being a hard-hitting street reporter who wrote about the crimes and corruption he uncovered. From that experience, he wanted to one day write mystery novels. But that just wasn't happening. He was shipwrecked in Lifestyle, and he'd gotten enough rejections on his novels to line the walls of this faux castle. Now here he was with yet another social elite who lived to have her photo spread here, there, and everywhere.

He pulled his pad out of the duffle bag and dug deeper for a pen. The chair opposite his scraped against stone, and Duke plopped into his own chair. "Your name again?" he mumbled. He would have been embarrassed that he'd forgotten, but he didn't care enough.

"Have I done something to offend you, Duke?" the blonde questioned.

Duke's head snapped up. "Excuse me?"

"You're acting like either you hate your job or you hate me." She examined her shiny fingernails, tipped in white polish, and then stared back at him. "Have I insulted you in some way?"

"How could you have done that?" Duke snapped. "I just met you."

"So you hate your job?"

"What guy in his right mind wouldn't?" Duke shot back before he could stop himself. "Humph!" he grunted. "The only reason I took a job in the society pages was to get a chance at an investigative reporting position, but when that came open did they give it to me? No! They promoted me to lifestyle managing editor instead."

Heather grinned. "So you don't enjoy the social scene at all?"

"No! I'm here because I like to eat and it pays the bills."

Her smile increased, and her teeth were so white Duke figured she'd probably had them bleached the day she bought the blue contacts.

"Well, off the record, I'm here because my family made me come," she said through a throaty gurgle. Then she leaned closer and whispered, "And I'd hate your job too."

Duke was a long way from being a naive schoolboy. He'd had his share of women flirt with him and a few who flung themselves at him. In his younger years he hadn't done much to stop them… to a point. But now that he was over 30 he'd decided to ignore any and all flirting and flinging. Duke wanted to get married like every other healthy guy, but he wanted a woman who wasn't ready to do the tango with every pair of pants she saw. Normally, on a good day, flirting didn't even faze him. Problem was, this wasn't a good day by a long shot. And she wasn't the usual debutante. Of all the society women he'd interviewed and photographed, few treated him with decent human respect, let alone looked at him with interest.

Duke realized he was gaping only a second before he heard himself say, "Do you wear contacts?"

She threw back her head and laughed out loud in a way Duke figured Mommy-O would say wasn't very ladylike.

"Not on your life," she finally said. "These baby blues are 20/20 all the way."

And for the first time in hours Duke smiled. "So…" He leaned back in his chair and tapped the end of his pen against the top of his tablet. "What's a nice girl like you doing in a place like this anyway?"

She lowered her head and looked at him out of the corners of her eyes. "Off the record?" she pressed and glanced toward the doorway.

"Absolutely." Duke swore, holding up his hand.

"I was born into it," she said and shrugged, "so I guess I'm stuck."

The sincerity in her words matched her forthright gaze. Duke realized he'd stumbled onto a diamond among a bunch of rhinestones. The terrace air charged with an electric spin that sent an expectant rush through him.

"What'd you say your name was again?" he croaked.

She reached across the table and tugged at his notebook. Duke let it slip from his grasp. When she held out her hand for the pen, he gave her that as well.

Her glossy lips tilting, the blonde scrawled something across the paper, handed the pad back to him, and stood.

Duke read, "Heather Winslow." He wondered how he could have forgotten such a great name. By the time her killer spike sandals clicked a beat toward the domed doorway, he realized her phone number was under the name.

"Hey!" Duke called. "What about the interview...and the photos?"

Heather turned to face him, her skirt swishing above her knees. Duke wondered how he'd missed that she was a long way from being an ugly duckling.

"Can it wait until tomorrow?" she asked.

"Well, yes," he said. "I already took several shots of the crowd and only need a couple of close-ups of you. My deadline's not for a couple days."

"Then call me tomorrow," she replied and opened the door. "Maybe we can meet for lunch or something, and then come back here for the pictures." Heather snapped the door shut behind her.

"Well, hello to you too," Duke muttered. He rubbed his thumb across the number. A light floral scent, uncomplicated and sweet, reminded him of his mom's peonies. Duke raised the slip of paper to his nose and absorbed more of the same scent. With the fragrance lingering, he realized that for one full minute he didn't hate his job. *This is a historic moment,* he thought and smiled for the second time in hours.

Heather sashayed across the great room and didn't even try to stop the smug in her grin. Duke Fieldman was everything Brittan and her mother said he was…and more.

On top of everything else, his brown eyes reminded her a little of Grandpa Morris'. That renegade oilman had been a huge player in the Kilgore, Texas, oil boom that turned a bunch of ordinary men into tycoons. But Grandpa Morris had never lost his down-to-earth manner. In some ways he'd been more of a father to Heather than her own dad, who'd been immersed in running Shelby Oil before Heather was ever born. Grandpa Morris had been the one to teach his granddaughter to play checkers and to experience the joys of eating double-butter popcorn while watching *Bonanza* reruns. Heather would never forget the kind light in his dark eyes—always approving, always welcoming.

She sidestepped a couple who were enjoying the music too much and spotted Lorna and Brittan near the beverage bar. Both sipped colas while appearing to chat about nothing beneath the hip-hop music and laughter. Heather knew their chat covered more than nothing. But even the scent of a new mystery couldn't hold her focus. Right now Heather was focused on tomorrow. She couldn't wait to get rid of this noisy party and see if Duke would take her up on her offer. She wasn't usually so forward with men, but she simply couldn't leave this guy to chance. He wasn't hard on the eyes by a long shot, but if that was all she wanted, she could snatch up one of the eligibles here tonight and live miserably ever after in a shallow world with a trophy husband.

But there appeared to be a lot more to Duke Fieldman than just a pretty face. He hadn't been the least bit interested in ogling her… hadn't even remembered her name…and that in itself intrigued Heather. Apparently the guy had other things on his brain besides chasing every attractive female he encountered. And that was exactly the kind of man Heather was interested in. The only thing left to be seen was whether or not the gold cross around his neck was decoration or indicated a faith as firm as hers. Tomorrow she'd find the answer to that.

When she was a few feet from Lorna and Brittan, they stopped talking long enough to notice her.

"Oh, hey there, you," Brittan greeted.

"Through already?" Lorna questioned and gazed around the room.

Heather glanced toward the domed doors. She figured Duke had taken the patio exit and wouldn't be back inside.

"Yep. All done...for tonight," Heather said.

"My, my, my, don't we look like a satisfied kitten," Lorna drawled.

"What happened? Did he already propose?" Brittan jested and adjusted her glasses.

"No." Heather's smile wouldn't stop. "I asked him out."

"You didn't!" Lorna gasped, her green eyes bugging like a frog's.

"Well, I actually gave him my number and told him to call me tomorrow. We're going to do the interview then...I suggested over lunch." She shrugged. "It's a perfectly logical choice, don't you think?"

"You go, girl!" Brittan breathed and toyed with her straw. "He's as yummy as fruitcake."

"Oh now *that* is a good comparison!" Lorna snorted and slapped Brittan's arm. "Sounds like something my grandmother would say. Get real!"

"Let's see." Brittan squinted and stared at the ceiling. As brainy as she was, the woman had her "duh" moments. "He's as yummy as...uh...fruit tarts!"

"Oh brother." Lorna rolled her eyes.

"Forget the yummy," Heather said through a chuckle. "I think he's just a really nice guy. And he has nice eyes. I'd like to get to know him better."

"I'm sure Yo Mama is gonna love that," Brittan drawled and wagged her head from side to side.

"Well, maybe what 'Yo Mama' doesn't know won't hurt her," Heather said and caught a waiter's eye.

The suit-clad man answered with, "Water with lemon?"

"You know me well, Geoff," Heather replied and gladly accepted the beverage.

"Look, we've got a dead mayor on our hands," Lorna said. "Let's forget Luke for now."

"It's *Duke*," Brittan corrected.

"Luke. Duke. What's the difference?" Lorna lifted her hand and raised her brows.

Lots! Heather thought and gazed toward the doors.

THREE

A familiar tune wheezed past the linen sheet and seeped into Heather's sleep. She squeezed her eyes tight and fought for a few more zzzs. But the theme song from *Bonanza* dragged her all the way to consciousness. She opened one eye and realized the tune was coming from her cell phone, charging on the nightstand. Wishing the whole *Bonanza* cast would go away, Heather fumbled past the layers of bedding topped with a newspaper.

One of her cats presented the final obstacle. Lucky meowed and placed his orange self between Heather and her phone. She reached past him, reaped an annoyed hiss, and figured the caller was either Lorna or Brittan. While the three had discussed getting together this afternoon and sneaking into the mayor's office or home, they hadn't set a time or figured out exactly how to accomplish their goal.

Heather flipped open the thin phone and mumbled a thick-tongued greeting into the mouthpiece while Lucky pressed his cold nose against her cheek and licked her hair. She accepted the apology and nudged the cat away.

"Heather Winslow, please," a masculine voice purred over the line.

Her eyes popped open. "This is she," Heather responded,

attempting to sound crisp. She only sounded slightly less sponge-mouthed. She grimaced and gazed toward the digital clock. Her eyes widened. *How could I have slept until eleven?*

"This is Duke. Are you still in bed?"

"Uh…" Heather swung her feet to the Persian rug and jumped to attention while her satin nightshirt slipped down her thighs. "No…not in bed. Just uh…"

Duke's chuckle was low and discerning. "What? Did you get up before you said that so you wouldn't be lying?"

Heather tried to stifle a yawn, but the yawn won.

The man's laughter increased and Heather giggled.

"You got me," she admitted and then imagined what he must be thinking: *rich, idle, boring.* "But this isn't a habit," she hastened to add. "We didn't get rid of everyone until after three o'clock, and I, like, uh…" the newspaper caught her eye, "I stayed up reading until five."

At least that was the truth. She and Brittan and Lorna had gone to an all-night convenience store and bought every newspaper from the area. Then they'd come back to her suite where they'd read the articles and searched the internet for as much information about the mayor and his murder as they could glean.

"Are we still on for lunch?" Duke asked, and Heather heard only expectation in his voice—no scorn.

"Sure," she said while rushing to the massive mirror covering the east wall. Heather gaped at her own image. She'd flopped into bed wearing her makeup and hadn't even brushed her hair. Mascara flakes dotted her face and eye shadow smudged below her eyes. The palatial surroundings emphasized her ridiculous appearance. She looked like a harassed raccoon wearing a blonde bird nest.

"May I pick you up in an hour?"

"An hour?" Heather croaked, imagining Duke driving up to her family's massive castle in a trusty Ford…or whatever it was newspaper reporters were driving these days. Next in her mental lineup was "Yo Mama"—a very disgruntled "Yo Mama"—who would want to know why Heather was going somewhere with a society reporter.

Heather's suite was in her own private wing of the castle, and it had its own exit and entrance. There was a chance her mom might not even notice. They would come back to the castle for photos later, but that was a no-brainer to explain to her mom. But if her mother saw her driving off with Duke, that was another thing altogether. Even though Heather had fought for and won her autonomy, she had yet to win the war over the boy–girl thing. And she didn't figure that victory would come until she married whom she wanted and her mother realized her cause was hopeless.

"Um, look…" she pressed her fingertips against her forehead, "why don't we just meet at—at Mario's downtown. You know the place?"

"You bet I do," Duke said. "It's one of my favorites."

"Mine too," Heather said through a big smile. The more Heather could hide Duke from her mom, the more appealing he became. "Can you give me an hour and a half?"

"Sure. Why don't I go ahead and get us a table?"

"That's too fab," she replied. Heather closed the phone, tossed it onto the bed, and was halfway to the bathroom before she realized she'd never told the guy goodbye. "Oh man!" she exclaimed and then waved off the faux pas. After all, she was the one who initiated this little rendezvous. No sense appearing *too* eager.

Heather hopped into the shower and out, wrapped herself in terrycloth, and was just turning off the hair dryer when her phone rang again. Certain this must be Brittan or Lorna, she scurried toward her bed and retrieved the phone from near the newspaper. This time she was awake enough to check the caller ID and note Lorna's name.

"Hey, babe," she said into the receiver.

"Babe yourself," Lorna said. "I've got us into the mayor's house this afternoon. Can you make it?"

"No way!" Heather said and plopped onto the side of the bed.

"Way!" Lorna quipped. "We're going in as florists."

"Florists?" Purring, Lucky pressed his head against her arm, and Heather stroked him.

"Yep. Florists. Remember that chain of flower shops my parents own?"

"No, but I never can keep up with everything they own." Heather cradled the phone against her shoulder, picked up the peony body lotion from the nightstand, and slathered the liquid onto her legs.

"Well, the latest news on the dead mayor is that there's going to be a memorial service for him at the family estate tomorrow."

"Okay." Heather rubbed lotion on her hands and set the bottle back on the nightstand.

"I did some checking this morning and found out the family has placed a big order at the North Parkway Shop for some plants to be delivered tomorrow morning."

"All right." Heather picked up the paper and gazed at the photo of the even-toothed mayor waving at a crowd after his recent land-slide election. Monroe J. Longheed looked like a cross between Bob Barker and a slick car salesman.

No wonder somebody shot him, Heather mused. Not that she had anything against Bob Barker, by any means. But there was more to it than the Bob factor.

"Anyway," Lorna continued, "I decided to, like, borrow one of the florist vans and make the delivery early."

Heather dropped the newspaper. "Brilliant!"

"I thought so too," Lorna agreed. "Only problem is, how do we borrow the van without creating suspicion at the shop?"

Heather checked her Rolex. Her eyes widened. She had an

hour to finish getting ready and get to Mario's. "Have you talked to 'The Brain'?"

"Uh-uh," Lorna answered. "Not yet."

"Call her. When you guys get it figured out, call me. I'm meeting Duke in an hour." She stood and walked back into the bathroom while fluffing her hair. "I've got to go."

Duke thanked the waiter for his iced tea refill and jabbed at the salad he'd ordered. He scrutinized the latest newspaper article. This mayor business had hooked and pulled him in all the way. Duke crammed a mammoth bite of dressing-drenched greens into his mouth, lifted the paper, and chewed while his stomach groweled for more. He'd skipped breakfast, thanks to his dog.

Jake had tangled his leash around Duke's legs this morning, yanked him flat, and merrily escaped across the park. By the time Duke found the dog and put him back into the townhouse, the reporter was nearly late for work. Breakfast had not been an option. Now his stomach was in the mood for one of Mario's famous pasta Florentines, replete with long slices of beef that a man could sink his teeth into. But he didn't want to order an entree until Heather arrived. His stomach wasn't buying the salad routine, despite the heavy layer of Parmesan. Duke crunched at another bite and looked at the article again.

The bullets struck the mayor smack in the heart. The guy had dropped on the spot and was dead by the time he hit the pavement. The shots had been fired from a mid-story office in the Henry L. Oswald financial building, apparently by Casper, the not-so-friendly ghost. The gunman had vanished. A photo of a shattered "Mrs. Mayor" was featured underneath her husband's.

She probably had him killed, Duke speculated for no reason he could validate. He tapped his fork against the top of the bowl as the thought that nibbled at his mind earlier turned into a hard bite. *What if I try to solve the case? Maybe solving a murder or two will give me a one-way ticket out of dullsville.*

"Knock knock!" a female voice called while the newspaper puffed inward several times.

Duke lowered the paper, and one look at Heather Winslow obliterated the mayor and his death. She wore a simple sundress and looked great. More natural. Less sprayed and splayed and painted.

"Hi!" He folded the paper, laid it aside, and was glad he'd stuck to his usual jeans.

The hostess who'd shown her to the table said, "A waiter will be with you shortly."

"Hello yourself," she quipped and plopped into the seat across from him. "Sorry I took so long. I had a couple of unexpected phone calls. You know how that goes."

"Sure," Duke responded and wondered if any of the callers were men. After last night he'd done a little research on Ms. Heather Winslow. The newspaper's archives were full of her, with reports of dozens of males after her. He'd also discovered she graduated from Princeton with honors and was a woman of deep faith who volunteered at St. Mark's soup kitchen. That fact turned his flicker of interest into an inferno. The whole scenario was almost too good to believe: beauty, wealth, brains, integrity, faith, *and* interest in him.

The reality of who he was merged with the knowledge of all those well-heeled suitors and spawned a whirlwind of doubts that multiplied with tornado speed. Duke realized the incredulity of this meeting. He was a mere "society pages boy," and she *was* society. He must have imagined her flirting last night.

"Have you already ordered?" she asked, eyeing his near-empty salad bowl.

"Just a salad," he explained. "It was either that or eat my napkin." He lifted a heavy paper napkin that resembled linen.

She laughed outright. Their gazes lingered, and she lowered her lashes. The air electrified just like last night.

Okay, Duke confirmed. *I wasn't imagining things. She really did ask me to meet her...and for more than just a wad of pasta and an interview.*

FOUR

🌹 "Great shot, Heather. Give me another grin just like that one."

Heather did the best she could at looking natural in the August heat while watering the silk ferns on the balcony and gazing into Duke's camera. She'd never aspired to be a model, and her smile felt as fake as the ferns. But he seemed satisfied enough to click another round of shots. Heather suspected the last 27 had been for himself. There were only so many the guy could use for the newspaper. They'd started in the garden and moved to the castle terrace before arriving in her rooms on the east wing and finally going to the balcony outside her den.

For some reason the camera loved her, and the Houston newspapers loved nothing more than plastering her photo all over the society section. A time or two Heather wondered if her mother lined a few palms to guarantee all the exposure. Marilyn Morris Winslow had been the "Queen of Houston" in her heyday, and she wanted the same for her daughter. That Heather was more interested in karate and working in a soup kitchen did nothing for mother–daughter harmony. And Heather couldn't even imagine all the different ways her mother would hit the ceiling if she learned her daughter and friends were developing an exciting, potentially dangerous hobby.

"Excellent." Duke lowered the camera and bathed her in a smile that said he meant the compliment for more than just the photos.

Heather's feminine instincts said Duke Fieldman was hooked. Even as exhilarating as the prospect was, she wasn't about to let herself get too excited until she knew for certain. One thing was sure: She was hooked. She liked this guy a lot...right down to the cocky little lift of his chin and his flippant remarks. He was her cup of tea and the sugar that went into it.

"Think that will give you enough pictures to choose from?" she asked, setting aside the watering can they'd found in the garden. She picked up one of her cats, Tigger, who'd wandered onto the balcony.

"Maybe," he hedged.

Scratching Tigger's neck, Heather walked beside Duke. As they neared the sliding glass door, she dared to voice what she was thinking. "Or maybe enough to line your wall with?"

"Would you mind?" His mouth barely lifted at one corner, but his dark eyes sparked with male appreciation.

Heather decided she liked this game and wasn't about to be too easy to catch. "Hmmm," she mused and opened the door. "I'll have to think about it."

"Maybe you'll think about seeing me again while you're at it," he hinted and tugged at her free hand.

Not even offering to pull away, Heather paused in the threshold while the chilled air from inside swept over her like a cold, Pacific wave that curled above and then covered her with delicious chills. A hint of uncertainty and longing mingled with the appreciation in Duke's eyes. Heather knew she had her man.

"I guess that all depends on what day you're thinking of," she teased.

"Is there a day that's not good?" he countered.

She laughed, pulled her hand from his, and sauntered inside. Heather heard him follow. She placed Tigger on the couch beside his best feline buddy, Miss Gray, and stroked Miss Gray's bluish fur before moving toward the massive beverage bar along the west wall. Even though she had Duke on the line, she didn't want to reel him in until she knew about the faith factor. She'd noticed he wore the gold cross again today.

Time to find out if it means anything to him, she decided. For her parents, the church and faith tradition was a social necessity, but somewhere along the way religion had turned into a relationship with Heather, a personal relationship with Jesus that meant more to her than any other.

After retrieving a couple of bottled waters from the fridge, she plopped Duke's on the counter and asked, "Do you do church?"

He put his camera aside and picked up the water. "Sure," he said. "I was going to ask you to go with me Sunday…" Duke unscrewed the water bottle and flicked aside the cap, "after the movie Saturday night," he added with a cocky little smirk.

"Oh, so you've got it all planned out?" she queried.

"Well…"

"Were you going to bother telling me?" If her smile had been any broader it would have hurt.

"I think that's what I'm trying to do," he admitted through a chuckle.

"Okay then."

"So is that a yes or a no?"

"For what? The movie or church?"

"Both."

"Why don't we go to the movie of your choice, and you do the church thing with me?" she countered as she removed the lid from her bottle.

"Works for me." Duke shrugged. "I'm just not sure I'll fit in." He looked down at his jeans, fashionably faded, strategically torn.

"Oh, you'll do just fine. My two best friends and I go to a tiny church north of Houston. We meet in a gym." Heather didn't bother to add that the very idea drove her parents insane. "Very warm and comfy and casual." She looked down at her striped sundress and spiked sandals. "Actually I'm probably a little over-dressed today."

"Oh really?" Duke's forehead creased. "That's interesting," he said with a hint of doubt.

"What?" Heather parried. "Not what you expected?"

"Well…" He glanced around the room.

Heather enjoyed a swallow of the cold liquid and followed his gaze. Granted, she'd used top-of-the line decorators. And her wing of the castle was replete with the finest brocade and the rarest of Monet. But when it came to matters of the heart, her preferences were of another vein.

"I enjoy real and simple when it comes to my faith," she explained in a practical voice. "What about you?"

Duke turned his amazed gaze upon her. "Yeah, me too." He leaned a bit closer and narrowed his eyes. "Are *you* real?" he questioned. "Or are you just a hologram my friend 'The Mike' is using to play a trick on me?"

Heather laughed out loud and then squeezed his fingers. "I'm real," she insisted, and he latched onto her hand.

"And is there…" he paused and stroked the back of her hand with his thumb, "anyone else?"

"No," she answered as a sad veil cloaked her heart. Heather ducked her head before Duke could detect the pain. She wondered if the memories would ever stop flaring at the most inopportune moments. She'd just been too young and too weak not to bend to her mother's whims back then. If only…but those "if onlys" had ended in a tragedy Heather still wondered if she could have stopped.

"What about you?" Her voice came out soft and full of hope.

"No. No one," Duke answered.

She raised her gaze and looked directly at him. "If you haven't already figured it out, I like you, Duke Fieldman."

"And I like you." He lifted her hand and firmly pressed his lips against her fingers. *"A lot!"* he added and peered into her soul.

A hard rap on the door preceded the invasion of the manor matron. Instinctively Duke sat straighter.

Heather disentangled her hand from his, set down her water, and moved from behind the beverage bar.

Holding a day planner, Mrs. Winslow swept into the room like the woman of the hour and began her spiel the second she spotted Heather.

"Listen, dear, I needed to ask—" She stopped on the spot and stared at Duke like he was a rare iguana. The Winslow matron wore a fire-engine red suit that dared anyone to cross her. Her knock-your-socks-off perfume would clear the sinuses of a gorilla. With her rhinestone reading glasses clinging to the end of her long nose, Duke figured all she needed was a crystal-studded scepter to round out her image. *Or maybe a broom and a green wart on the end of her nose,* he amended.

"Hello again." He turned on the stool and lifted his water bottle in a salute.

"It's you!" she gasped and darted a hard-faced glare at Heather. "What's *he* doing here?"

"He was just taking some more photos for the article," Heather explained and nonchalantly covered a yawn. "Did you need something?" Heather's high heels tapped against the stone floor as she moved to her mother's side.

The tiles must have been imported from the moon or somewhere equally exotic, Duke decided. Once again he was reminded of the differences in their worlds. Whether he could fit into Heather's realm remained to be seen. Meanwhile he wasn't so daft that he missed Marilyn Winslow's disdain and Heather's attempt to cover the sparks that zipped between him and the debutante.

And Duke didn't like the taste of her covering it. If Heather thought he wasn't good enough for Mommy-O, then there was no sense in taking the relationship one inch farther. The last thing he wanted was to be some rich chick's novelty that she tossed aside when she got bored. Duke was too old to play games with any more fickle females.

He slipped from the stool at the same time the theme song from *Bonanza* erupted from across the room.

"That's my cell. Just a minute," Heather requested. She scurried across a wool rug as green as thousand dollar bills toward a purse that looked like it cost as much as Duke made in a week. And the price of the leather loveseat where the purse sat probably came closer to what he made in a month.

"So you were here taking photos." Clutching the day planner, Marilyn stalked closer and removed the rhinestone spectacles from the end of her nose like a theater mama in the middle of a grand finale.

"Yep." Duke took a long swig of the water and stared straight into eyes as blue as Heather's, except Heather's were soft and inviting and this broad's were as hard as lapis.

"Are you through?"

"With the pictures? Yes."

"Then it's time for you to leave." She pointed toward the doorway.

Duke narrowed his eyes and gazed at Heather, who worriedly glanced at her mother's back and then offered a weak, although encouraging smile. But Marilyn's back was turned. Duke wondered just how encouraging Heather would be if her mom could see her.

"But I haven't said goodbye to Heather yet," Duke said in a slow, even voice. "Back in West Texas, it's not polite to leave without saying goodbye," he added and figured if he were Jake every hair on his neck would be at attention. Duke inserted his hand into the pocket of his baggy jeans and balled his fist.

"Okay. I'll be there just as soon as I can." Heather's urgent voice pierced the taut moment.

"Don't think I don't know what's going on here," Marilyn snarled under her breath, her red lips curling away from teeth every bit as white as Heather's.

Must be a family thing, he thought. *A weekly bleach and blab session or something.*

"And exactly what would *that* be?" Duke asked. "Do you think I'm a cave man who's going to drag 'er off by the hair or what?" His tone sounded like it did just before his sister would whack him over the head with his baseball bat when they were in high school.

Mrs. Winslow didn't have a bat. Instead she lifted her chin. Her lips stiffened in a pucker.

Duke barked out a laugh. The woman couldn't have been fifty yet, but she reminded him of an 1820s prude…or was that a prune? Not that she *looked* like a prune. *More like she's been drinking prune juice,* he decided and laughed again.

"Listen, you–you *newspaper* boy!" Marilyn waved her glasses. "If you're even *thinking* of touching my daughter, I'll—"

"*Mother!*" Heather snapped while hustling forward. "*Please, Mother! This is too much!*"

Marilyn turned on her daughter. "Heather, I've already told you once—"

"Yes. And I'm twenty-three years old. I can choose my own friends."

Mrs. Winslow stared down at her daughter like a mother superior dressing down a wayward novitiate.

Her chin set, Heather stared up at her mom.

"Are you saying—" Marilyn began.

"I'm saying we're going out this weekend." Heather crossed her arms and tapped her white-tipped toes.

Duke's shoulders relaxed.

"Well!" Marilyn huffed. "Just wait until your father hears about this!"

"Daddy has my cell number," Heather retorted and marched toward her purse. She scooped it up, slung it on her shoulder, and tossed her hair away from her face. "Have him call me." She strode back toward Duke and grabbed his hand.

"Come on, Duke. You can walk me to my car," she commanded and propelled him toward the doorway.

"Just a minute! My equipment." He gathered his camera and duffle bag, all the while feeling Mrs. Winslow's scrutiny. A naughty streak suggested he offer to let the wench search his duffle just in case he'd stolen something, but Duke decided it was best not to go there. Instead he followed Heather out the door and stopped himself from giving Mrs. Winslow a parting shot. After hurrying down the narrow hallway, the two exited the door they'd come in. Duke never imagined he'd embrace Houston's suffocating heat, but it was a welcome reprieve from the frigid atmosphere he'd just exited.

Duke followed Heather across the paved drive to her new Porsche, which looked absolutely lovely next to his used Chevy pickup. He cut a glance toward the castle, sprawling upward and outward like a giant hovering on the hillside. He figured he could fit four of his family's ranch house in that place. An acre of royal green surrounded the palace, and Duke recalled the dust and long-horns back home. The sprinkler system here probably used more water in a month than his parents used in a whole year.

When Heather pivoted to face him, Duke rubbed his forehead and decided a gracious bow-out was probably the best option at this point. Even though he was glad Heather stood up to her mother, his doubts about fitting in were mounting by the second.

Despite the fact that Duke was trying to talk himself into settling down, he'd purposefully avoided ladies since he'd pursued his dreams by moving to Houston a year ago. The last twenty-four hours had shown him just how much he missed feminine company

and awakened him to the fact that perhaps he should start contem-
plating finding a wife. However, he would be far more practical
and way better off if he found a nice gal in his league—maybe a
teacher, or a court reporter, or somebody at the newspaper, or a
member of his church. He wasn't so naive that he hadn't noticed
a few women taking second…and ninth…looks.

"I'm sorry about Mom," Heather said and placed her hand on his
arm. "She can be a control freak when she wants to be."

"No joke," Duke returned and then cleared his throat. "And I
thought my dad was bad. He still can't wrap his mind around the
fact that I'd rather write than chase longhorns, but at least he's
giving me the space to do my 'thang.'"

"Well, I do my 'thang' too," she replied and gazed away. "For
the most part, I guess."

"Obviously," Duke said. "Uh, look, Heather," he hedged, "I
guess we both got a little carried away. Maybe you and me…" he
pointed at her and then at himself. "Maybe this isn't such a good
idea after all. I hate to cause problems between you and your folks.
Maybe it's best…"

Before he could even think of what to say next, Heather stood
on her tiptoes, leaned close, and whispered, "I'll *see* you Saturday
night. Pick me up at six. My mother will just have to deal with it."
Her warm breath brushing his ear wove its spell, nullified Duke's
logic, and sealed the date.

When she pulled away, it wasn't far…at least not far enough to
stop the whole countryside from tilting. Duke scrambled around
in a mad attempt to remember why he'd been about to cancel the
date. He couldn't come up with a scrap of memory in the face of
the temptation to kiss her. The invitation in her eyes suggested
she wouldn't mind in the least. Still, he stopped himself. No sense
moving too fast. While Heather Winslow was as alluring as all-
get-out, she was eight years his junior and totally living in another
universe.

Even though thoughts of Saturday night were too appealing for him to further resist, Duke hoped he had the strength to keep things slow and easy. He was getting too old to get his heart tied up and then dumped because a rich twenty-something decided she wasn't in the mood for newspaper reporters anymore...especially when Mommy-O wasn't *ever* going to be.

FIVE

"Wow!" Heather said as she boarded the elevator leading to Brittan and Lorna's penthouse in the downtown Shay Complex. Her head was still spinning with that near-miss kiss, and she couldn't imagine what she'd do if Duke ever *did* kiss her.

Probably faint! She chuckled. *The guy just has it!*

Heather found herself more and more certain that their relationship held potential. Now that the thrill of hiding the relationship from her mother was blown, Heather knew her attraction was driven by her fascination for Duke himself. Now if she could just keep him hooked. Heather had resorted to being forward to retain the date for Saturday night. After the "Yo Mama" episode she didn't much blame Duke for backing away. But he was still willing so maybe the attraction was as strong with him as with her.

Please guide us, God, she prayed. As the elevator opened, Heather reminded herself that she'd always gotten what she wanted in life and never questioned that it was God's will. *Well, I've almost always gotten what I wanted,* she qualified and decided not to dwell on that right now.

She'd only taken two steps out of the elevator when her cell phone rang. Heather dug it out of her purse's side pocket and glanced at the screen to see one of two names she suspected: Brittan Shay.

When Lorna called earlier, she'd informed Heather they had nabbed a van that was now full of plants, and they were ready to go to the mayor's house. Heather hadn't asked the particulars on how those two had pulled it off, but she never doubted they would come up with a plan.

She flipped open the cell phone and said, "I'm right outside the door."

"Gotcha," Brittan replied.

The penthouse door whipped open and Brittan stood on the threshold, wearing off-white coveralls, her cropped hair stuffed under a red baseball cap. "What took you so long?" she demanded. "We're supposed to leave in thirty minutes!"

"I told Lorna to tell you I've been with Duke," Heather explained and shoved her phone back into her handbag. She hurried forward and entered the ultra-modern living room. The building belonged to the Shays, like several others surrounding it, and Brittan and Lorna's rent was as free as Heather's wing in the castle.

Brittan snapped the door shut behind her. "Yes, she told me. But I was beginning to think the two of you eloped or something."

"In my dreams." Heather dropped her handbag on a settee.

"So things are going well?"

"We're going out Saturday night."

"No way!"

"Way, girlfriend."

She noticed Lorna near the window, the cordless phone pressed to her ear. Lorna waved at Heather and then focused on the Houston skyline. Like Brittan, Lorna was dressed in a pair of coveralls. Her hair was in a ponytail. She wore no makeup. A baseball hat sat on the back of a nearby chair.

"Here," Brittan said and reached toward a table where a pair of coveralls were topped with black work shoes. She handed them to

Heather and whispered, "This is what we're going into the mayor's house in. You need to get rid of the makeup and do something about the hair." She eyed Heather's blonde locks.

"Okay. Okay." Heather accepted the coveralls.

She kicked off her heels and headed toward the hallway that led to the restroom. Before exiting the room, she turned back to Brittan and whispered, "Who's she talking to?"

"Right now, the mayor's wife," Brittan quietly replied. "Lorna called to confirm the delivery, but I think they're having a counseling session or something. I heard Lorna telling her she'd pray for her." Brittan shrugged.

"Go figure," Heather said. "We're about to sneak into her house to snoop around and Lorna's on the verge of having chapel with the homeowner." She snickered and Brittan covered her upturned lips.

"Stop it!" Brittan admonished. "And go get changed so we can get outta here!" She playfully shoved Heather toward the restroom.

"Wait!" Heather held up her hand. "How did you guys get one of the florist's vans?"

"We didn't," Brittan said. "You've got to learn to think outside the box." She tapped her temple. "Why did we need a van from that particular florist shop? Why not just rent a van and have a magnetic sign made to attach to the side and then go buy all the plants we need?"

"But don't those signs take time?"

"Not when you've got the right amount of money." Brittan rubbed her thumb against her fingertips, and her smile couldn't have been more satisfied.

"There's a reason we call you 'The Brain,'" Heather affirmed and shared a soft high five with Brittan.

An hour later the three friends rolled to a stop in front of a colonial-style home, replete with wraparound porch and a collie lying on the top step. The green lawn stretched to rolling meadows fenced and full of horses and cattle. A Mercedes sat in the circular driveway next to a Jag.

None of the scene was a surprise. Last night the three had learned Monroe J. Longheed had been born into a family who made a mint via a chain of import stores. The mayor had taken the family fortune and invested wisely.

"What's his wife's name again?" Heather asked from the backseat.

"Mrs.," Lorna quipped. She put the van into park and pointed an exaggerated wink at Heather.

"Ha, ha." Heather shoved at a ficus branch that was seriously invading her space while a fern tottered on her lap. How she'd landed in the back with all the foliage was still a mystery.

"Her name is Terrell. Terrell Longheed," Brittan supplied looking over her notepad.

"Terry for short," Lorna explained. "And yes, she told me to call her Terry." She unlatched her seat belt and adjusted her baseball cap.

"So remember," Brittan said, "we all go in with the plants. While Lorna gets Terry distracted, you focus on the staff." She pointed at Heather. "I'm going to look for the Internet Protocol address of the mayor's PC first. Then if there are any other computers, I'll get those IP addresses too...along with anything else I have time to go through. And meanwhile, you get any and all house staff involved in the plant business." She pointed at Heather, who was batting at the ficus, which was tickling her ear. "And find out any tidbits from them you can."

"Speaking of which," Heather dryly added, "these plants and I are a little more intimate than I'm comfortable with."

"I'm a bit uneasy," Lorna said, gazing toward the home. "Terry broke down and cried on the phone earlier and told me all sorts of things about her husband. I wound up offering to pray for her. I feel like a conniving snitch right now."

"Get a grip on it," Brittan admonished and shook her pen at Lorna. "A good detective uses whatever opportunities she can pull from the air. This one fell into your lap. Use it. For all we know this 'shattered widow,' " she drew invisible quote marks in the air, "might have arranged her husband's murder."

"She's pretty upset," Lorna said and shook her head. "Enough to break down and sob with a total stranger. I mean, I'm a *plant deliverer* to her and nothing more. I can't imagine she'd murder her husband."

"I'm ready to murder a plant back here," Heather groused and blew at a stray leaf.

"Okay. Okay. Let's get out of here," Lorna ordered.

Heather opened the van's sliding door. The afternoon heat blasted her despite the gathering clouds blotting out the sun.

"Looks like rain," Lorna commented as she rounded the van.

Duke walked through the *Houston Star's* maze of editorial cubicles and desks and employees doing their things. When he passed the office for the star investigative reporter, he came close to kicking the door in but refrained. He didn't think God would appreciate that little display of temper. He headed toward the Coke machine and tried to convince himself he wasn't developing an attitude problem. But thoughts of how great that door would look with his footprint on it dashed aside his momentary introspection.

So, I've got a 'tude or two. Who hasn't at one time or another? He stopped in front of the pop machine, shifted his duffel bag to the other shoulder, and dug into his hip pocket for his billfold. Duke was seriously ready for an RC but they were scarce in this office. He settled for a Dr Pepper and was pulling the bottle out of the machine when a squeaky female voice floated from behind him.

"Hello, Duke. Are you going on break?"

He glanced at his watch and then at the woman—blonde, tall, but not half as attractive as Heather Winslow. She was Tisha something-or-other who worked in circulation and had a voice that ranked right up there with fingernails scraping chalkboard. Duke had crossed paths with her several times the last couple weeks... more than usual. He wouldn't have remembered except every time she spoke to him he wanted to scream, "Stop!"

He unscrewed the lid on his pop and hoped the dame wasn't after him. "Nope. No break," he replied. After a quick swallow, he stepped around her, only to receive a blast of perfume that rivaled Marilyn Winslow's.

Where do women get this stuff? he wondered. *She smells like a perfumed skunk.*

"No rest for the weary," he quipped. In an attempt to be at least half civil, Duke paused and shot a tight smile past her. "Been out. I'm heading to the office to do a final write."

"Oh, well...uh..." she sighed and focused past him a little too long to validate a casual glance away.

Duke's internal alarm system blasted so forcefully he almost dropped his soda. The skin on the back of his neck crawled like someone was watching him. He glanced in the direction Tisha was looking and saw another gal from circulation, whom he caught in the act of a gesture he didn't need a psychiatrist to help him understand.

"Well, I was thinking that maybe we could uh, do lunch soon or...or something," Tisha said, and Duke noticed the top button on her blouse was strategically breaking the company dress code. He wondered if it had been demurely buttoned until he came on the scene.

Not interested, he thought. *Not at all.* When he looked away, he knew his accountability partner, Mike Mendez, would be proud.

"I've got a girlfriend," he mumbled and wondered if having one date with Heather could officially classify her as a "girlfriend." Dismissing this minor detail, he walked toward the office with his nameplate on it. He didn't look back when he snapped the door shut. Hopefully Tisha would take herself and her annoying voice and hunt down another pair of pants in the office.

Duke dropped his bag in the center of his desk and knocked over the photo of his folks. He shifted his soda to his left hand and picked up the picture to gaze into the faces of the weathered couple with gray in their hair and light in their eyes. Momentarily he wondered if he should just do what would make his father happy—stop chasing his rainbows and start shouldering his part of the family heritage. While his parents' whole life savings would never touch what Heather's family had, the ranch wasn't a bad deal by anybody's standard. His elder sister had hauled off and married a doctor and moved to Memphis. And that left Duke as his father's one and only hope. But instead of staying on the dusty plains, he'd hightailed it to the big city to be a writer.

Some sort of writer I've turned out to be, he grumbled and placed the photo on the desk. Duke stepped to the first-story window and gazed into the Houston hubbub. By now he'd been certain he would be an applauded street reporter with at least one mystery novel under contract. But so far his novels were headed to nowhere-ville, and he was applauded, all right...as an ace society reporter. He was so good they'd even put him in charge of the whole Lifestyle Department and bestowed a real office upon him. Duke wondered if giving his best and excelling was sealing his longevity in the spacious office that went with the fluff-pages job.

The passing thought from this morning barged upon him. Houston's mayor was deader than dirt, and so far nobody knew who killed him. Duke took a long swallow of the soda and enjoyed the burn enough to repeat it. This time the speculation from lunch became a real possibility.

"Why not me?" he demanded and figured there was no swifter

route to the investigative offices than solving a high-profile murder. A slow smile crawled over his face. Duke shifted from the window and dropped into his rolling chair. He'd knock out this article on Heather and then spend the rest of the evening on the Monroe J. Longheed case. That guy looked about as honest as the mafia. There had to be more than one person who wanted him dead.

SIX

So far the plan was progressing beautifully. While Lorna chatted up Terry Longheed, Brittan asked for the location of the restroom and never returned. Heather occupied the housekeeping manager and yardman with multiple trips to the van to retrieve plants. Now, on the last haul, Heather suddenly realized that although the plants were wrapped in foil and ribbon, they lacked a florist's seal.

Hopefully, no one will notice. And what happens when the real flower shop delivers plants later today? she wondered. *By then it won't matter,* she decided. *We'll be long gone.*

Heather eyed the lanky man who pulled the final ferns from the back of the van. His gray eyes were as dull as his faded overalls. Even though Heather didn't figure he'd come close to realizing the lack of seals, she wasn't so certain about Mrs. Longheed's housekeeper.

Ironically named Lilly, the woman acted like Hitler and looked like a cross between Aunt Jemima and Einstein. Terry Longheed, on the other hand, gave credence to every airhead blonde joke ever invented. When they arrived she'd been looking for her glasses, which were perched atop her head. Even though the mayor's wife was as scatterbrained as she was vulnerable and shattered,

Heather held no doubt that Lilly possessed every scrap of insight Terry lacked. Furthermore, not one speck of dust could be found in the house.

If I were dust I'd run in terror, Heather decided as she observed the six-foot hulk of a female.

"Is that the last of them, Norman?" Lilly's formidable voice boomed from the front porch steps.

"Yes'm," the yardman replied.

Carrying a poled ivy in a decorative glass pot, Heather followed the man whose gait resembled a giraffe's long, lanky strides.

She swallowed a giggle that was as much a product of nerves as the sight of the giraffe-turned-yardman. The cyber-virus case had involved behind-the-scenes work and nothing more. This was the first time the friends had attempted a civilized version of breaking and entering. This venture was going too fast and felt anything but safe. As exasperated as her mother was over her flirtation with Duke, Heather couldn't imagine what she would do if her only daughter were arrested.

In the aftermath of her distraction with Duke, Heather hadn't even thought about being nervous until she started unloading the plants and looked into Lilly's all-seeing, sharp eyes. If they got out of here without Lilly sensing something was up, it would be an act of God.

Keeping her head ducked, Heather traipsed up the steps past Lilly. She hoped Brittan was working swiftly because there was little else she could do to delay this process. With the yardman and Lilly helping, what the debs hoped would take twenty minutes had only taken fifteen.

Now what? Heather wondered as she entered the house and walked through the foyer toward the back hallway that led to a large room now turned into a family chapel.

Hitler's firm footsteps vibrated behind while Heather discreetly searched the immaculate house for any sign of Brittan. When she noticed the ivy quivering, Heather moved the plant to the crook of her arm and carried it against her torso. Hopefully her shaking was less visible this way.

"Where's your friend?" Lilly accused from behind.

Heather jumped and hoped it was subtle enough that Lilly didn't notice. "Um, I thought she went to the restroom," she wheezed out.

"She should be through by now, shouldn't she?" The house-keeper paused by the doorway that led toward to the restroom.

Unfortunately the restroom door stood ajar. The light was off. And there was no sign of Brittan.

"That's odd," Lilly mumbled.

When she stepped toward the restroom, Heather's pulse throbbed in her throat and her palms went sickly moist. In a frenzy of "what-to-dos," she decided an accident was in order. After a wild glance around to make sure no one was watching, she turned the ivy upside down and violently shook it. Once the plant was plummeting to the tile, Heather released the glass pot. The resulting crash was exactly what she'd hoped for. Italian tile was just as hard as her own castle's imported stone.

"Oh my goodness! I'm so sorry," Heather shrieked and then decided to throw in some theatrics for good measure. She dropped to her knees and began crying. "I can't believe I've done this!" Somehow Heather managed to squeeze out a few tears and a sob or two.

"For cryin' out loud!" Lilly bellowed. A pair of industrial strength shoes appeared near the scattered dirt and shattered pottery.

Heather hunkered down and feigned a terrified glance up at the housekeeper. "I'm *so*, so sorry. I'll start cleaning it up now," she whimpered and scooped up a handful of dirt while struggling to stand. When a piece of glass pricked her palm, Heather shrieked again and released the dirt all over Lilly's shoes.

"You little klutz!" the housekeeper barked. "What is *wrong* with you?"

"Oh no! Oh no!" Heather wailed and stumbled to her feet. "Where's the broom? Is there a broom somewhere? I'll clean it all up in no time." She scooted her feet through the dirt while hurrying toward the kitchen, shoving the mess in all directions.

I should get an Oscar for this, she thought as Lilly belched out a commanding, "Stop! You're trackin' dirt everywhere!"

Hunching her shoulders, Heather pivoted toward Lilly. Seeing the woman in full-blown army sergeant mode, Heather nearly saluted and hollered, "Ma'am! Yes, ma'am!"

By now Norman had appeared from the back of the house, and Terry Longheed was hustling into the hallway with Lorna and Brittan in her wake. So was a Saint Bernard. The dog's friendly bark preceded its loping toward Lilly, right through the dirt, and planting both paws on the housekeeper's midsection while licking at her face.

"Get down!" Lilly sputtered, staggering to keep her balance. "You brute! There's broken glass everywhere. You'll cut your paws!" Lilly's protests incited the dog to more eager attempts at affection.

"Here! Here!" Norman growled while hurrying forward, but the loose dirt on slick tile acted like tiny wheels beneath his shoes. He crashed into Lilly and the dog, and the three tumbled into a heap of arms and legs and tail wagging and delightful barks that said, "Playtime!"

Heather covered her face with both hands and camouflaged her laughter by wailing, "It's getting worse!"

When she got control of her hilarity, Heather looked up. Brittan was biting her lips, and Lorna couldn't have been paler. Lilly lay sprawled on the floor with her skirt hiked up, her control top pantyhose saying "Hello!" to the world. The Saint Bernard hovered above her face, blissfully slinging slobber in affectionate swirls. Norman, clutching his back, struggled to sit up while mumbling something less than appropriate.

"Benji! Benji! What is the matter with you?" Mrs. Longheed fretted and scrambled toward the dog. After several tugs on its collar, the canine obeyed its master and sat beside her.

Lilly pulled her massive frame upward while sputtering, "Look what that idiot did!" She motioned toward Heather and the dirt.

Both Lorna and Brittan peered at the mess and then eyed Heather. Lorna's widened gaze said, *What in the name of common sense were you thinking?* But Brittan offered a discreet thumbs up before mouthing, "Let's get out of here."

"I'm so sorry, Mrs. Longheed," Heather babbled. "I can clean it up myself, if you'll just—"

"No, I'll clean it up!" the housekeeper snapped. "You've already caused enough trouble. Just go, will you?"

"Don't be so hard on her, Lilly," Terry said and knelt beside the pooch. "I'm sure it was just an accident. Cheryl has been such a help to me—just letting me talk." She gazed up at Lorna with a quivering smile. "It's worth several broken pots."

The red-eyed widow buried her face into the dog's fur and choked out, "I know Benji's upset too. That's why he's being so aggressive. He already misses his daddy. Last night he wandered all over the house whining." Terry fished a tissue out of the pocket of her big-legged pants and mopped at her mascara-smeared face.

"This has all been so terrible. Who would want to kill Monroe? He was such a wonderful man. Our whole church is in shock."

A flash of disgust marred Brittan's features and made Heather wonder exactly what her friend had found in those fifteen short minutes.

Lilly's face hardened. She struggled to her feet and stomped past Heather toward the kitchen. "I just mopped that floor this morning," she muttered and punctuated her claim with a piercing glare that made Heather shudder. Given Lilly's reaction to dirt, she'd hate to see what happened to the person who really crossed her.

Maybe the mayor knows, she thought with a covert glance at the housekeeper's retreating form. *At least the spilled plant worked. Lilly forgot she was wondering where Brittan was.*

"Well, if the plants are all inside, we need to go," Brittan said. "We've got a lot to do."

"You've been such a help to me, Cheryl." Mrs. Longheed stood and grasped for Lorna's hands. "God works in mysterious ways. My sons haven't arrived yet, and I needed someone to talk to. You've been a jewel."

The Saint Bernard, now free, romped toward the dirt again.

"Come here now!" Norman commanded and grabbed the dog's collar while wincing and stiffening. "I'll put him in the backyard, Mrs. L.," he grunted. Norman clutched at his back and urged the dog from the room.

"Thanks, Norman." Terry sniffed and focused on Lorna again. "Please give me the name of your boss," she urged. "I want to call and tell her what a joy you've been. You deserve a bonus or a raise or something."

Heather balled her fists in her overall pockets and stifled a gasp. Brittan didn't look like she was faring much better.

Without a pause Terry continued, "You've been such a help to me."

Lorna held Terry's gaze and never wavered. "It was my pleasure," she said and patted the widow's hand like a middle-aged nursemaid.

"It's like I've already met you somewhere, but that's impossible," Terry rambled.

Looks like I'm not the only one who should get an Oscar, Heather noted and nonchalantly meandered toward Brittan, where she had a clear view of the living room. A large painting of Monroe J. Longheed hung over the fireplace. The artist had managed to leave out the crooked car salesman impression and go more with the Bob Barker look. Half a dozen votive candles burned on the mantel beneath the painting and lent an eerie aura to the man's image.

The longer Heather stared at the painting, the weirder it became. Soon she was overcome with the impression that the man's eyes could see her.

She jerked her gaze away, held her breath, and recognized the discomfort for what it was: guilt. Like the man in Poe's "Tell-Tale Heart," Heather was beginning to feel the weight of her deed. She and her friends had entered this home under false pretense, and who knew *what* Brittan had gotten into. If not for the fact that their journey was for the ultimate good of justice and society, Heather would back out.

"It's time to leave now," Brittan said again under her breath.

Hedging closer to the door, Heather nodded and looked over her shoulder in hopes of cuing "Lorna-the-Nursemaid" that it was time for a swift exit.

"I will pray for you like I promised, Mrs. Longheed," Lorna was saying as she followed her friends. "I know this has been such a horrible shock. I can't even imagine…"

Brittan opened the door. Mrs. Longheed stepped toward it and gripped the handle like a good hostess. She once again reached for Lorna's hand and held on like she wasn't about to let go. "Yes, it's been just dreadful," she said, letting go of the door and clutching the neck of her house dress.

Heather gripped Brittan's arm. No one had expected this odd turn of events. Lorna's girl-next-door freckles and guileless green eyes often got her into conversations with total strangers that she never solicited. Now this!

For the first time, Heather noticed an odd glimmer in the widow's big brown eyes—almost like her Great Aunt Mary had. She had a chemical imbalance that made her do unusual things when she failed to take her medication. Heather's mind raced. The mayor's wife might be grappling with a chemical imbalance…or she was a lonely woman who grasped at any human being within a ten mile radius…or both.

Finally the three extracted themselves from Terry's company and hurried toward the van in tense silence. By the time she was halfway across the lawn, gooseflesh began at the small of Heather's back and crept to her shoulders. Memories of Mayor Longheed's accusing eyes in the painting made her want to race to the van and crawl under the backseat. Instead Heather ducked her head and purposed to keep her gait nonchalant. When she reached the van, she stood with her hand on the sliding back door, waiting for Lorna to unlock the vehicle. Her heart pounded. Her breathing was far from natural. And her knees had stopped being steady the second she stepped off the porch.

The sound of the door's unlocking couldn't have been sweeter or more welcomed. Heather flipped the handle and slid the door open. Before dropping into the backseat, she cast one last glance toward the mayor's manor just in time to see Lilly turning from the front window.

Heather's guilt was annihilated.

The second the three women climbed into the van and slammed the doors, Brittan blurted, "I hit pay dirt," while Heather sputtered, "You—you nearly got caught," and Lorna asked, "What was the deal with the broken plant?"

SEVEN

"Lilly was starting to get suspicious about Brittan since she wasn't in the bathroom." Heather leaned forward in her seat and gently punched Brittan on the arm. "Why did you leave the door open with the light off?"

"I left the door open?" Brittan's eyes widened. "I thought I shut it. I know I shut it!" She lifted both hands.

"Maybe it wasn't shut well and swung open." Lorna glanced into the rearview mirror, looked side to side, gassed the van, and headed down the driveway.

"Probably," Brittan said, "because I *do remember* shutting it."

"Okay. Whatever." Heather scooted back and snapped on her seat belt. "Lilly was about to go investigating, so I created a diversion."

"She wound up showing her control tops rather than going after me," Brittan said through a chuckle.

Lorna laughed outright. "I nearly died when I saw what was happening. I couldn't imagine what you thought you were doing, girlfriend." She glanced toward Heather as she paused at the country lane, turned on her blinker, and pulled out.

"Yes, I know. You should have seen your face!" Heather exclaimed. "Brittan was giving me the thumbs up and you were going white!"

"Ha!" Brittan clapped. "I love it! And what gives with Terry calling you Cheryl?" She peered at Lorna.

"Did you think I'd tell her my real name? Get real!" Lorna switched on the windshield wipers as a fine mist began dotting the glass. "Don't you guys remember? Cheryl is what my dad wanted to name me because that's what my grandmother wanted. It's her name. My mom refused. My dad's mother calls me Cheryl to this day. She refuses to call me Lorna."

"Okay, okay," Heather admitted. "I remember that now."

"Hey, I say whatever works," Brittan added.

"Not trying to change the subject here," Heather said, "but does anybody else think Terry Longheed might not be quite balanced?"

"Whatever gave you *that* impression?" Lorna teased.

"She latched onto you—a mere flower deliverer—like you were her best friend. She'd never even seen you before," Heather commented.

"Oh, she's seen me before," Lorna admitted. "I've mingled at a few of my dad's parties with her there. She just didn't recognize me without makeup and in this gear." She touched the tip of her baseball cap. "We've talked several times, and she's always liked me."

"Whew! You're a brave one," Brittan said. "If she'd recognized you, now that would have put a real damper on our little investigation."

"Yep," Lorna replied.

"So, Brittan, what'd you find out?" Heather asked.

Brittan removed her baseball cap and fluffed her short hair. "First thing, that computer I got the address on has a log that's full of internet porn sites. It was in their bedroom and has Monroe's name as the owner. So I'm putting two and two together."

"I'm sure that church where he's so 'respected' doesn't know about that little piece of info." Lorna lifted a hand off the wheel and drew invisible quotes in the air.

"Yep," Brittan agreed. "Or the fact that the guy had a mistress."

"How'd you find that out?" Heather asked and strained forward against her seat belt.

"I found a pile of letters on the nightstand. One was dated just two weeks ago. I skimmed it." She puckered her lips. "Not good." Brittan pulled a folded piece of paper from her pocket. "I'm thinking Terry found the letters and has been reading them. This one looks to be written in gel ink and it's all smudged—like somebody has been crying over it."

"You took one?" Lorna shrieked and gaped at the letter.

"Watch the road, will you?" Heather demanded.

"Sorry!" Lorna snapped and pulled the van back into their lane.

"I scanned it into the computer and printed out a copy. I wanted all of them, but I only had time for this one. It's got the name and address of the other woman, as well as more than enough evidence that the two were intimate."

"Is anybody else thinking maybe Mrs. Longheed had him killed?" Heather asked.

"Now why would you say that?" Brittan drawled.

"I think she's definitely got some problems," Lorna said.

"Yes, and then there's that article we found this morning about her being arrested for domestic violence." Brittan took off her glasses, pulled a tissue from her pocket, and gingerly rubbed at a spot before holding the glasses up to the light.

"What?" Heather asked.

Lorna nodded. "We were going through some of the *Houston Star's* online archives and found this article about it. She beat Monroe up with a fireplace shovel about a year ago."

"Why didn't I know this?"

"You were with that Luke guy," Lorna said.

"It's *Duke!*" Heather insisted.

"Luke. Duke. What's the difference? Right now he's just a

distraction. He'll go away in a week or two, and you won't be any better or worse. But this murder rules!" Lorna balled her fist and tapped the steering wheel.

Maybe he'll go away, and maybe he won't, Heather mused and smiled. Thoughts of this coming weekend certainly weren't going away. Saturday was only four days away...and counting.

"Okay," Brittan said, "I did get the computer's IP address. So the next thing we do is boot up my computer and prowl around in Longheed's files to see what we can see."

"And what about contacting the guy's mistress? What do you think of that?" Heather asked.

Brittan and Lorna looked at each other in stunned silence like Heather had just suggested they rob a bank.

"Watch the road!" Heather croaked. "There's a curve coming— and a car!"

Lorna jerked her attention back to the road.

"I think your idea rules, Heather!" Brittan exclaimed.

"Yes, you would," Lorna chided. "And exactly how are we supposed to pull this one off?"

"I don't know," Heather said, "but the quicker we move the more likely we are to solve this. It's looking like it might be a no-brainer for the police. If we're going to get credit, we need to hurry."

※ ※ ※

A rhythmic knock rapped against Duke's office door. He glanced away from his computer screen and called, "Come in."

The door opened and Mike Mendez peered inside. "Working late?" he asked.

"Uh...yeah," Duke said and minimized his browser. *If you can call trying to solve the mayor's murder working,* he qualified. And the bits of information he'd already gleaned made Duke hungry for more.

"Whazzup, man?" Duke leaned back in his chair, pushed his

desk with his boot, and allowed his chair to roll until it hit the wall.

"Not much. Just seeing if we're still on for the run this evening." Mike pointed toward the window. "It's getting late."

After a glance toward the window, Duke looked at his watch. "Yikes. Eight already!" He sat up straight. "What are you doing here so late?"

"Just had a long day," Mike explained over a yawn, and Duke noticed bags under the guy's eyes. "Lots to cover with the mayor checking out like he did."

Duke cut a glance at his computer screen and back at his friend. They'd been running together ever since Mike came to work at the *Star* six months ago. He covered city news. Aside from running and an insatiable love of sports, the two also shared their West Texas roots...and their faith. When Duke invited Mike to his church, the friends had joined the men's Bible study and agreed to be account-ability partners.

Idly Duke wondered if Tisha had been after Mike yet. Even though Duke wasn't an expert on who was considered good-looking in the male department, he'd heard enough of Mike's stories to know a few women liked Latin blood.

Or maybe a few thousand, he added to himself. Mike was trying hard to fly straight, but he had some stories from his wilder days that made Duke glad his own dad had been so strict once upon a time. No telling what he'd have gotten into. Way more than he did, that was for sure.

Thankfully Duke could look into a mirror, hold his own gaze, and honestly say, "I've never been drunk. I've never been high. And I've almost never tried tobacco." That "almost" involved a cud of chewing tobacco, a hot summer day, a junior high baseball game, and a bunch of scrawny-kneed boys who dared each other to chew the stuff. They'd also all been green within the hour. Duke had lived through the joy of puking.

Mike angled toward Duke's desk, his broad shoulders slanting with every stride like a basketball jock exiting a hard game. "So are we on or not?" he asked, his voice less than enthused.

"Why don't we skip tonight?" Duke asked and stretched.

His attention roamed back to the computer. He'd like to spend another hour or so fumbling around the *Houston Star's* archives. So far Duke had gleaned all sorts of interesting facts about the mayor and his clan—like the story of how his psychotic wife had been arrested for domestic violence last year. According to the story, she'd gotten mad at "Mayor dear" because he came home late. She assaulted him with a fireplace shovel. Their yardman, Norman Grayson, had called the police. This tidbit added fuel to Duke's gut instinct that Mrs. Longheed might be behind the shooting. Whatever the guy did to deserve a shovelbeating just might get him shot as well.

Maybe that Grayson guy wouldn't mind answering a question or two, Duke mused.

"Yo!" Mike's bark jolted Duke back to the present. "What's got you so distracted?"

"Uh…" Duke blinked and mumbled, "Sorry. I guess I'm zoning out."

"Yeah. I feel yo pain," Mike said and glanced down before covering a gigantic yawn. Then with a low wolf whistle he picked up one of the digital shots of Heather that Duke had printed out. Mike eyed the photo of her leaning on the terrace's handrail, looking away from the camera with her hair draped over her shoulder. Her smile held a hint of secret. "Is this the reason you're so zoned?" Mike held up the picture, and his grin couldn't have been broader. "You holding out on The Mike?" he chided and rested his fingertips against his chest. Sitting on the edge of the desk, Mike picked up a few more photos and sorted through them.

"Nah…not exactly." Duke shook his head, stood, and stretched.

"Seems like I recognize her." Mike narrowed his eyes. "But I don't know why."

"She's a society chick I suffered through interviewing today." Duke chuckled under his breath.

"Oh you did, did you?" Mike dropped the photos atop the rest of Heather's pictures. "Looks like you suffered a lot." He stood and hiked up his jeans.

"Actually we're going out Saturday," Duke said and had a serious flashback to the college locker room the day he'd landed a date with the head cheerleader. As much as Duke wanted to be mature about this, he couldn't deny the awe in Mike's eyes did something for his ego. He'd love to say he didn't have one of those things, but it was kinda hard to deny it when the attitude regularly stomped through his psyche.

"Where'd you find this castle?" Mike asked and pointed to the top photo.

"She lives there," Duke explained. "It's northeast of Houston."

"She lives in a castle?"

"Yep."

"How'd that happen? I mean, did her family build it or what?"

"Don't know," Duke answered and gazed at the photo of Heather standing alone in a meadow with the castle in the background. All she needed was a renaissance dress to look like a damsel waiting for her knight to fight off the latest dragon. Duke had been so focused on the woman he'd not asked about her home.

"Maybe I'll find out soon," he added.

"Humph!" Mike shook his head. "You know how to attract the rich ones, that's all I know."

"Whaddaya mean?" Duke questioned.

"All the rich babes are after you. How do you do it?"

"What other rich babe—"

"Tisha McVey."

"From circulation?"

"Yeah, man. And word has it she's out for you." Mike picked up a pen, tapped the edge of the desk, and his head began to bob to an unheard tune. The guy was a drummer in their church band, and sometimes he just didn't stop.

"Tisha's rich?" Duke asked.

"Her uncle owns this rag," Mike informed and never missed a beat. "She's cycling through the different departments to get the feel of the whole shebang. She's supposed to be working on her master's degree in something, and it's helping her to be here."

"Oh!" Duke said and raised his hands. "Now ya tell me."

Mike laughed. "What happened? Did you slap her or something?"

"Physically no. Verbally…maybe. I just wasn't interested, and I wanted her to really know it. So…" Duke shrugged.

"Does her being a Shay niece mean you're now interested?"

"Not!" Duke touched the back of his neck. "She's got a voice that hits me right here. I don't care how much money she has. I'd pay her to shut up."

Mike released the pen, threw back his head, and laughed.

"But at least I could have let her down easier." Duke placed his hands on his hips. "Nothing helps with a promotion like a mad niece," he groused.

"But what do you care?" Mike chided. "You've got a potential sugah mama eating out of your hand."

"I wouldn't go that far," Duke hedged. "And it's not about money for me anyway. I'm just playing it by ear. It's just one date. And I don't have a clue if it's going to work out." As much as Duke's ego-guy enjoyed telling Mike about the date, his more practical side shoved Mr. Ego out of the way and dumped a load of logic into the mix. Regardless of how attractive and inviting Heather Winslow was, Duke still had his doubts. And on the off-chance that the future had him moving back to the family ranch, he needed a wife who could adjust to West Texas dust, longhorns, and hair mussed by dirt devils. And then there was the hard work associated with being a rancher.

This was just one date. No harm done. If it worked, he'd be glad. If it didn't, it didn't. Despite the logic, his attraction meter was registering high, that was for sure. And Duke wasn't so certain he'd wait for the second date to kiss her. He picked up a large foam basketball from a nearby bookshelf, perched it over his head, and then propelled the ball toward the net hanging on the back of his door. On the days when the society doldrums just wouldn't stop, that basketball hoop was better therapy than a session with the company counselor. The ball hit the outside of the rim and zoomed to the floor.

Mike lunged toward the ball, scooped it up, hopped into the air, and tossed it sideways. The ball swept through the net like a dream. Mike thrust his hands into the air and cheered, "Two points for The Mike Man. Zero for The Duke."

Duke retrieved the ball, faked a few dribbles, went in for a layup, and sank it. "Two-to-two," he hollered.

EIGHT

After the business with the mayor's wife, Heather had gone to a department store. She purchased black, thick-framed, clear lens glasses and cleaning-lady garb—a pair of navy blue slacks with a matching shirt.

With several hours left in the afternoon, Heather went to City Hall and meandered through the building disguised as a cleaning woman. She found a mop and bucket in a ladies' room closet and pushed it around a while...listening...just listening. She heard nothing of use.

When a man in worker garb came up and said he didn't remember hiring her, Heather didn't give the tubby guy time to ask more questions. She abandoned her mop, ran from the fifth floor to the third, and hid in a musty closet full of Christmas decorations. When she figured the coast was clear, she slipped from the building. "Mr. Tubs" was nowhere in sight.

※ ※ ※

This morning Heather decided to give City Hall another shot. A burning drive in her gut insisted she might get as lucky today as

Grandpa Morris had in Kilgore, Texas. She'd given up the cleaning woman routine and was now posed as a maintenance employee who was changing air conditioning filters. Wearing no makeup gave her a pale, wan look. Now she stood in a ladies' room on the first floor of City Hall. She looked at herself in the mirror. The reflection assured that she was unrecognizable. This morning she'd used a temporary rinse on her hair that took it to strawberry blonde. She'd also slicked her hair back into a tight bun. She was ready. She planned on some heavy-duty eavesdropping and more aggressive snooping.

Brittan and Lorna were doing their own detective work. Brittan was at her penthouse finishing her perusal of the mayor's computer from her computer, while Lorna was pursuing contact with Monroe's mistress.

As with Brittan and her computer search, Heather held no agenda on what she might find. She was simply here to discover or uncover any information that might lead to the murderer. She washed her hands with soap that smelled like stale mint, dried them, and slipped her arm through the shoulder pack strap. The canvass bag held a complete change of clothing, along with cosmetics and a hair brush…just in case she needed to change her look to escape. She'd also included a miniature digital camera, video recorder, and audio recorder. Heather exited the ladies' room and went to the immediate task at hand.

She walked across the bustling lobby to the elevators and pressed the up button. The first floor she planned to penetrate was the one that housed the mayor's office. According to the directory, all city officials were on the fourth floor. She hunched her shoulders, inserted her hands into her pockets, and eyed the marble floor that dated to the early seventies.

A klatch of men wearing suits and scowls stopped near the elevator. Two of them stood as erect as toy soldiers, but Heather sensed there were no childhood games on their minds. Keeping her head lowered, she cut another discreet glance toward the three. The shorter one looked like one of the Blues Brothers without the sunglasses. His companion was tall and wiry, with bulging eyes, a broad mouth, and slumping shoulders. The third guy was as tall and dark as Magic Johnson. The wiry guy eyed him like he was afraid for his job…or his hide. He reminded Heather of a possum—and an ignorant one at that. When his companion glanced at "The Possum," Heather doubted his expression could be any more exasperated. Intrigued, Heather decided she'd follow these suits and see what she could see. Along the way she'd remove a few air vent filters to make it look like she was doing her job.

This morning the man at the hardware store gave her a short seminar on changing air filters. According to him, the return air vents held the filters. All Heather had to do was unscrew the quarter-turn wing nuts, open the air vent, and she'd immediately see the filter. He also told her sometimes the vents required a screw driver. So Heather bought a set of various sizes and packed them into her bag.

The elevator door sighed open. Two women strolled out. One, a sour-faced matron, the other, a young, cute brunette who wore a low-cut blouse and high-cut skirt designed to make a man look twice. All three of Heather's stone-faced companions ignored her. Heather figured either they were committed to their marriages or the meeting that had them so tense was big enough to block their vision.

As Heather boarded the elevator, the smell of cigars entered when the men did.

"Magic" pressed the button for the fourth floor, and Heather was even more intrigued. "That's my floor too," she mumbled.

The second the elevator hissed shut. "The Possum" said, "I just thought it was best to be honest."

"I told you to keep your mouth shut!" Magic snapped. "And that means *now* too!"

All three glanced toward Heather.

She made eye contact with Magic. He tightened his lips and stared straight ahead. Heather cut her gaze downward and tried her best to project a "maintenance" persona while hiding the fact that her legs were trembling. This crime-solving business had certainly taken a more challenging turn this time. Heather again felt out of her element.

Between the first and fourth floors, she prayed no one would suspect her and then realized she was asking God to cover her duplicity. *But there's a murderer at large, and it's for the good of our city,* she justified and continued to pray. This time she added a request that God would also lead her to clues.

The elevator dinged at the fourth floor. Heather waited in hopes the suited gang would exit first. Her hopes were fulfilled. She nonchalantly strolled into the hallway that had several offices branching off. She glanced up the hallway and down, in search of a return air vent.

Heather saw none and deliberated what to do. Finally she decided to meander in the direction the suit gang was heading. Lagging behind, she watched as they turned into a doorway. She steadily moved toward the office the men had entered. Unfortunately the door was now closed. Heather placed her hand on the knob and silently turned. It didn't budge.

It's locked! She read the nameplate: Willdruff J. Freidmont, City Attorney. Based on his obvious authority and command of the office complex, Heather speculated Magic's real name might be Willdruff. A rich voice boomed on the other side of the door, but as much as Heather strained, she couldn't decipher the words.

In her "seminar" this morning at the hardware store, the clerk had mentioned that sometimes rooms shared return air vents. She might be able to go into the next room and eavesdrop through the vent. It was a long shot, but worth a try.

Heather hurried to the next doorway. It was marked "Men."

"Oh no," she breathed and eased down the hall a few feet before halting.

If nobody's in there, I could slip in, check for a return air vent, and come right back out. Heather wandered a few more feet and checked ahead for signs of anyone. She nonchalantly turned around and peered down the other end of the hall. With no witnesses in sight, Heather slipped into the men's room, held her breath, and hovered by the door. The facility was silent.

She hedged around the wall that blocked the view of the room, bent, and looked under the stalls. Releasing her breath, she stood and scanned the room for any signs of a return air vent. There wasn't one.

"Well great!" she whispered and noticed a door in the middle of the wall opposite the stalls. Yesterday she'd discovered a small storage closet in the ladies' room. That's where she'd gotten the mop and bucket. This door looked identical to the one in the other restroom. But just in case it might lead to the other room or a vantage where she could easily eavesdrop, Heather hurried forward and tried the knob. The door opened easily to reveal a small storage closet. Cleaning supplies, toilet paper, and paper towels lined the shelves. A mop sat in an industrial bucket in the corner.

"The famous mop," she groused.

Heather shut the closet door at the same time the restroom door opened. She snatched open the closet door, stepped inside, and glimpsed two of her elevator companions before quietly shutting the door. Breathless, Heather turned the lock on the knob. The only light in the closet was seeping through the vent grating on the bottom half of the door. She dropped to her knees, opened her canvass tote toward the strips of light, and groped through the bag for her digital recorder.

"I told you he was going to be mad," a bass voice growled.

"Well, what exactly did you expect me to do?" the other man replied.

Heather recognized "The Possum's" voice. He had a drawl like a cowboy and a faint lisp on top of that.

"Act like we had the land secured when we didn't? We'll lose the deal anyway if we don't get the land."

Come on…come on… Heather pulled out the video camera. She set it aside and dug deeper for the recorder. Instead she dragged out the camera. After fumbling with it, Heather slipped her hand through the camera's strap and finally pulled out the recorder. She held the device to the vent and pressed the record button.

"All I know is now we both look bad. And our jobs may be history. You know that plant was supposed to bring millions to the city." A stall door slammed.

"So what do we do? Just fake it 'til we make it? Come on! It's better to be honest now than have to eat crow later." Water hissed out of a faucet.

"I don't think Friedmont agrees with you. He's probably still screaming to himself."

"The guy's going to have a heart attack and die over this."

"And that's bad?"

Both men chuckled. The automatic hand dryer wheezed on and drowned all noise except the sound of the door thumping to a close.

Heather pressed the stop button on her recorder and slumped. The suit gang didn't have anything to do with the murder. All their tension was related to a land deal that had something to do with a company coming into Houston.

"Shoot!" she mumbled and prepared to stand.

The restroom door opened again. Heather hovered on her knees and waited. When she started out this morning, she hadn't exactly daydreamed about eavesdropping in the men's room. She pulled off the glasses, rubbed her eyes, and began to think she should have chosen to interview the mayor's mistress rather than snoop at City Hall. Connecting with the mistress had been *her* idea. But City Hall had seemed so much more adventurous. Now, after two days of nothing but dead-end leads, Heather was growing weary.

The day is still young, she encouraged herself and slid the glasses back on. *And there are still a lot of air vents to change.*

A series of faint beeps preceded the latest guy's mumbling, "Hello." A stall door bumped closed. A lock slid into place.

Heather leaned forward, clicked on the recorder, and strained for the man's words.

"Shirley?" he said, his voice low.

Oh brother, Heather thought. *It's Romeo.*

"I thought I told you not to call me until noon. I'm still at City Hall. This is risky."

Risky? Maybe this isn't a Romeo deal after all.

"Yes, we've got the money."

Money?

"He's in the Bahamas right now, taking care of everything. It'll be electronically transferred into your Swiss account as we agreed. I've just gone through his office. There's no evidence of anything."

Her eyes widening, Heather shifted her weight to her left knee.

"The money should be accessible today by three."

Heather glanced at her watch and strained to see it was just past ten-thirty.

"I already told you that!" the guy said through gritted teeth. "It will be from Hines, Drieb, and Associates... Yes... Yes..." he clipped and then paused.

A drop of sweat trickled down Heather's temple. She swiped at it.

"Your work was *excellent*," the guy snapped. "But calling me like this is beyond dangerous. The media—*everyone*—is clueless. Let's keep it that way," he hissed. "Remember, murder has a lifetime sentence...or death. We're in Texas. Capital punishment is still on. If we go down, you're going with us."

Murder! The digital recorder trembled in Heather's hand. Her disdain for the men's room vanished. *Maybe I should hang out in men's rooms more often,* she decided and swallowed a heady giggle.

"We plan to use you every time we need to get rid of someone," the guy hammered out softly, "but not if you're going to take any more risks like this." A faint snap indicated the call was over.

Even though Heather couldn't be one-hundred-percent certain, chances were significant she'd stumbled onto someone associated with the mayor's murder. What other murder was taking over the media right now?

The man finished his business and paused long enough to wash his hands. Heather dropped the recorder into her bag, wrestled the camera from her wrist, and waited for the right moment to open the closet door and snap a photo. She held the camera to the grill and used the limited lighting to check the flash icon. It was off.

She waited to open the door when the hand dryer kicked in so it would cover the door's click or rattle. When the dryer swooshed on, Heather unlocked the door and slowly turned the knob. She held her breath, cracked the door, lifted the camera toward the slash of light, and strained for a peek. The man had his back to her. At her vantage point she could see the man, but he would only see her if he turned directly toward the closet. The mirror was blocked by the stall walls, so he couldn't detect her reflection. The guy appeared clean-cut and well-dressed. His hair was light; his body slender. Without so much as offering a profile shot, he walked toward the exit. Heather wildly clicked the tiny camera until the guy disappeared.

She snapped the door shut, fell back, snatched at every breath, and decided the whole episode must have been divine intervention. *Maybe God wants this murder solved as much as we do,* Heather pondered and was glad she'd persevered.

Eager to view the fruits of her labor, Heather stood and relocked the door. She fumbled on the wall near the door until she found a light switch. Flipping it on, Heather eagerly pressed the "preview" button on her camera. According to the number on the upper left of the tiny screen, Heather had captured eight photos. *Eight!* she cheered to herself. *Count 'em—eight!* But her smile went stale as she scrolled through each one and saw clear shots of the bathroom wall…and nothing else.

"Ah man," she whispered and wilted against a cabinet. A bottle of glass cleaner toppled back, and Heather turned to right it. Then she gritted her teeth as she pressed the scroll button again to view the final photo. While she hadn't gotten a full picture of the guy, at least she had captured part of him—his right hand on the door as he was exiting. And on that hand was a ring.

"Yes!" Heather hissed.

The bathroom door opened. Heather jumped and snapped off the closet light. Footsteps neared and stopped. The doorknob rattled. Heather's mouth fell open. She had a hunch this just might be "Mr. Tubs" from yesterday. He'd probably throw her out by her hair today or have her arrested. She shoved the camera back into her bag as her heart rate jumped into the violent zone.

Keys clinked. Heather held her breath through several keys grinding against the knob. Then a familiar male voice floated through the door. "I told Tony I didn't think I had the right key. I'm going to have to call a locksmith. I oughtta make him pay for it."

It's him! Heather grabbed her throat.

He continued to grumble while moving away from the closet. The bathroom door opened and clapped shut.

Heather counted to sixty, seized her shoulder pack, and hustled out of the men's room. She entered the hallway with her head down, hung a left, and nearly ran headlong into a man. Certain he must be the janitor, Heather yelped and gazed upward. Instead of "Mr. Tubs" she peered into the eyes of Duke Fieldman.

NINE

She gasped and nearly blurted, *What are you doing here?* but stopped herself when she saw no sign of recognition in Duke's eyes.

"Excuse me," he mumbled. "I didn't see you coming." He pointedly eyed the men's room.

"No problem," Heather wheezed. "Housekeeping."

Duke said something she didn't catch and continued on his way. Heather darted a glance over her shoulder and spotted him entering an office three doors down. Curious, she turned and followed. The sign on the door said "Herman A. Soliday, City Manager." A secretary's desk sat in an outer office, but no one was behind it.

Heather hovered at the door and watched Duke's every move. Slipping on a pair of latex gloves, he went straight to the door marked "Herman A. Soliday." Duke tried the knob. When he found it locked, he pulled a leather-covered sheath from his pocket and extracted a long, thin tool that looked like something a dentist might use.

Furtively he glanced over his shoulder, and Heather backed off the door. She held her breath, counted to three, looked up and down the hallway, and eased back. Duke bent over the knob, inserted the tool, and manipulated the lock. Within seconds he opened the door and stepped inside. Heather noted the room he entered was as dark as the utility closet. She retreated into the hallway.

The city manager is out, Heather deduced and wondered if his secretary was too. *Maybe he's on vacation, and when the cat's away, the mouse will play.*

Two laughing women appeared at the end of the hallway. Each held a Styrofoam cup, and Heather suspected they were employees coming off break. She eased into the office and searched the walls for a return air vent. She spotted one along the wall opposite the manager's office.

Why couldn't it be on the side with the manager's office? she fumed and walked over to the task at hand. She fumbled to unscrew the tight wing nut and was nearly ready to give up when it budged. Another hard twist accomplished her goal. The other wing nut was less ornery. The air filter was exactly where the hardware store clerk told her it would be—housed in a vertical shelf just inside the return air vent. She pulled out the dusty filter, closed the air vent, and sneezed.

"Bless you!" a pleasant female voice chirped from behind.

Heather feigned a bad case of shyness. Keeping her head ducked she said, "Just changing the air filters."

"Wow! That's a mess, isn't it?" the secretary exclaimed.

Heather eyed the dusty object and sneezed all over again. *At this rate I'm going to have a full-blown allergy attack.*

"Bless you again!" the secretary said.

Heather noted the nameplate on her desk read "Betty S. Moreillon."

She looked toward the city manager's office and wondered what Duke was going to do. *Maybe he's snooping around like I am...for the same information,* she conjectured. Heather recalled his disgust with his job and how he'd admitted wanting to be an investigative reporter. *If he found a link to solving this case, maybe he'd get moved out of the society section and smack in the middle of where he wants to be. But why is he looking in the city manager's office? Has he stumbled onto something we missed?*

"Excuse me. Is there something else you need?" Betty asked.

Heather pivoted toward the secretary. "Oh, uh, s–sorry," she stammered and looked down. "Are there any more return air vents in there?" She pointed toward the manager's office. "Or anywhere else that you know of?"

"No, that one's it, I believe."

"Okay, thanks," Heather said. She put the used filter on a filing cabinet. After replacing the vent screen and putting on the wing nuts, she retrieved the old air filter and scurried out the door. Taking a hard right, she marched straight around the corner where a sign with an arrow read "Ladies' Room." She hit the door, entered the oversized handicap stall, dropped the air filter and her shoulder bag, and began tearing down her hair.

If she hurried, she might intersect Duke as he left the building and nab him for a lunch date without him realizing he'd been kidnapped. Their official date was still three days away, which seemed like an eternity. The chance of spending time with Duke was worth the interruption of her investigation. *Besides, I have to eat,* she rationalized.

Within five minutes she'd changed into the denim skirt, cotton T-shirt, and spiked sandals she'd brought just in case. After cramming her glasses and uniform into her shoulder bag, she waited through two women's visits and then left her stall once they exited.

Heather propped the air filter inside the maintenance closet and planned to return for it later. She'd scrape the dust off and put it back where she found it. She hurried to the mirror and made sure her hair hung around her shoulders and swung free. Heather grabbed lip gloss from her bag's inside pocket and finished her

makeup with a slathering of pink on her full lips. She shoved the
gloss back where it came from.

With the transformation complete, Heather was satisfied no
one would suspect the mousy maintenance gal was the same as the
chic woman in denim. The only similarity was her hair was still
strawberry blonde. At closer inspection, Heather realized the pink
gloss that nicely complemented her true hair color now clashed a
bit with the new tint.

Oh well. She fluffed her hair.

Heather stepped from the ladies' room and strolled around
the corner. Hopefully Duke was still in the city manager's office.
Slowing when she neared the office, Heather glanced inside. The
secretary sat at her computer, absorbed in work. Heather peered
at the manager's closed door. Her gut instinct suggested the guy
was in there for the long haul—at least until lunch or the secretary
left her desk for another reason.

Heather continued walking and glanced at her watch. Lunch
was an hour away. Her stomach growled. She'd grabbed an apple
on the way out this morning, which she ate on the road while
sipping her coffee. She'd been too uptight to think of eating anything else. While she wanted to dash to the first restaurant she
spotted, Heather purposed to wait for Duke to come out, at which
time she would "conveniently" run into him. Hopefully he'd be as
glad to see her as she was him.

As she boarded the elevator and planned to settle on one of the
benches just outside City Hall, Heather recalled watching Duke
enter the city manager's office. The guy had picked that lock in
no time. How he acquired the tool and skill was anybody's guess.
Apparently he'd known what he was doing from experience. That
was one more thing Heather would put on her list to discover about
this fascinating new man in her life.

✳ ✳ ✳

Duke clenched the tiny flashlight between his teeth while he fumbled through the file cabinet. Fully aware of every squeak of the secretary's chair, he tempered each breath and made certain the whisper of his latex gloves against the paper files was kept to a minimum.

He'd decided to search the city manager's office on a hunch last night after finding an obscure article that suggested friction between the mayor and manager. The mayor had publicly hinted the manager was abusing alcohol, but the city manager had hotly denied the claim. No evidence had been found to support the mayor's accusation. While the conflict wasn't usually the stuff murders were made of, Duke itched to follow the lead.

So far his quest had unearthed nothing. He hadn't even discovered anything of concern on the manager's computer. While the guy was a slob in his office, the computer files were void of anything out of the ordinary. Even his email files had been purged.

And this stupid file cabinet is just as bad, Duke thought. *Either Soliday has nothing to hide or he's really good at covering his tracks.* Duke hadn't thought anything could rival his closets at home, but he'd finally run into someone who just might be worse than he was. Even though the files in the cabinets appeared to have started out in alphabetized order, the current system of organization defied logic. Duke silently slid the drawer back into place, removed the flashlight from his mouth, rubbed his forehead, and sighed.

The final frontier was the guy's desk, and it was as insanely disorganized as the file cabinet. The huge desk held a wad of tangled papers that might take years to get to the bottom of. Duke flicked the flashlight onto his Timex: eleven-thirty. He figured the secretary would go to lunch at noon. Duke planned to make his exit fifteen minutes after that. Hopefully the halls would be nice and empty...if everyone left for lunch at close to the same time.

He had forty-five minutes to fumble through that vast unknown on the desk.

* ✻ *

Heather sat on a wooden bench in Hermann Square and observed the City Hall entrance. She munched the granola bar she'd bought from the newsstand down the street. Heather had stepped into the shop for a newspaper and couldn't resist the health bar and a bottle of water. At least it was stopping her from gnawing her own shoes or violating her vegetarian diet and pouncing on the hot dog stand near the road. That smell alone was making her stomach growl.

A young guy was buying a chili dog. He'd barely pocketed his change when he crammed the creation into his mouth. Chili smudged his cheeks. He didn't even bother to wipe it off before going for another bite. Heather's taste buds ached. She forced herself to look away. She'd be having lunch with Duke soon. Checking her watch again, she noted noon was swiftly approaching.

Picking up the paper, she scanned the headlines while checking the entrance every few seconds. As she suspected, the latest news was no news. The headlines declared there were still no leads on the mayor's murder. Heather wondered if Brittan was gleaning any hot info from the mayor's computer. She dug her cell phone from her bag and pressed Brittan's speed dial number.

Her friend answered on the first ring. "Whazzup, girlfriend?" she quipped.

"Are you still in his computer?" Heather asked, her voice low.

"Yep."

"Look for someone named Shirley," Heather said.

"Will do."

"Oh, and see if you can find any reference to Hines, Drieb, and Associates."

"Got it," Brittan said.

"Also any connection between the city manager and you know who."

"I already know they hated each other," Brittan supplied.

"Oh really?" Heather responded and eyed the sporadic pedestrians to make sure no one was giving her undue attention. Even though the passersby barely glanced at her, Heather kept her voice low, her face impassive.

"Follow that lead," she encouraged.

"Where are you?" Brittan quizzed.

"Outside City Hall waiting for Duke to come out."

"Duke? How'd he get in the picture? You didn't tell him did you? I mean, about us?"

"No way. Don't even go there. You know we have a pact of silence! I'll explain everything later," she supplied and then continued without missing a beat. "How's Lorna doing?"

"Haven't heard. But she decided to go in as a carpet cleaner."

Last night Lorna was brainstorming options for connecting with the mayor's mistress. Heather had left early this morning and hadn't heard Lorna's final decision. "A carpet cleaner?" Heather repeated.

"Yes. Last I heard."

"I guess we'll see how that one goes," Heather replied through a snicker. "I can't imagine Lorna steam-cleaning anything. She's liable to suck herself up."

Brittan chuckled. "Yeah, but neither of us thought you'd be able to change an air filter either."

"Hey!" Heather exclaimed and squared her shoulders. "I'm a pro now." When a young woman pushing a baby carriage looked toward her, Heather realized she'd allowed her voice to get too loud. She hunched her shoulders, lowered her head, stared at the thick grass, and scolded herself.

"No telling what we'll learn to do before this is over," Brittan observed.

And Heather couldn't wait to find out. This case was turning into one big adrenaline rush. The more moves they made, the more exhilarating it became.

"Well, I've got to get back to the computer. I'm finding out lots. We'll need to put our notes together tonight. Maybe we'll have this bagged in a day or two."

"That would be too cool," Heather said before the friends bid adieu.

She dropped the cell phone back into her bag and downed the rest of her granola bar. Heather was on the last swig of water when Duke sauntered out of City Hall like he'd been taking care of the most mundane business on the planet. When he neared Heather, she stood and fell into step beside him without saying a word.

After about eight paces, she felt his glance and cut him a saucy, sideways glimpse. "Hi," she said.

"Well, hello there!" Duke replied and slowed to a stop.

Heather halted as well and put enough energy into her smile to dazzle a dozen men.

Duke's huge grin assured her he was thoroughly smitten.

"What's a girl like you doing in a place like this?" he asked.

Caught off-guard, Heather groped for an explanation and finally came up with a lame excuse. "Well, you know. Just hanging out."

"Oh," he said and glanced at her paper. "You enjoy current events?" he questioned.

"Sure. Who doesn't?" Heather replied. Her stomach rumbled.

"Whoa!" Duke backed away and gazed at her waist. "Was that you?"

"Afraid so," Heather drawled.

"Sounds like somebody better feed you. Hey, I'm off today. Would you like to—"

"Yes," Heather answered.

Duke laughed. "Yes? But you didn't even let me finish."

"Yes to whatever you were going to say."

"I was going to ask if you'd like to go to the city zoo and wrestle alligators."

"Hey, I'm good for alligator wrestling." Heather lifted her hand. "As long as we can eat them when we're through."

Duke laughed out loud. "Actually I was thinking more in terms of lunch."

"That's what I was thinking too," Heather replied. "And again, yes, I'd be delighted."

"Great! There's a burger joint a block down." He pointed east. "Nothin' fancy, but their food is so terrific you'd slap your grandma if she got between you and your hamburger."

"I'm so hungry I don't think I'd stop eating long enough for grandma to get that close!"

He chuckled and grabbed her hand. "Come on."

One man officially nabbed! She fell into stride beside him.

TEN

Lorna yawned for the third time in fifteen minutes. She'd been awake half the night trying to decide how to approach the governor's mistress. The debutante wasn't certain whether she should be sneaky or use a more direct approach and strike up a conversation with the woman. Finally Lorna decided sneaky worked with Terry Longheed, and sneaky was best. She also knew the plant delivery gig yesterday had given them only a few minutes inside the Longheed place. But if she could enter Eve Maloney's apartment under the pretense of doing an assigned task, she would have the advantage of being able to snoop more.

By six this morning Lorna decided steam-cleaning or shampooing the carpet in a whole apartment could take hours. She'd run the plan by Brittan, who said it was perfect. The only problem was convincing the mayor's mistress that her apartment's carpet needed to be cleaned.

Eve Maloney. Rhymes with baloney, Lorna thought as she wrestled the steam cleaner out of the elevator. She maneuvered the equipment across the short hallway that four luxury apartments opened onto. The one marked 212 was supposed to be Eve's.

Lorna had dressed in the coveralls and cap from yesterday and bought the cleaner outright because she didn't want to have to deal with any rental people—especially if she broke the machine. The specialty shop had given her a short session on operating the Steam Monster III, but Lorna still had her doubts as to whether the monster would man her or she would man it. A test run at the penthouse had seemed easy enough. She'd already filled it with water and added liquid cleaner. Soon she would learn if it was going to suck up stains like it did at the penthouse or somehow ruin the carpet. Lorna wondered if this endeavor would be the stuff nightmares were made of. Nevertheless, she was game.

She decided to steam clean the landing first. Then she could knock on Eve's door and ask if she could plug in the steamer in her apartment. If the woman agreed, that would mean the cord would keep the door from completely shutting. And if Eve left, Lorna would have easy entry into the apartment. Or maybe, after a while on the landing, she might be able to coax Eve to let her clean her carpets as well, especially if she assumed it was an official mandate of the management. If Eve cooperated it would be amazing. Lorna prayed for a miracle.

She examined all the knobs and whatsits on the Steam Monster III and double checked the cylinder that was filled with a mixture of water and carpet cleaner. "Looks like it's ready to go," she said on a prayer and hoped for the best. Even in college, she'd had a housekeeper. Lorna had never even run a vacuum cleaner. While the steamer and she had gotten along beautifully for a trial run at her place, nothing in her Inter-Disciplinary Studies degree at Princeton covered steam-cleaning carpets. And until today Steam Monster III sounded like something from a horror show.

Lorna approached 212 and rang the doorbell. When nothing happened, she rang the bell again and hoped the woman was home. She had no idea what she was going to say—only how she would say it. Lorna had been told by her theater professor that she possessed an uncanny ability to mimic voice styles. Now was the time to exercise that skill.

Finally soft footsteps approached the door. Lorna gazed straight ahead and sensed that she was being examined through the peephole.

When the door opened, a tall, thin woman of mixed heritage stared her eye-to-eye. Lorna was stricken by her unusual beauty—exotic, almond-shaped eyes and fine bone structure. She looked like royalty from India, except Lorna suspected she was probably Native American.

She pictured Terry Longheed, that disoriented blonde who seemed to care little for her physical appearance. And while Lorna didn't condone the mayor's affair, she recognized the fascination he might have had for this woman.

"Is there something you need?" Eve finally asked. Her diction was as perfect as her features.

Lorna held up the steamer cord. "I'm hare to shampoo de carpet," she drawled in the worst Texas accent she could conjure. "I'm gonna start widda foyer first." Lorna pointed over her shoulder.

"Oh, great!" Eve said. "I've never been so glad of anything in my life. My neighbor's dog got out last week and soiled the carpet. I can still smell it!"

Lorna gave a slight sniff and tried to detect any hint of dog waste, but she only noticed a faint whiff of new paint as she glanced at the bright beige walls. *Who cares if it's really there or not? That dog's accident just might be my ticket.*

"Well, I wus jus' wonderin' if you'd let me plug this hare steamer in yur 'partment," Lorna drawled and spotted a plug in the foyer about six feet from Eve's door. Her shoulders almost stiffened, but she caught herself. She held her face impassive, and hoped Eve didn't recall the plug's location.

"Sure. Whatever." Eve agreed.

Lorna relaxed.

Eve opened the door wider and pointed to a plug near the entry. "Use that one."

Lorna stepped inside and was hit with the overwhelming scent of potpourri or diffuser oil. *Eve must soak the reeds in fresh oil daily,* Lorna decided, trying not to gag.

A black Persian cat reclined on a velvet couch. A queen who had been thoroughly disturbed, the feline lifted her head and observed Lorna.

Deciding to take her chances, Lorna eyed the cat and then her owner.

"Ya know," she offered, "I'd be glad ta shampoo yur carpets too. Management ain't told me to or nuthin', but what with that cat, you might have a few odors in hare too."

"Do you smell something?" Eve delicately sniffed the air.

"Uh…" *Not unless you count scented oil so strong it's clearing my sinuses.*

"I would just die if my apartment started smelling." Eve hurried toward the corner, her satin pants flopping around her ankles. She paused near a silk tree and inhaled. "Muffin was digging in the tree's basket a few days ago. I was worried then."

Lorna gazed around the apartment. The place looked like an advertisement for Ethan Allen Furniture Gallery, right down to the marble statuette of an Egyptian cat sitting on the coffee table.

"Look, just go ahead and shampoo it." Eve shoved at her sleeve and examined a watch that had more diamonds than even Lorna's mom's. "Is it possible for you to shampoo it now though? I've got to leave in an hour."

"That's fine," Lorna said. "But I ain't sure I cun be dun by then."

"Oh well." Eve waved aside Lorna's concerns. "If you aren't through when I leave, it will be okay. You can make sure the door is locked when you leave. I've never had trouble with any maintenance people at this place. I won't be gone long. I've just got an appointment for a fitting for a new suit." Her eyes shifted. "I've got a funeral tomorrow," she explained as if she were reciting a grocery list.

Lorna nodded like she couldn't care less. "I see," she said. "Every-thang sounds jus' fine." She yawned without covering her mouth and then scratched at her midsection.

Eve's nose quivered. Her lips turned down.

Lorna figured her theater professor would probably give her an A-plus for this performance. She forced a loud burp. For that matter, Lorna was ready to give *herself* an A-plus.

"'Scuse me thare," she said and finally got around to plugging in the steam cleaner.

"Yes, well…" Lifting her chin, Eve looked at Lorna like she was a worm.

Lorna ducked her head to keep from laughing. Truth was, Lorna's family could probably buy Eve Maloney several times over, but today Lorna was a carpet steaming lady and nothing more. And that only if she could make the machine work.

"You won't need to vacuum first," Eve said as she sashayed out of the room.

Vacuum? Lorna thought. *Nobody told me to vacuum first!*

"My maid was here late yesterday," Eve continued. "So you should be good to go."

"Okay, ma'am," Lorna said and tugged on the rim of her cap. "I'll take care of it fur ya."

The second Eve disappeared down the hallway, Lorna gulped and eyed the Steam Monster III. "Okay, listen you," she threat-ened under her breath, "I'm the one in charge here, and don't you forget it."

A soft gravelly sound enveloped the room. Lorna raised her brows, backed away, and then realized the growling was not coming from the machine but from the cat on the couch. Lorna observed the yellow-eyed feline, who in turn opened her mouth, showed her fangs, and hissed straight at her.

For some reason most cats hated Lorna. She had no idea why. Maybe it was her odor or they just didn't like brunettes. Or maybe they sensed she was a dog person and resented the injustice. Whatever the case, this cat was no different from any of the others she'd endured. Lorna figured she needed to let this black fur ball know who was boss.

"Don't mess with me," she threatened. "Or I'll steam clean your tail."

ELEVEN

Duke couldn't remember a better-tasting burger *ever*. But then he'd never had such a charming companion either. The two of them had done nothing but talk about him. Or, rather, Duke talked about himself. Heather asked the questions. All sorts of questions. Like where he grew up. What life was like on a West Texas ranch. And exactly how many tornadoes *had* he been through anyway.

"So there I was," Duke said, "stuck out on the back forty—literally—with nothing for shelter but my horse and my saddle. The lightning was terrible. I'll never forget it. I was all of seventeen and scared out of my mind." He widened his eyes for effect.

"I think anyone would be at *any* age," Heather said. She placed her elbow on the table, rested her chin in her hand, and wholly focused on Duke, which made him feel like he was the only man in the crowded restaurant.

He struggled to concentrate on his story and was sorely tempted to embellish a bit more—just enough to make him sound like a bigger-than-life hero. The temptation finally grew too strong. Duke went for it.

"Then all of a sudden..." he extended his hand toward the large window, "I saw it. A tornado dropped out of one of the blackest clouds you've ever seen and not more than fifty feet in front of me."

Heather's focus intensified. "What did you do?"

"I'll tell you what I did, lady," he said and cocked his eyebrow. "I did the only thing I could do. I charged that tornado like a bull after a red cape. And when I got within ten feet of it, I moved to the side, grabbed it by the tail, and shook the living daylights out of it. The whippersnapper went yelping back the way it came, hopped into the clouds, and never came back."

Heather narrowed her eyes and lifted her head. "You know, I've heard that Houston smog can affect your thinking, but I didn't believe it until now."

Duke chuckled and rubbed his chin. "You mean you don't believe me?" He rested his hand against his chest and leaned back in his chair. "I'm crushed—absolutely crushed!"

"Yes, I bet you are," Heather drawled and picked up her bottled water. "And to think you had me going there for a while." She took a long swallow of water. "I really thought you had a one-on-one with a tornado."

"Actually I did." Duke drummed both hands against the table's edge. "But it wasn't half as glamorous or as big as my Texas-sized tale." He picked up a small onion ring, popped it in his mouth, and smiled while he wiped his fingertips on his napkin. "I was seventeen, like I already said. And I had been out wandering around on the back forty. No horse. Just me and my camera and nature. It was my hobby then, and still is."

He paused and covered her with a lazy grin. "Especially when the subject is fascinating." Duke never had considered himself exceptional with lines, but he gave himself a cool 100 points for that one. It was good. Really good. And it reaped the exact results he'd hoped for.

Heather acted like he'd just dumped a bucketful of honey right into her soul. She beamed for a while and then settled down to a flattering glow.

"Go on," she urged.

"Oh yeah...the story," Duke said. "I forgot there for a minute."

She looked down and then held his gaze with a warm rush of adoration that made Duke forget she was a blue blood.

Heather looked as good today as she had yesterday—except her hair was different somehow. Less blonde? More red? Maybe he just didn't remember right. There seemed to be more to her than what he'd detected in their previous encounters. A hint of a secret that heightened her appeal. Duke hoped to discover that secret and with it, learn that maybe they really were compatible.

Fleetingly he wondered what she would say if she knew he'd been prowling around in the city manager's office. Granted, he hadn't found one thing—except a flight itinerary that said the guy was now in the Bahamas. After searching the mountain of paperwork on his desk and perusing any computer files that looked suspicious, Duke saved the man's Palm Pilot files that were backed up on his computer but protected by a security code. He was glad he knew this trick and hoped The Mike could hack into the files later. The memory stick he'd brought just in case had paid off big. Now tucked safely in his billfold, Duke looked forward to the chance to inspect the files. If they didn't reveal anything suspicious, then either the city manager was as pure as bleached cotton or a pro at covering his tracks.

Duke tossed around the idea of telling Heather he was turning stones, but he decided against it. The fewer people who knew, the better. He cleared his throat, looked away, and focused on his tornado story.

"Anyway," he continued, "a storm did come up—some wind... a few clouds...a little lightning. And I was scared. When the sky turned green, so did I."

Heather sobered. "No joke this time?"

"No." He held up his hand. "Scout's honor."

"Okay, so what happened?" She leaned forward.

"Next thing I knew, the weirdest thing I'd ever seen in my life dropped out of the sky." He held up both hands. "I promise. It was a tornado that wasn't much bigger than a fat jump rope." He made a circle with his index fingers and thumbs. "Like I already said, I had my camera with me. I was on a hill—"

"Right up there where the lightning could *really* get you," Heather emphasized.

"You got it!" Duke laughed. "But I forgot all about that. I had my 35 millimeter going and took all sorts of shots before it broke up."

"Sounds like a bad girlfriend experience," Heather said.

Duke snickered. "Yep. You get the point. Anyway, after the tornado did its thing, the hail came. I ran to the bottom of the hill and got into a cave. And I use the word 'cave' loosely. It was more like a hollow spot under a short cliff in the side of a short hill. Just enough shelter to keep me from getting beaten half to death."

"I can't imagine." Heather's eyes reflected her honest intrigue, and Duke still felt like a hero even though he really didn't grab a tornado by the tail.

He sat a bit straighter and couldn't deny the surge of something that made him want to have Heather Winslow look at him like that every day. "Once the hail and rain stopped, I went to the stretch of land where the tornado had done the hokey pokey. I took all sorts of shots of the ground. There was a long, narrow, ditch-like trail, not more than a foot across and about six inches deep."

"Very odd," Heather injected.

He nodded. "The local paper thought so too. I wrote up a story and submitted the photos with it. The whole shebang made the front page of the *Lubbock Times*. Next thing ya know—bam—it hit the syndication trail. My photos and that story wound up being published all over the U.S."

"No way!"

"Yep. From then on I made it my business to find all sorts of odd things that interested the local rag. By that summer they'd hired me part-time. It got into my blood. I wound up studying journalism at Texas Tech. I worked on my dad's ranch for several years before finally chasing my dreams. Now here I am." He grimaced. "A society reporter for the *Houston Star*." Duke twirled his index finger in the air. "Whoopee!"

"I guess taking pictures of women like me is dull and boring compared to chasing tornadoes and hail storms," Heather admitted.

"Oh, I wouldn't go so far as to say *that*," Duke said through a smile. He slumped back in his seat, picked up an extra straw, and tapped it against the edge of the table. She looked good enough in that T-shirt and denim skirt to plaster on the cover of a magazine, and Duke decided to tell her so.

"Fascination comes in all shapes and sizes," he said. "Sometimes it's a long, skinny tornado. And sometimes it's an exquisite woman. And, well, I'll take the woman any day." *Okay, that one should be worth another hundred points,* he thought and knew The Mike would be very, very proud.

"You're really laying it on thick now, aren't you?" Heather teased.

"And you don't like it?"

"No, not at all," she said and again rested her elbow on the table, her chin in her hand. "Not in the least," she gurgled while her dancing eyes said, *Lay it on thick some more, baby.*

Duke reached across the table, tugged on her fingers, and wondered if he was moving too fast...for her sake and his. But no matter how he cautioned himself, he couldn't stop. He hoped what he was feeling really was for the woman and not the mere adrenaline rush that comes with a new romance.

He enjoyed "the conquer" just as much as the next guy. But if he and Heather became a pair, there had to be something to hold onto.

He eased away from her fingers. That was something only time would tell. He reminded himself he'd barely gotten to know her and nothing lasting could ever be based upon surface attraction.

"So, enough about me," Duke said and straightened. "Tell me about you. What do you like to do in your spare time?"

Heather looked down, toyed with her veggie burger's wrapper, and said, "Oh, you know. This and that. My mom is always after me to serve on all these social committees. I do what I have to do. Did I tell you during my interview that I'm the regional spokesperson for the Animal Rescue Society?"

"No, you didn't." Duke shook his head.

"Well, it's comprised of people who love animals and want to make sure they aren't abused. They believe in the rescue work enough to plunk some serious money behind it. It's very rewarding, and I enjoy it." Heather popped a fry into her mouth. "Maybe I like it so much because I'm a cat fiend," she continued. "I have six."

"Six!"

"Yes." She raised her fingers and counted off the cats. "Lucky, Tigger, Miss Gray, Miss Stripe, Sam, and Socks—all but one from the animal shelter. So the Animal Rescue thing is right up my alley.

"Then, like I told you," she continued, "I volunteer in a local soup kitchen. Really, I'd rather do that than be on a committee any day. So my volunteer work and church activities keep me busy. I also *adore* traveling," she added.

"Great!" Duke said. He found himself caught up in her energy. He hoped they had a few things in common. He also suspected she might be a vegetarian because of her veggie burger. That was interesting, since his father raised Herefords to be slaughtered for eating. Duke decided to sort that one out later.

"I'm big on always getting my pets from the humane society. I adopted my dog from there when I moved to Houston. And I try to volunteer for a missions trip with my church every year." He looked upward and brainstormed for another possible area they could connect. "Let see. Do you...enjoy reading?"

"A little." Heather shrugged.

"What's your favorite?" he prompted. "I love mysteries." He hoped she'd agree.

"I like mysteries. They're okay." Heather smiled. "I remember you saying you want to be an investigative reporter, so I'm guessing you like real-life mysteries. Right?"

"Absolutely." Duke nodded.

"So..." She glanced away, tore the edge of a napkin, and went on. "Do you ever go after any mysteries in your spare time?"

Duke blinked. For a second he wondered if she suspected what he was up to. *But that's ridiculous. There's no way she can know,* he reasoned. Duke revisited his decision not to tell her and decided to stay with the plan. Telling her was risky. Heather might know someone who knew someone involved, and she might innocently leak his info.

"So do you?" she prompted.

"I did a little of that in college actually—part-time," he said in the most nonchalant voice he could conjure. "I was an investigative reporter. But I knew my dad wanted me to take over the ranch one day and I..." he toyed with the straw in his Styrofoam cup, "decided to give that my best shot. So after graduating I moved home. I lived in the extra house on the ranch and was my dad's right-hand man.

"A couple years ago I realized I was dedicating my life to my dad's dream, and I really didn't have my own life. We went to a small, country church three times a week and that and the church get-togethers were about all the social life I had—unless you count a few meaningful relationships with some longhorns."

Heather chuckled.

Duke didn't expand on the number of single women in that country church who'd made a blatant play or two or twelve for him. He wasn't into being chased; he'd rather do the chasing. His sister told him he was too old-fashioned. Call it what you like, but the second a gal did what Tisha at the paper had done, she was scratched off his list—if she ever made it on the list in the first place. Heather had made it very clear she was available for the chase, but she hadn't crossed that fine line. Besides, there was something different about her. Something that intrigued him. Something he couldn't put his finger on yet.

"I guess that country church had a shortage of young, single women?"

He laughed. "No, I wouldn't go that far," he admitted. "It runs a couple hundred people. So there is a pretty strong singles program."

"Oh." Heather's eyes sparked, and Duke could almost read her mind. He figured she was dying to know about any women in his past. But that wasn't anything he'd be sharing. Not yet, anyway.

The *Bonanza* theme erupted from beneath the table, and Heather reached down. "Sorry. That's my cell," she said. Once she extracted the phone from her bag, she examined the caller ID. "It's my friend. I need to take this one," she said. "Do you mind?"

"No, not in the least." He lifted his hand. "By all means, go ahead."

Duke was thankful for the interruption. It gave him a chance to regroup after the vein of their conversation. He hadn't elaborated that he simply hadn't found a gal yet who could hold his interest past the second or third date.

His mom said he was too picky.

His sister said he had commitment issues.

His father told him to hold out for the best.

Duke was holding.

None of them understood the devastation he'd endured when Sarah Jenkins dumped him for the star quarterback. A senior in high school could be all the way in love and all the way destroyed. That was part of the reason he'd been on the back forty the day he encountered the rope tornado. Duke had been so depressed he'd wanted to be alone. He'd covered his emotions at the time and publicly shrugged it off. He'd even attended Sarah's wedding a year later and congratulated the bride *and* groom...when he really wanted to drop kick their fancy-schmancy wedding cake right through the church's stained glass windows—in Christian love, of course.

Now that Duke was a grown man, he was beginning to see that part of his wife hunt problem involved not wanting a Sarah repeat. At some point, he knew, he was going to have to take a chance. Now that he was alone in Houston, his townhouse seemed more and more empty.

Sure, Jake was there. The poor pup had been a special-needs orphan who'd lost an eye to a cat who didn't appreciate a puppy's nose in her face. Duke had rescued him the day before he was going to be euthanized, and their bond went deep. Nevertheless, a bull-dog did little to fill the void of a man ready to be married. As much as Duke enjoyed Jake, the mutt couldn't kiss worth a flip.

"Really?" Heather shrieked and then laughed so loud the neighboring diners focused on her as swiftly as Duke did. Her eyes bugging, she covered her mouth, got control of herself, and then checked her watch.

"Okay. Yes. I think I can be there in fifteen minutes. I'm downtown anyway. Near City Hall." She pulled a pen from her handbag and scribbled on a napkin. "Yes. Right. Got it. Tell her I'm coming." She bid farewell and snapped the phone shut.

"I'm sorry, Duke. I've got a friend who's in a pickle. I'm going to have to go."

"That's all right." He scooted back his chair. "I understand."

Heather giggled and pressed the cell phone against her lips.

"She's been trying to run a carpet shampooer steamer and it's a disaster!"

"If there's some way I could help..." Duke stood.

"Do you know about them?" Heather asked.

"Well, my mom owns one. And when I lived in Lubbock she was always roping me into steaming her carpets. She always got me to her house with a home-cooked meal promise and then, wham, I was attached to that baby before I knew what hit me. I don't know a lot, but maybe I could help."

Heather looked at Duke like his offer was as complicated as reading ancient Egyptian. "I don't know..." she hedged. "On one hand," she dropped her cell phone into the canvass bag. "But then, on the other hand..." She tilted her head and Duke was certain he heard her brain's gears clicking.

"No pressure." He held up both hands. "Just trying to be a good scout."

"Come on." She jerked her bag onto her shoulder. "We've got to hurry." Grabbing his hand, Heather yanked him toward the doorway. "This has got to be quick." They hit the glass doors and bustled onto the busy sidewalk.

"Just promise me one thing." Heather pointed at his nose.

"What?"

"Don't ask any questions," she said. "This is a really weird deal, and there's all sorts of stuff I can't tell you. Okay?"

"Okaaaay," Duke drawled and didn't believe anything about a carpet steamer could be all that secretive. *Oh well,* he decided. *I'm game.*

"The only thing you need to know is that my friend Lorna has gotten herself into a fix. She needs to be bailed out as quickly as possible and then we've got to scram. Understand?"

"No questions. Fix steamer. We scram. I can do this," Duke promised. He'd barely gotten the words out of his mouth when she grabbed his hand and took off. He had to run to keep up.

"Whoa!" he said through a laugh.

"We don't have all day," she hollered.

As they paused at an intersection, Duke couldn't imagine what kind of secret Heather Winslow and her friend might hold. *Whatever it is*, he thought, *it can't be half as important as she's acting. What could a rich debutante be involved in that's top secret anyway?*

TWELVE

Two blocks later Heather spotted the luxury high-rise where Lorna was supposed to be. Rockworth Plaza was sprawled across the portico, under which sat a Rolls Royce, a limo, and a Lamborghini.

"There it is." She pointed toward the skyscraper covered with black windows. She began digging through her bag. "Just a minute." Heather pulled out her cell phone, and they stopped at another intersection. "Let me call Lorna and tell her we're on our way up."

She smiled into Duke's eyes and tried to act as innocent as a pup. But Heather's fingers shook so fiercely she could barely punch in Lorna's speed dial number. Once the task was complete, she placed the cell to her ear and eyed Duke to make certain he hadn't noticed. The guy was gazing up at the black building and didn't appear to have a clue.

Likewise, Heather had no clue if she should have accepted Duke's offer to help. She'd weighed the options and then weighed them again. If she did accept his offer, he might figure out what the three of them were up to. But without him, Lorna might be in a crisis too big for Heather to help her out of.

Like I know anything about carpet shampooer steamers, she thought as Lorna's breathless voice came over the line.

"Lorna," Heather said, "I've got Duke with me. He's going to help. We're right across the street and should be there in just a few."

"Duke?" Lorna exclaimed. "Are you crazy? Did you tell him what we're doing?"

"Absolutely not!" Heather insisted. "Trust me on this one, okay? I don't know any more about carpet steamers than you do. Duke's mom owns one at least. I'm thinking he can get everything going and we can get out of there before…um…your client gets back." Heather darted a discreet glance at Duke.

He stood with his hands in his pockets, gazing at the traffic zipping by.

"Okay," Lorna said. "I'm desperate. I don't have a choice. Just make sure he doesn't find out."

"It's taken care of," Heather said. "Believe me, I'm as concerned as you are. Don't worry." She snapped the cell shut and realized as soon as she dropped it into her bag that she hadn't even said goodbye. *Lorna should be used to that by now,* Heather decided.

"She's watching for us. Let's go," she said as the pedestrian light turned green. They crossed and entered the building, found the elevator, and were soon exiting on the second floor. Heather approached the door marked 212 and rapped. Lorna whipped open the door.

"I'm between a *serious* rock and a fireplace," she blurted.

"Do you mean a rock and a *hard* place?" Duke questioned.

Lorna huffed and rolled her eyes. "Whatever."

Heather nearly burst into laughter.

Her friend had wet spots all over her coveralls and a dot of suds hung from a tuft of brown hair peeking beneath her cap. When Brittan said the thing blew up on Lorna, she must have meant it. Heather bit the insides of her cheeks and told herself that laughing could lead to decapitation. Then she caught sight of suds all over the front of a couch that looked like it cost as much as her own furniture did. A black Persian was perched on top of a bookshelf. Her fur wet, she glared down at the steam cleaner like it was a fiend from Hades.

"Go ahead and laugh, why don't you?" Lorna squeaked out, her eyes turning red. "But it's not funny!"

Heather's initial attack of humor dissolved. *This is serious,* she reminded herself. *As serious as hiding in the men's room and recording conversations.*

"What happened?" she asked.

"I don't know." Lorna looked at Duke. "It just started foaming like crazy and then the stuff blew everywhere. I need to be out of here before the owner comes back, and now I've got a mess the size of Europe." She opened the door wider and motioned toward the steamer. A large puddle of suds resembling a pond marred the forest-green carpet.

Heather swallowed a giggle and sternly told herself she was probably going to get slapped if she didn't get a grip.

Duke stepped inside and sneezed. "My word, what's that smell?"

"It's some kind of scented oil, I think," Lorna said.

"Smells like it," Heather agreed.

"It's lethal," he complained and sneezed again before examining the apparatus. "Steam Monster III," he said under his breath. He punctuated the comment with a third sneeze.

Heather crossed her arms, rocked forward, bit her lips, and stared hard at the carpet.

Duke mumbled something and then observed Lorna. "Have you ever done this before?"

She shook her head.

"Well, it looks like you've put in way too much cleaner fluid. Now you've got a suds revival on."

"No joke!" Lorna said.

His forehead wrinkling, Duke studied Lorna for a full five

seconds and then said, "Why are you doing this professionally if you don't know—"

Heather cleared her throat and then coughed outright.

Duke darted his gaze to her. "Right. No questions." He sighed. "Okay, I think the best thing to do is clean up the mess." He pointed to the front of the couch and the coffee table. "I'll empty out the cylinder and put in plain water. I'll use that to get rid of this soap lake."

Heather pressed her fingers against her mouth.

"Maybe you could get some towels from the bathroom, Heather," he suggested and then pointed toward the couch.

"Oh sure." Heather walked toward a hallway and spotted a rest-room at the end. On the way, she allowed a few chortles to leak out and realized the laughter was as much a product of her stretched nerves as the suds swamp. *This is some day!*

Near the bathroom Heather passed a large bedroom, every bit as immaculate and well-decorated as the living area. She ducked inside and took a quick peek, just to see if anything might offer a clue. At first glance, she saw nothing. But then she neared the dresser and examined the framed photos lining the top. Most included a fine-boned woman with dark skin and eyes, whom Heather assumed had ensnared more than her share of males. She figured the woman must be Eve. In one photo Eve stood beside a man who greatly favored her and appeared to be twenty years younger.

Probably her son, Heather deduced.

The final photo featured Eve next to a tall, sandy-haired man. They sat on a couch, and he had his right arm loosely around her shoulders. Heather assumed he must be her husband...or boy-friend. When she spotted the ring on his right hand, Heather's eyes bugged.

She scratched through her canvass bag and dug out her digital camera. After turning it on, Heather scrolled to the last photo she'd taken—the guy's right hand on the men's room door. Careful not to touch a thing, she bent within inches of the photo and scrutinized the ring. Next she studied her photo. She zoomed in on the hand until the ring was as large as she could get it. Then she went back to the photo on the dresser.

"It's the same ring," she whispered, and her mind whirled. Heather reached for the frame, but stopped herself. *No fingerprints,* she thought and then realized she could snap a picture.

"Brilliant," she whispered after the final photo, "even if I have to say so myself."

"Heather?" Lorna's voice floated down the hallway.

She scurried out of the room and spotted Lorna. Heather held her finger to her lips and pointed toward the bathroom. Lorna followed her inside. She grabbed a washcloth from a wall shelf, wrapped it around the doorknob, and closed the door.

"No fingerprints," she whispered.

"Right." Lorna held up both hands. "No touchy."

"Listen, I've stumbled onto some big stuff," she hissed. "Just stay cool. But I think we're on the verge of nabbing our murderers. Heavy on the plural."

"Already!" Lorna exclaimed.

"Yep." Heather shook her head. "And I think this lady might be involved." She pointed downward to emphasize they were standing in the very apartment of a potential murderer.

"Then we need to get out of here before she comes back." Lorna grabbed a couple of towels from the rack. "I'm not in the mood to be murdered."

"You got it." Heather nodded. "But, remember, I've always got your back when you're with me."

"That's assuring," Lorna said, her green eyes wide, "but no karate on the planet would have saved the mayor."

"Right," Heather said and smiled. "But put me in the same room with 'em, and they're history." She sliced her fist through the air.

"I'd rather just run," Lorna said and mimicked Heather's air-slicing.

Heather wondered what Duke would think if he knew she wasn't half as defenseless as she looked or that she volunteered at a Christian school to teach junior high girls self-defense. She'd withheld that tidbit from him because she'd learned the hard way that some guys were too intimidated by a man with a black belt… much less a woman. And then developing a romantic relationship with her? Ha!

"How's Duke doing in there?" she asked, pointing toward the living room.

"He's all over it. I just hope…" Lorna checked her watch. "Eve's due back in, like, twenty-five minutes," she fretted. "I was faking it fine until she left. I kept going for a few minutes, just to make sure she really was gone before I snooped around. And right when I was ready to turn off the thing it all went south." She pointed her thumb down.

"Well, come on!" Heather covered the doorknob with the washcloth and opened it as the whir and wheeze of the steamer floated up the hallway. "We've got to do what we've got to do. If we have to leave the suds swamp, then that's what we have to do."

"But she'll get suspicious," Lorna protested.

"Come on," Heather urged. "We'll worry about that when the time comes."

Heather invaded the living room with Lorna close behind. Duke had already emptied the cleaner's cylinders and was sucking the suds out of the carpet like a pro. She bent close to his ear. "We need to get out of here ASAP," she urged.

He gazed up at her, and more questions bounced between them. Heather shook her head. Duke sighed and went back to his task. Within fifteen minutes the suds were no more. Heather and Lorna had dried the spots off the couch and removed the glob of suds off the cat statuette on the coffee table. The black Persian refused to move from her spot on the bookshelf and glared at them. "Touch me and you're dead meat," she seemed to say. They decided to let the cat be and Eve could just wonder how the critter got so wet..

Holding the used towels, Lorna trotted to the bathroom and came back empty handed. "Let's get out of here," she urged as Duke stooped to wrap the cord around the casing on the side of the steamer.

Keeping her eye on Duke, Heather pulled her City Hall shirt out of her canvass bag and wiped off the inside knob before opening the door. She shoved the shirt back into her bag as he was turning for the door. The three ducked into the hallway, and Duke bent to retrieve the rebellious cord that had fallen out of its casing.

Heather leaned close to Lorna's ear. "Wipe off the outside doorknob with your shirt," she whispered before Duke straightened.

Lorna nodded.

Grabbing Duke's arm, she dragged him toward the elevator. "Thanks so much, Duke," she said and was overcome with gratitude. When they paused to await the elevator's arrival, Heather impulsively planted a kiss on his cheek. Immediately she gasped, "Oh my word! I can't believe I just did that!"

"Neither can I!" Duke exclaimed, his face flushing. "How dare you!"

Heather's stomach knotted, and she would have gladly drank a whole gallon of invisible potion.

"You left this side out!" With a mischievous grin, he turned the other side of his face toward her.

Her stomach went from a clench to a flutter. "Well, that can be remedied," she asserted and stood on tiptoes to complete the task.

"Would you two stop it!" Lorna scolded and pressed the elevator's down button.

"Oops. Sorry," Heather said.

"But are you really?" Duke asked, leaning closer.

Laughter gurgled in Heather's throat, and she barely registered the elevator's ding. "Actually no!" she answered.

"Good!" Duke said and raised an eyebrow. "Neither am I."

The door began opening.

"Come on," Lorna insisted and pulled Heather's arm.

"I guess one day you'll tell me what all this is about," Duke drawled as they boarded the elevator.

"Probably not," Heather said with a grin she hoped appeared frivolous.

Duke grunted and shook his head. The elevator doors opened on the first floor. He pushed the Steam Monster III out of the elevator and onto the marble floor.

"Now what?" he asked. "Are we going to steam clean the sidewalks or something?"

"Not!" Lorna said. "I'm donating that beast to Goodwill!" She pulled off her baseball cap, and her hair spiked in protest.

THIRTEEN

That night at Brittan and Lorna's penthouse the three debs began putting together the puzzle pieces each had collected. A large pizza and a bowl of salad claimed the center of the glass-topped breakfast table as the friends alternated eating with snapping in pieces of the mayor's murder.

Heather took a long drink of her bottled water and reached for another slice of pizza. She went for the cheese half and avoided the hamburger side. As much as she tried to get Lorna and Brittan to convert and become good vegetarians, she never won. While Brittan was health conscious, she had no plans of giving up meat.

Lorna, on the other hand, was a hopeless cause on all counts. She was what Heather dubbed a food disposal. And while Lorna wasn't bone thin by any means, Heather wondered how the woman kept herself down to a size fourteen considering some of the food she consumed. Her countless hours of tennis were her only salvation.

Lorna picked up her Diet Coke, laden with aspartame, and shamelessly guzzled before saying, "Do you guys think we need to take our clues to the *Star* tonight or wait and see if we can figure out who Shirley is?"

"I don't know," Brittan said.

"I want to make sure we get the information in before the police find everything. This murder is an easy one, and it shouldn't take them long to figure it out," Heather asserted. "If we want The Rose to get credit, we might need to move fast."

"Well, maybe," Brittan said. "But then they've probably got enough red tape tangling them up to keep them off the trail another month. I think it seems so easy to us because we moved in fast and landed in the right places at the right times." She munched a bite of salad and gazed across the room. "Or maybe we had some divine help on the deal."

"The truth is, we don't know what the police know," Lorna said. "And I say the sooner we spill the beans the better."

"I'm with you," Heather said. "But do we have enough information to make sure the key players are nabbed?" She took a bite of her pizza, stood, and stepped toward the breakfast bar where all their evidence was laid out. As she eyed the different documents, the kitchen tile cooled her bare feet, which were protesting all the blocks she'd walked in those killer spikes today.

After she left Duke, Heather had gone back to City Hall, changed into her maintenance gear, scraped the dust off the air filter, and put it back where she found it. The secretary never suspected that Heather had recycled the old filter. Once at the penthouse she'd changed back into her skirt and T-shirt, but longed for floppy shorts like her friends wore.

"I think we're in good shape," Lorna said, moving to stand near Heather.

Brittan joined on the other side. "Maybe," she asserted.

Heather swallowed her pizza and eyed the photo of the sandy-haired man lying near a printout of him from the City Hall website. They'd discovered his name was Victor McIntosh and that he was the assistant to the city manager. Heather's zoomed-in photo of his hand lay beside the one of him and Eve Maloney. Next to that picture lay another zoomed-in snippet of his hand resting on Eve's shoulder. As Heather suspected, the rings matched. The man who was involved in the mayor's murder was a close friend of the mayor's mistress, which made the mistress a likely suspect.

The other half of the bar contained printed information that Brittan had gathered from the mayor's computer. According to her, she had delved into files that had been deleted from the recycle bin. Even though Lorna and Heather had dubbed Brittan "The Brain," Heather wondered if "Computer Houdini" would be a better nickname. This time Brittan's abilities had produced amazing fruit. One expletive-filled email from the city manager left no doubt that the two hated each other. Another email from Mayor Longheed threatened to "reveal all" if the manager didn't cooperate with his plans for economic expansion. That message was dated a week before the mayor was gunned down.

"I'm sure this information and the recording I got today will give the *Star* some serious fodder they can either do a hot story on or take to the police." Heather reached for her piece of pizza.

"I think if they're smart they'll take it to the police first," Brittan added and dabbed at a dollop of pizza sauce on the front of her T-shirt. "If they run a story that implicates the murderers, chances are high they'll fly the coop. Right now the criminals are still hanging around."

"Everybody except the city manager," Heather commented. "He wasn't in his office today at all." She bit her pizza, and her stomach thanked her.

"Where is he?" Lorna questioned.

"I have no idea. But I'm seriously wondering if he's the guy in the Bahamas. She picked up the digital recorder that held the conversation referencing someone transferring funds from the island.

"Could be," Brittan asserted.

"I just wonder what the mayor was threatening to reveal. Apparently, the city manager is up to his neck in something not quite kosher."

"Ya think?" Lorna quipped.

"I say we go ahead and take this information to the *Star*," Heather decided. "And why not leave it on Duke's desk? He wants to be in the investigative camp so bad he snuck into the city manager's office today. I don't know what he found, but chances are high he can put this information with what he found and come up with some killer leads. Then he can do what he wants with it from there."

"You really like this guy, don't you?" Brittan peered at Heather. Her dark-framed glasses highlighted the circles under her eyes, which attested to the hours of intense work she'd put in today. Despite that, Brittan's brown eyes were as piercing as if she were fresh.

"Yes, I do." Heather nodded. "I like him a lot. And I want to leave the information in his office this time, rather than in the managing editor's. Is that okay with you guys?" She looked from Brittan to Lorna.

"Works for me." Lorna shrugged. "I don't care who gets the information, as long as it's used to arrest the murderers."

"Ditto," Brittan said and sipped her bottled water.

"Do we go in tonight or keep snooping for clues?" Heather asked.

"I vote for tonight," Lorna said.

"I'm fine with what you guys want to do," Brittan added. "If they don't take what we give them and solve the case, we can pull together some more information and hand it off to them in a week or so."

Heather smiled and glanced toward the window. Evening shadows already clung to the skyscrapers surrounding the penthouse, but she knew from the previous case that they'd wait until after midnight to deliver their clues in a sealed envelope topped with a single red rose. Except this time, the delivery would be far more exhilarating.

❋ ❋ ❋

Duke sat at his home computer, scrolling through the city manager's Palm Pilot files. Getting past the security code had been a challenge, but The Mike circumvented the whole thing. Duke asked no questions, but he was beginning to suspect that Mike's past might involve more than just partying and women. Duke was just glad his friend had pulled it off.

At first Mike had helped Duke peruse the files. But when nothing exciting popped up, he turned his attention to the tube. He was sprawled in front of Duke's big screen with a Houston Astros' game in full swing while Duke read the files. Jake rested his head on Duke's leg. Occasionally the dog nipped at Duke's running shorts, and Duke responded with an ear scratch.

So far nothing unusual stood out in the files—except the fact that the manager was rather well-heeled for the title he held. His bank files revealed a six-figure balance and some hefty cash flow going on. Many deposits were labeled Hines, Drieb, and Associates, which made Duke wonder if he'd invested in a company that hit the big time.

"Ah, man! He's not out!" Mike yelled.

Jake jumped and barked.

Duke turned toward his friend, who had scattered popcorn all over the couch. The look blended well with last night's soda cans strewn on the coffee table. Mike stood in the middle of the room glaring at the TV. To say the guy took his baseball seriously was an understatement.

"That's it!" He raised his hands. "The game is over!"

Duke eyed the TV and tried to zone in on the controversy. Normally he'd have been butting heads with Mike and wailing about the injustice of insane refs. Mike usually wound up screaming something about all of them being on drugs while Duke diagnosed them as having dementia.

But this time Duke was pulled back into the files. He was sure he was close to something important. Problem was, he didn't know what.

The smell of Mike's popcorn finally got to him. *When all else fails, eat!* he thought.

He stood and strolled into the kitchen at the back of the town-house. This place wasn't huge by any means, but Duke liked it and there was enough room for a single guy and a few of his buds. Jake trailed him as he entered the kitchen and flipped on the light.

He peered down at the one-eyed dog The Mike said was a collie in the body of a bulldog. Other than his understandable hatred of cats, Jake never showed any mean tendencies—unless licking your face off was considered aggressive.

"Wanta share some popcorn with me?" Duke asked and pulled a bag from the box on the microwave.

The dog woofed, licked his chops, and whacked the cabinets with his wiggling rear end. The dog loved popcorn even more than Duke did.

Once the bag was being nuked, Duke meandered back to the computer and typed, "Drieb, Hines, and Associates" into his browser. Strangely, no applicable listings came up.

Interesting, Duke thought. *Either they don't have a website or they don't exist.*

The microwave bell dinged. Jake, who'd never made the break from the kitchen, barked. Duke stood and moved toward the smell. After dumping a third of the bag into Jake's bowl, he enjoyed a few kernels on his way back to the computer.

FOURTEEN

Midnight shadows cavorted along the Houston streets like phantoms of the night. The three friends rode in silence as Brittan steered the rented Honda toward the building that housed her parents' newspaper, one of three successful newspapers that belonged to the Shay publishing empire. The friends had laid out a plan identical to the other rose delivery.

The first step involved parking the car in an all-night, self-service lot two blocks away. As Brittan put the car into park, Heather lifted the single-stemmed red rose to her nose and inhaled the fragrance. The petals were as soft as velvet. Adrenaline coursed through her veins. Tonight couldn't be matched, not even by sneaking into City Hall or the mayor's home…or the last time they delivered a rose to the *Houston Star*. This time they were going to make a huge impact on Duke Fieldman's career. Heather smiled and thought toward Saturday night. Life couldn't be more perfect.

"Okay, we're here," Brittan said and clicked off the engine.

Heather exchanged silent glances with her friends, whose faces were swathed in splotches of light oozing from the street lamps.

"Let's get this over with," Lorna said. From the backseat, she tossed dark knit caps into Brittan and Heather's laps and then slipped hers on. All three wore black—slacks, socks, canvass shoes, and long-sleeved shirts.

Heather slipped on her hat and stuffed her ponytail under it. She retrieved three small flashlights from the glove box and handed one to each friend. Then she pulled out a couple pairs of dark purple latex gloves and extended them as well. Heather already wore her gloves and had since before she stuffed freshly printed pages into an envelope. As before, The Rose took no chances on leaving any tracks—or prints—behind.

Lorna opened her door and got out. Once she stood beside Heather, Brittan snapped her door closed and activated the vehicle's alarm system.

The three friends put their flashlights in their back pockets, headed out of the parking lot, and clung to the shadows near the buildings. The summer night was as heavy as the suspense pulsing through Heather's veins. Even though her head perspired beneath the knit cap and sweat trickled near her ear, Heather would rather be doing this than attending a debutante party any night. She wiped at the perspiration.

Once they neared the *Houston Star*, they waited until the outside security guard walked to the front of the building. They ducked down the side of the building and around the back. Before the last rose delivery, Brittan had accessed her family's computer files and done her research. There was a back doorway that required only a simple security code to enter the building. Furthermore, there were three hours every night between midnight and three when no inside employees were on duty. Those were the hours of The Rose.

Lorna and Heather followed Brittan, carefully keeping their heads down and altering their gaits as they scurried up the loading ramp and straight to the warehouse door. Brittan slipped on the latex gloves before pressing the code into the strip of numbers beside the doorway.

Leaning toward Lorna, Heather whispered, "Do you have your gloves on?"

Lorna raised her hands and wiggled her fingers ensconced in purple.

The doorknob rattled. Brittan peered over her shoulder. "Remember," she whispered, "give me time to deactivate the alarm system before we go in. Otherwise…"

She opened the door to a warehouse room that Heather recalled housed newsprint, some ancient Linotype machines, and other paraphernalia that the shadows cloaked.

Brittan turned on her flashlight and leaned into the room a few inches. She pointed the light on the wall to the right and took a remote out of her hip pocket. She pointed the device toward the wall where the guts for the company's alarm system and surveillance cameras hung. Once the task was complete, she smiled over her shoulder.

"Ownership has its privileges." She lifted the remote to her lips and blew over the top as if the device were one of the pistols she was so adept at using.

Heather swallowed a giggle.

"Let's roll!" Lorna pulled her flashlight out. Stepping into the room, she clicked on the beam and gazed around.

Heather followed. When the door closed, it blocked out the last traces of weak light. The darkness hung thick; the tension mounted.

"Not scared are you, girlfriend?" Brittan asked.

"No, just cautious," Lorna admitted.

"I'm having the time of my life," Heather whispered.

"I will be too—*after* we pull this off."

"Relax," Brittan said and strolled ahead of her friends. "There's nobody here right now."

"Except that outside security guard who does have access to the surveillance cameras and just might notice the things are off," Lorna warned like a grade school principal.

"Come on," Brittan said through a smile. "Let's take care of business and scram before he notices."

Brittan led the way through a doorway that opened into a hallway.

As they passed the executive editor's office, the cool air hit every bead of perspiration along Heather's neck and sent a delightful chill down her spine. "Feels good in here," she said.

"Yes," Lorna agreed.

"Duke's office is up here on the right," Brittan whispered. She soon paused in front of a door marked "Duke Fieldman, Lifestyle Managing Editor."

She tried the knob, but it didn't budge. "Just what I figured," Brittan said.

"Do you still have the master key?" Heather asked.

"Of course," Brittan asserted through a sly smile.

"The Brain thinks of everything," Lorna drawled.

"Don't forget it!" Brittan wiggled her brows. She opened Duke's door, and the three friends went inside.

The city lights oozed through the blinds and slashed the room with strips of gauzy glow. Entering Duke's office was like stepping into his mind. Heather pulled her flashlight out of her hip pocket and darted the beam across the room in search of anything that would better acquaint her with this new man in her life.

She gazed around the room, absorbing as much as possible in the brief time she had. The office held little decor. The wall behind Duke's desk spoke of hours of photographic artistry. The pictures ranged from black-and-whites of snow-covered trees to full-color explosions of farmers putting their souls into their land. Then, smack in the center of the whole spread, were several shots of a rope-like tornado carving a narrow ditch along dusty earth. Beneath the photos hung a framed article from the *Lubbock Times*.

Heather smiled.

"Wow," Lorna said from beside Heather. She directed her beam onto the photo. "That's what I call a weird tornado."

"Let me see," Brittan said from behind. Her light joined Heather and Lorna's, and the tornado appeared luminous and alive in the dark room. "Oh cool."

"Duke told me about this twister earlier today—or was it yesterday over lunch? He was just seventeen when he took the photos and wrote the article. It wound up being nationally distributed." Heather couldn't stop the hint of pride in her voice.

"I love it," Lorna breathed and touched the frame with her gloved finger.

"Yep, but what would you say if it were in your backyard?" Brittan asked.

"I'd die like a frog," Lorna admitted.

"It's die like a dog," Heather corrected through an indulgent smile.

"Whatever," Lorna said. "I think I'm as fascinated by tornadoes as I am afraid of them."

And I'm fascinated with the photographer, Heather confessed. She relived those two kisses yesterday. *He asked for the second one,* she remembered and wondered if he might kiss her on the lips Saturday night.

"Well, we probably need to take care of business and get out of here," Lorna declared.

"Right," Brittan agreed. "No sense asking for trouble."

Heather turned and flipped her beam toward Duke's desk. She placed the envelope in the center of his desk and then lifted the rose to her lips. After a light kiss to the fragrant petals, Heather laid the flower on top of the envelope.

The three friends turned as one and went through the door. Once Brittan locked Duke's door, Heather led the way down the hallway. The sound of firm footsteps echoing from an intersecting corridor stopped her in her tracks. Lorna bumped into her, and Heather braced herself to keep from sprawling to the floor.

"What is it?" Lorna whispered.

Heather whipped around, placed her finger to her lips, and pointed toward an open walkway that led into another section of the building. Her friends ducked through the doorway with her and plastered themselves against the wall. All three turned off their flashlights as one.

The footsteps grew closer. "I don't know what happened," a man's whisper was barely discernable. "The surveillance cameras have shut down. So has the alarm system. I'm looking through the building, but I don't see a sign of anyone."

He passed the walkway through which they'd ducked, and Heather could have touched him. In the shadows she detected a communication device held to his ear.

Probably a cell, Heather conjectured.

"Yes. Might be a fuse," he whispered. "But I think it would be good to send in some backup just in case. I don't see anything or anyone, but I feel like someone's been here. I'm going to keep my eyes peeled."

Lorna's cold fingers wrapped around Heather's. And Brittan could feel her two friends silently screaming in unison, "What are we going to do now?"

Beads of sweat dotted Heather's hairline, and she squeezed Lorna's fingers as tightly as Lorna squeezed hers.

The guard continued up the hallway. "Right," he whispered, his voice fading. "Just let me know when the backup gets here. We'll get the alarm and cameras going again."

Brittan appeared in front of Heather. She placed her hands on her friends' shoulders and whispered, "We've got to make a run for it now. Once backup gets here, we're history."

She didn't give Heather or Lorna time to agree. Brittan grabbed their hands and the friends quickly tiptoed up the hallway. Heather glanced behind every few steps but detected no sign of the guard. All was well until they slipped through the doorway that led into the warehouse. As hard as Heather tried to silently close the door, it produced a click that sounded like a bomb.

"Oh no!" Lorna wheezed.

"Run!" Brittan hissed.

The three raced past the piles of newsprint and stopped at the final doorway. Brittan nudged it open at the same time the door they'd just clicked sprang open. All three unceremoniously shoved their way through the exit.

"Come back here!" the guard screamed. "Stop or I'll shoot!"

Heather banged against the brick wall as all three stumbled their way across the driveway.

"Follow me!" Brittan said over her shoulder, and Heather didn't have to be told twice.

The building's back door banged open. "Stop now!" the security guard bellowed.

Like he thinks that's going to make us stop? Heather almost laughed as she rubbed her burning elbow and ran.

She ducked behind the building and blindly followed Brittan around the corner with Lorna close behind. A side door proved their destination. Brittan pulled out her keys, inserted one into the lock, and opened the door.

Heather stepped into a dark room that smelled of cleaning fluid and dust. Lorna moved beside her. Brittan snapped the door shut.

The sounds of three women snatching at every breath filled the room. Heather had never prayed so hard in her life.

Five seconds stretched into eternity. Then feet pounded past the doorway.

Heather grabbed Lorna's hand on one side and Brittan's on the other.

The footsteps faded. "We've got to get to the car before the backup gets here," Brittan whispered.

"This was a bad idea this time," Lorna snapped. "I didn't feel good about this from the start! Next time we've got to do something different. I don't care if I have to dress up like a man and deliver a box in broad daylight," she huffed. "Anything is better than this."

"Shhh!" Brittan hissed. "This is no time to get feisty." She cracked the door open, stuck her head out, and gazed up one way and then the next. "Let's go!" she whispered.

Heather nudged Lorna ahead and closed the door behind them. Brittan ran straight to the next skyscraper and scurried down beside it. Before they turned onto another street, Heather glanced over her shoulder. No sign of the guard or his backup. The three wove their way to the parking lot where the rental vehicle awaited them.

The deed was done. The rose had been delivered. Now they wait.

FIFTEEN

 "Have you heard about the break-in?" Tisha asked as Duke meandered down the hallway to his office.

When he'd seen Tisha, Duke planned to be civil but not encouraging. And he certainly had no intentions of stopping. He stopped anyway.

"What break-in?" he asked. "Where?"

"Here." Her eyes wide, Tisha pointed down. "Last night. Whoever it was, they turned off the surveillance cameras and alarm system and got in and out with no signs of breaking and entering. The security guard said he saw someone running out of the warehouse and then around the side of the building, but he didn't get a look at him."

Duke's eyes widened. That explained why he'd felt a sea of tension when he entered the paper this morning. Three months ago the surveillance cameras had been turned off, and that's when The Rose made a visit. But that time no one had seen her. He'd decided long ago that The Rose was a woman because no guy would leave a rose.

"Is he sure it was a man?" Duke asked.

"Well, I just assumed." Tisha shrugged.

"Hmmm," Duke mused. He noticed Tisha wore a sensible jacket

and slacks today. He'd compliment her for her choices, but he figured she'd take it the wrong way. Despite her professional look, she still smelled like a perfume skunk. Duke sniffed back a sneeze.

"Anyway, management is telling everyone to make sure to check to see if anything is missing."

"Missing?" he repeated and had a hunch this wasn't about what had been taken, but what had been left. Something red maybe. A thrill zipped through Duke. Last time Mr. Gude had received the rose. Duke wondered if he'd be the recipient again.

"Has Mr. Gude made it in yet?" he asked, walking around Tisha.

"Yes." Tisha said. "He's been here a while. You'll see a note in red taped to your window. Everybody's getting one. He's the one who sent them out."

Duke's boots scuffed the short-piled carpet as he hurried to his office. Sure enough, a message printed in red was taped to the office door. Eagerly he ripped it off and skimmed it. Apparently Mr. Gude thought this time the prowler had been there to take something. He was asking every employee to see if they had anything important missing.

Well, Duke reasoned, *if Gude had gotten a rose, he wouldn't have sent this announcement. So much for that!*

He unlocked his door and entered the office. Duke figured there wasn't anything in his corner of the universe anybody would want, but as he stepped into the room, something didn't feel right. He stood on the threshold and eyed his haven in search of who knew what. It was almost like someone was in the room watching him. His gaze darted from one corner to the other.

Everything was exactly where he'd left it—right down to the keepsake photos hanging on the wall. Finally Duke decided the power of suggestion was getting to him. A spirit of unease hung about the place, and Duke was as affected as everyone else. No one liked the thought of a thief in his space.

Then his attention rested on his desk. Right in plain view lay a single red rose on top of a manila envelope. Duke's eyes widened. He lunged for the desk, snatched up the rose, set it aside, and grabbed the envelope. With only a clasp holding the flap down, the envelope opened with ease. He dumped the contents onto his desk as someone strode down the hallway.

He looked up to see a flash of Tisha's blonde hair. Duke sprang toward the door, closed it, and turned the lock.

Back at the desk he settled into his chair and scanned each incriminating item. His heart thumping, Duke booted up his computer and inserted the memory stick. According to the typed notes from The Rose, the recorded conversation belonged to the person whose hand was on the door. On that hand was a ring that matched one the assistant city manager—Victor McIntosh—wore in the photo with the mayor's mistress, Eve Maloney.

Duke narrowed his eyes and scrutinized McIntosh. The guy looked familiar. Duke thought he might have seen him recently, but where?

Oh duh! he thought. *Probably at City Hall when I was prowling around.*

With that dilemma solved, Duke refocused on the clues. In the digital recording The Rose included, McIntosh mentioned a payment for murder from Drieb, Hines, and Associates.

"Drieb, Hines, and Associates is connected to the deposits the city manager made," Duke whispered. "Holy Toledo!"

He picked up the red rose. This time The Rose had chosen him.

Why me? he wondered, and then figured it must be a purposeful randomness to help her hide her identity.

"Whoever you are, I love you." He kissed the rosebud, now wilting for lack of water.

A plan cavorted through his mind. While these clues by no means fully solved the mayor's murder, they presented enough tips, leads, and direction for the police force to seriously get to the bottom of the case...and fast. Duke decided to first approach the managing editor and tell him he'd had a visit from The Rose. Then he would insist that the only way he'd relinquish the information was if he was assigned the story. Next he'd go to the police and trade the information for permission to be the only press on the scene when they made their arrests. He'd be a first-hand witness and take first-hand photos. The story would be a headliner. And hopefully his career would take a serious change for the better.

He twirled the rose in his hand and whispered, "Thank you, thank you, thank you," while fresh fascination with this elusive female began a slow burn in the center of his soul.

In the middle of his musings, a new thought barged into his mind: *Am I sure The Rose is a woman? Tisha thought the person was a man.*

Duke blinked and stared out the window. He placed the rosebud on top of the envelope, leaned back in his chair, crossed his arms, and squinted. Duke had no way of knowing, other than the simple assumption that a guy wouldn't leave a flower with the clues. Most "regular" men would just drop the information off and be done with it.

But what if it's not a regular guy? Duke grilled himself.

He closed his eyes and tilted back his head. Duke thought hard and then went with his gut. The Rose was a woman. Had to be. His instincts insisted she was a woman. The fact that roses were a feminine symbol made a huge statement about the gender of the sleuth and indicated she was the same person who'd left clues about the internet hacker who had shut down Houston banks a while back. Leaving the rose was like a criminal leaving his mark so he could get credit for his daring in the media. Serial killers tended to do this.

The Rose is a serial sleuth. Duke laughed outright. "A serial sleuth," he said aloud. "I like it." He picked up a pencil and rapped the side of his desk with a steady beat. *And it makes a great title for an article!*

* ✳ *

Heather sat straight up in bed and almost knocked Lucky into next week. An orange-striped guy who thought he ruled, the cat growled and glared at Heather before jumping from the bed.

Covering her quivering face with clammy hands, Heather whispered, "Oh no. Oh no. Oh no." She gripped the sheet, wadded it against her lips, and stared across the bedroom. Her black clothes from last night lay on a settee. The flashlight sat on her nightstand. The triumph of how the three friends successfully slipped back to the car undetected by the guard had lulled her into a pleasant sleep. But her sleep erupted into the conscious awareness that she'd made a dreadful error.

She'd been responsible for putting together the packet of information they passed on to Duke. In her eagerness to give him as much evidence as possible, she included the photo of Eve "the mistress" Maloney with Victor McIntosh. A copy of the letter from the mayor's mistress was there as well. And that was *after* she'd dragged Duke to Eve's house to help Lorna.

Heather slammed her palm against her forehead and flopped back. "Brittan will kill me if he pieces it together," she said. The Brain thought of everything and expected everybody else to as well.

Last night on the way home, she'd even cautioned Heather against mentioning that the two of them were friends. "If Duke finds you hang out with Leon Shay's daughter," Brittan said, "he just might suspect we're The Rose. Eventually somebody's going to figure out that whoever The Rose is, she's got keys and a remote to the alarm system. Who better to have it than the owner's daughter and her girlfriends?"

Heather recalled her coming out party and every subsequent conversation with Duke. She doubted he'd seen her and Brittan together at the party, and she had no recollection of mentioning Brittan to him. "Except that I asked him to church with me Sunday morning," she said and groaned. *I'll have to somehow change the plans and go with him,* she decided. If Heather continued to be careful, she could hide the link between her and Brittan. And maybe he wouldn't connect the dots on the Eve Maloney business.

At least Eve's address isn't on the copy of the letter, Heather encouraged herself. *And I didn't include a copy of the envelope. So the only way Duke will be able to put it together is if he somehow sees the mistress' address or has to go to her apartment for some reason.*

Heather's stomach relaxed. There was a fairly good chance that Duke just might miss the connection. She sat up, flopped over, punched her pillow, and buried her head against the soft folds.

A few minutes later Heather opened one eye and glared at the digital clock. Eight o'clock. After she, Lorna, and Brittan had left the *Star,* they'd gone back to the penthouse and hung out until the adrenaline rush wore off. Heather had then headed home and hit her bed, but she didn't sleep until three-thirty. She groaned and begged the sandman to zap her again—at least until eleven. Heather volunteered on Fridays at a Christian school where she taught karate to junior high girls. She didn't have to be there until one. But then she thought of Duke finding the rose and clues this morning. Her eyes snapped open again. Heather threw aside the covers and paced across the room while giddy excitement swept aside her worries.

"He's probably reading the information now," she mused and had never been so simultaneously thrilled and terrified.

※ ※ ※

Duke approached the managing editor's office and paused

outside the open door. Solomon Gude sat hunched in front of his computer, his fingers pecking at the keyboard like a hungry hen. His shirt was as rumpled as if he'd slept in it. A few wiry hairs sprang from his ruddy scalp. And, as always, his blunt nose and bulging eyes reminded Duke of one of his dad's stocky Hereford bulls.

Clearing his throat, Duke reached inside and knocked on the door.

Mr. Gude looked up and stared a greeting like a Pharaoh ready to drown the person who intruded his royal territory. "Fieldman!" he barked. "What is it?"

For a second or two Duke nearly got intimidated but decided not to go there. *I'm the one with the trump card this time,* he reminded himself.

"Mr. Gude," he said and entered Pharaoh's court without being summoned. "I've got some very important information." He turned and snapped the door closed.

Gude's eyebrows flexed. "You do, do you?" he mocked.

Duke stepped forward and dropped the wilting rose onto the center of his boss' desk. "I don't think the intruder last night came to take anything," he stated. Crossing his arms, Duke rocked back on his heels. "Whoever it was left information about the mayor's murder that the police can use. And I figure they'll want it bad enough to give the *Star* front row seats when they make their arrests."

Mr. Gude's widened gaze moved from the rose to Duke. "You?" he gasped. "Why you this time?"

Duke shrugged. "Who knows. Maybe she's choosing someone different every time, and I'm her guy this round."

The tyrant stood and snatched at the rose. Duke whisked it out of his grasp.

"Where's the information?" Gude flattened his palm against the desk. His jowls set, he silently dared Duke not to tell him.

Duke took the dare. "It's in my possession."

"Hand it over."

"No."

Gude's face flushed. "I said hand it over!" he bellowed.

"I'm taking it to the police myself." Duke lifted his chin. "But only if I'm given the right to cover the story."

"But you're the *lifestyle* manager," Gude shouted.

"Exactly," Duke replied and never blinked. "And I want to be on the investigative team." He decided he had nothing to lose at this point so he might as well stick it out. "If you remember, I've mentioned this in every review I've had."

A tinge of wary respect merged with the irritation in Gude's watery gray eyes. His cheeks paled a bit. "You better not be lying to me, Duke Fieldman!" he challenged.

"Not a chance." Duke's lower lip protruded and he shook his head.

Solomon narrowed his eyes.

"With your permission, I'd like to take the information to the police now," Duke requested.

"Do I have a choice?" Gude snapped.

"And I'm going to tell them I'll trade the information for first rights at the story."

"You're serious, aren't you?"

"As a heart attack." Duke uncrossed his arms and inserted his hand into his jeans' hip pocket. "Do we have a deal?"

Mr. Gude barely nodded. "Deal," he said.

"Good." Duke held up his hand. "But there's one other deal I want to make."

"What?"

"If this all flies like I think it will, I want to be moved to investigative reporting."

"There are no openings." Gude shrugged.

"Make one," Duke replied.

Solomon Gude's jowls went as scarlet as the rose. Duke's gut quivered despite his determination for it not to.

"You want me to create a spot for you?"

"If that's what it takes," Duke agreed.

"You've got a lot of audacity, Fieldman," Gude growled.

"And that's exactly what it takes, isn't it?" His throat went tight. He swallowed but refused to reveal one trace of angst.

Gude stared at Duke for several seconds and then released a dry laugh. "Yep," he said. "That's exactly what it takes." He squinted and observed Duke like he was looking at a new acquaintance. "What's next? Are you going to ask me to sign a contract in blood?"

"No." Duke shrugged and considered whether or not he should ask for a written agreement. "Tell you what," he said. "Let's keep this simple. I keep up my end of the deal. You keep yours." Even if Solomon Gude *did* have a short temper and liked to throw around his weight, he was fair. He was a man of his word. Duke had never caught him in a lie, and neither had anybody else as far as he knew. "It's that easy. All I ask is the right to cover the story. If you're happy with my work, I get a spot on the investigative team. If I blow it, I'll go back to Lifestyle." *Or back to the ranch,* he added to himself. "Oh, and one more thing. I want to do a series of follow-up articles on The Rose as well. I think Houston residents will go nuts when they find out she's behind this case—especially if I tell our readership I'm determined to find out who she is. That oughta help subscriptions."

"I think I just might have underestimated you, Fieldman," Gude grumbled.

"So we have a deal?" Duke stretched out his hand.

Gude observed Duke's hand and finally extended his. "You drive a hard bargain," he said with something that almost resembled a smile. "But I like your style—and your ideas."

"I guarantee you'll never regret this, Mr. Gude!" Duke declared.

He hurried from Pharaoh's court and back to his office. Duke gathered the information, slammed it into a duffle bag with his camera, and maneuvered down the hallway to the back exit.

SIXTEEN

"Wow! You look great!"

Heather stepped out of the castle and beamed up at Duke. "Thanks!" She closed the castle's door behind her, double-checked the locked knob, and smoothed her hand along the front of the beaded denim jacket she'd bought at a boutique. After her rude awakening yesterday morning, Heather had taken a brisk shower and decided she needed to do something to shake off her worries about Duke discovering The Rose's identity. So she'd gone shopping, gotten her nails done, and indulged in a new makeover. By the time she got to her karate class, Heather looked like she was ready for an evening out. "Her girls," as she dubbed them, had interrogated her about who the new man was. Heather had gently shrugged off their comments. Then she promptly pulled a calf muscle while sparring with one of her star pupils.

Heather had so wanted to be her best for this date, so she periodically massaged her calf all afternoon until she hoped she could walk without a limp. At least the ache had taken her mind off worrying about whether or not Duke had any suspicions about her being The Rose. Now, looking into Duke's admiring eyes, she sensed he wasn't even close to thinking about the mysterious informant.

Duke took her hand. A daring glint in his eye, he leaned closer and brushed his lips against her cheek.

Heather's lids slid shut, and she drank in the warmth that even the summer heat couldn't touch. She opened her eyes and looked at Duke.

His lips curving into an audacious smile, Duke said, "I say we start this date off right."

"By all means," Heather agreed, "except you left this side out." She pointed to the other cheek and faked a flirtatious pout.

"Well, we don't want that side to feel lonely, do we?" Duke replied, his voice thick with mirth. He leaned in for another kiss that lingered and rocked the earth while his fingers slipped between hers for a squeeze.

When Duke pulled away, a question hung between them. Heather debated whether to give him the cue to go ahead with a *real* kiss. An eager voice insisted she live daringly, but then she recalled something her mother once told her: *Remember, Heather, no matter what anybody says, a man still enjoys a good chase. Don't be too eager.* This advice had been mingled in with references to making sure the guy had a fortune too.

Heather reminded herself that she was the one who initiated their first lunch meeting and decided to give Duke something to anticipate. She glanced down and inched back.

"You look great yourself!" she said, admiring his sports coat and new-looking Dockers.

Duke tugged on the front of his jacket. "My mom would be proud," he said with a smirk before checking his watch. Sobering, he tugged her hand and they strolled toward the passenger side of his truck.

"Listen, Heather," he hedged as they paused between her vehicle and his.

She looked into his troubled face. "Yes?" she prompted.

"I've got a huge favor to ask. And I've got to tell you before I ask that this isn't my usual MO. Something has come up with my job."

"Oh?"

"Yes." He shook his head. "I'm expecting a phone call, probably around eight." He looked at his watch again.

Heather followed suit, and her simple-but-elegant Rolex said exactly six o'clock.

"And I might have to cut our date short. Once I get the call, I'll probably have to scram." He snapped his fingers. "So I was thinking... My church has a cafe of sorts where singles can hang out or even take dates. Instead of going to a movie and dinner, would you mind going there?" His brown eyes were full of silent pleas for her understanding. "It would give you a great opportunity to meet my friend The Mike," he added.

"Sounds great," Heather said.

A veil of relief eased away the lines of worry. "Great. And one more thing." He glanced toward her Porsche. "Would you mind..."

"Of course not!" Heather said and swallowed a heady giggle. *This must have something to do with the mayor's murder.*

"I'll take my car. I don't mind at all."

"Are you sure?" Duke rested his hand on her shoulder.

"Definitely."

"I feel like a royal jerk, but I just can't get around this."

"You're anything but a jerk," Heather said through an approving grin.

"Well, for what it's worth, this is very important," he said. "Right now it's top secret, but you probably wouldn't believe me if I told you."

"You never know," she said in a singsong voice. "Maybe you should try and see."

Duke inserted his hands into his pants pockets and gazed toward the distant woods.

Certain he was going to confide in her, Heather held her breath and waited.

"Once we get to the cafe, you need to tell me about your castle," he said.

"The castle?" Heather repeated, dull disappointment dashing aside expectation.

"Yep." Duke lowered a delicious smile at her. "Did your parents have it built or was it already here? If they had it built, what possessed them? If it was already here, who owned it before you bought it and what possessed them to build it?" He motioned toward the sprawling home.

"Well sure. I'll explain," Heather replied and tried to sound at least halfway interested. Talking about the castle was beyond anticlimactic in the face of a breaking story about the mayor's murder.

She lowered her head, dug her keys out of her bag, and pressed the button to unlock the car. Duke opened the door for her, and Heather settled into the smell of new leather. When she reached for her seat belt, Duke placed his arm along the edge of her door and hovered over her. Heather gazed up into his face.

"You really are unbelievable!" he declared.

"Hold that thought," she teased.

"No, seriously. A lot of women would not be a happy camper with a last-minute change like this." His gaze settled on her lips, and Heather swallowed. "Since I'm probably going to have to leave early, we won't get to end our date in the traditional way, will we?" His gaze traveled to hers. His eyes said, *I want to kiss you now.*

"And what's the traditional way?" Heather rasped, wondering if she sounded as inane to him as she did to herself.

"Maybe I should just show you," he suggested.

"Maybe," she agreed.

He lowered his head and his lips pressed against hers. Kissing Duke Fieldman was like skydiving...exhilarating and cool and dangerous. He tasted of mint and heaven and smelled of something subtle and spicy. Heather reveled in the rush of dizzy adrenaline while trying to catch her breath. She suspected she had met a man she could safely give her heart to. Heather hadn't felt this way since Tyler…but then she'd lost Tyler. And that was the scary part.

When Duke abruptly broke away, she crashed to earth without a parachute. Suddenly Heather realized she was clutching his jacket's lapel. She released the coat.

Duke remained only centimeters away. Silently he peered into Heather's eyes and waited. Mesmerized by his nearness, Heather held his stirring gaze and could think of nothing more than repeating the kiss.

"Nice," he finally said and straightened.

Heather blinked. *Nice? That's all? Just nice?* "Nice" was in the same category as "okay," which was only one rung above "blah." She wondered if the kiss had meant way more to her than it had to him. Maybe she'd imagined his eager response and the glowing aftermath in his eyes.

Duke turned, walked to his truck, got in, and started the engine. Heather closed her door, cranked her Porsche, and gripped the gearshift until her fingers ached.

Mmmm, Duke thought as he drove from the castle's driveway and relished the kiss. *Now that's what I call a liplock supreme!*

"Here's to kissing!" he mumbled and checked out her reflection in his truck's side-view mirror. The castle loomed behind her, a blaring testimony of her family's wealth. He'd learned before interviewing her that the family *was* Shelby Oil. They probably could shred thousand dollar bills and use it for mulch. *But you'd never know that by the way Heather acts,* he noted. *Not only is she sweet, she tastes sweet.* He wiped his lips and came away with a blur of pink lip gloss. Duke smiled and rubbed his fingers together until the stuff went away. He was glad now that he hadn't forgotten the date. And Duke would never admit to her that he nearly had.

The meeting with Mr. Gude yesterday had catapulted Duke into an immediate conference with Police Chief Rob Lightly. He had grudgingly agreed to Duke's terms before warning him that the case was dangerous. Duke assured the chief that he fully understood the fallout of being on the scene during an arrest. Sometimes those about to be arrested didn't go without a fight. Nevertheless he was ready to take that chance. And the second chance was happening tonight at eight, according to his four o'clock phone call. The city manager was arriving home from the Bahamas, and the police had enough evidence from his "loyal conspirators" to arrest him at the airport.

They'd arrested Victor McIntosh and Eve Maloney at two o'clock. The two had conveniently been together at Victor's home. Duke was there and snapped photos for the paper. Soon after taking them into custody, the pair began telling all and bargaining for plea agreements. Duke was in the throes of his front-page article at five when by some miracle he remembered his date with Heather.

The article could wait until after the eight o'clock arrest. It was going to be a headliner in Sunday's paper. The story on The Rose would be the second lead. So far both features were the best writing he'd ever done.

Duke picked up the limp rosebud from his seat and smelled it. He'd accidentally left the flower in his truck yesterday. Somehow he couldn't throw it away. By the time Duke drove into the parking lot of Christ Community Church, north of Houston, his mind was wholly focused on the article about The Rose. His tag line was already fixed, "Serial sleuth strikes again. Who is The Rose?"

Whoever she is, he decided as he pulled the truck into a parking place, *she's got what I want in a woman.* Duke needed a wife who shared his interest in criminal investigation—or at least enjoyed a good mystery novel and understood his passion. He also wanted her to have enough spunk to hunt down a criminal, whether she ever actually did or not. He put his truck into park, eyed the rose again, and turned off the engine. Two spots over, Heather was getting out of her Porsche. She was pretty enough, that was for sure. And that kiss had given him something to think about. But he wasn't sure she had the initiative and gumption he was looking for.

Duke touched the withering rosebud and ached to know the female behind it. Clever. Resourceful. Brilliant.

The Rose had once again penetrated the newspaper offices by turning off the alarm system and the surveillance cameras, all without signs of breaking and entering. According to the digital files, the cameras had been deactivated a little past midnight. Whoever she was, she knew how to operate the company security system and was very observant. She'd struck during the only three hours that the newspaper office was vacant. She probably also had access to a key and the remote to deactivate their security devices. Duke believed she might be closer than anyone realized.

Maybe she's an employee at the Star, Duke mused. *Maybe I see her every day. But why would an employee hide behind a rose?* he countered. *Whoever she is…is she single and in my age range?*

He glanced across the parking lot. Heather was walking toward his truck, the wind lifting her hair from her shoulders. Duke hadn't noticed the crook in her nose until after he kissed her, but he saw it now and probably would every time he looked at her. The imperfection added extra character appeal. Duke wondered how the crook happened—whether from birth or an injury of some sort.

Heather is real, he firmly told himself. *The Rose is just a fantasy right now. I might find her, and then again, I might not. There are no guarantees. If I do find her, she may already be married…or old enough to be my mother.* Duke groaned. No sense getting carried away with a fantasy woman. While he was whipping Houston into a frenzy over the "serial sleuth" and hopefully driving newspaper sales higher, Duke needed to love the one he was with. Or at least give love a chance.

SEVENTEEN

Her left leg aching, Heather approached Duke's truck and wondered why he hadn't gotten out. He'd been sitting there since she drove up. An awkward uncertainty slowed her pace. She bent and massaged the pain away as she debated whether to approach his truck or just wait behind the Ford next to his vehicle. She straightened and slowed when she got to the Ford as fresh worries about the meaning of that "nice" kiss assaulted her again.

Maybe Duke wasn't as hooked as she'd hoped. She was the one who initiated their first meeting. And, she'd waited for him outside City Hall, which resulted in their second lunch date. Even though he had asked her to lunch, she'd made herself very available. *What if he thinks I'm throwing myself at him, and he's just coming along for the ride?*

She stopped, crossed her arms, and examined the black asphalt, oozing an evening heat that testified to the intensity of a Texas August. Using every scrap of logic she could scrape together, Heather tried to talk herself down from her growing fascination with Duke Fieldman. She wasn't in love yet by any means, but Heather knew beyond doubt that she could go there with this guy. But she wasn't in the mood to have her heart broken this year...or next. The loss of one love in a lifetime was enough.

Eyeing the massive, pillared church, Heather resisted the urge to run into the sanctuary, fall at the altar, and beg God to show her exactly what to do.

Duke's door opened. Heather looked up. His face thoughtful, he slid out of the vehicle, slammed the door, and pressed the remote lock before noticing Heather. His features relaxed, and his easy smile reminded her why she liked him so much.

"Did I mention you look great?" He stepped to her side, took her hand, and gazed down at her like a man who'd been kissed into a new realm of interest.

Soft laughter gurgled out of Heather, and her worries tottered off. Maybe the verdict of "nice" meant way more to him than it did to her.

"Because if I didn't," he continued and leaned closer, "I think it's high time, don't you?"

"I don't think you mentioned it," she said through a huge smile and tightened her grip on his hand.

"I think you'd look good if you dyed your hair green and blackened your teeth!" he declared.

She tried to stop the cackle but couldn't. Her mother had warned her from childhood that her laugh was too loud, too big, and just plain too much. She'd gotten it honestly via Grandpa Morris. And like him, Heather never was able to harness the honker, especially not with a comment like that one. *Oh well, Duke doesn't seem to mind,* she noted with glee.

A convertible Mustang zoomed across the empty side of the parking lot and screeched to a stop. Music blared from the car's stereo, and Heather recognized the tune as "Jesus Freak," the decade-old hit from dc Talk. The music stopped and an attractive Latin guy got out.

He called, "Yo, Duke!" with a big wave.

"Oh no. It's The Mike," Duke said. "Brace yourself."

"I already have," Heather said through a chuckle.

Mike wore floppy basketball shorts, a tank top, and a pair of athletic shoes. He trotted toward them, pointed at Heather, and said, "Hey! I recognize you!" Mike stopped. "You're that gal Duke had about a hundred pictures of all over his desk."

"Do you always have to tell everything you know?" Duke asked, punching his friend in the arm before shooting a glance at Heather that bordered on embarrassment.

Heather bit her bottom lip and decided she'd take Duke's verdict of "nice" any day.

"Heather, meet Mike Mendez," Duke drawled. "If you talk to The Mike for an hour, he'll tell you everything he's ever known. And that's about all it will take too," he added.

Mike focused on Heather. "Listen, The Duke has his opinions, and they all stink. Just remember one thing about me. If he doesn't treat you right, you call me, okay?" He pressed his fingers against his chest. "I keep him in line." He dragged out the last word and wagged his head from side to side.

"Okay, I will," Heather said.

"And if you get ready for a real man, you call me then too." He cocked his eyebrows and added a flirtatious wink. "I know how to treat a lady."

Heather covered her lips with her fingertips and glanced toward Duke.

Her date leaned close and loudly whispered, "Just ignore him. He'll go away. He always does."

Mike tilted his face toward the cloudless sky, lifted his hands toward the heavens, and said, "And would somebody please tell me why I keep taking this treatment?"

"Because you love me, man," Duke said and gripped his friend's shoulder.

"Get your hands off me!" Mike shoved at Duke's hand and moved to Heather's other side. "I've got important business here," he said as the three walked toward a metal building adjacent to the church. "Listen, Heather, tell me about this castle you live in."

"Hey, I'm supposed to be asking that!" Duke challenged.

"Too late!" Mike shot back.

Heather laughed out loud. "You two are nuts! You remind me a little of me and my two friends, except I think maybe you're crazier."

"Nobody's crazier than him," Mike and Duke said in unison while pointing at the other.

They arrived at the building's doorway. A cute, twenty-something gal carrying a tray piled with sandwiches neared from the side, and Mike stepped forward to open the door.

"Allow me, m'dear," he said.

When she offered a shy smile, Mike turned toward his friend, wiggled his eyebrows, followed her inside, and closed the door on Heather and Duke.

"Well!" Duke said. "So much for us, right?"

Heather giggled. "He's sweet," she said.

"Sweet!" Duke's forehead creased. "The Mike is one of my best friends. I hang with him all the time. I've heard him called a lot of things, but never sweet."

He opened the door. Heather took one step and her calf muscle knotted. Sharp pain zipped up her leg. She stopped and hissed as she sucked in her breath.

"What's the matter?" Duke asked.

Heather bent to knead the muscle. "I pulled a muscle today in PE," she said.

"PE?"

"Um, yes. I volunteer at a Christian school on Fridays," she explained and debated whether or not to mention the karate. Her muscle easing, she straightened and decided to wait. No sense scaring the guy off. "I teach a PE class to junior high girls," she explained. "I guess I got a little too rambunctious today."

"Are you going to be okay? We can go ahead and sit down." He motioned into the building that was emitting a pleasing blast of cool air.

"I'm fine," Heather said and walked forward. "Don't worry about it. I'm good."

"Well, okay," Duke said and placed a supportive hand along her back. "But let me know if standing gets to be too much."

Heather smiled up at him and enjoyed the protective concern in his eyes. Yes, for now it was best for him not to know she could probably beat him to a pulp before he could blink. Men enjoyed feeling needed, and Heather enjoyed being pampered. Once their relationship had progressed, she'd tell him. But for now ignorance was his bliss and her blessing.

She stepped into a large, well-lit building crowded with young adults who ranged in age from about twenty to thirty-five. Contemporary Christian music floated through the room at a comfortable volume level. Heather realized this was actually a multipurpose building that could be converted for numerous uses. Basketball nets hung at each end of the room. On the far half a small skirmish for the ball was underway. The section closest to the door held round tables and a couple of pool tables where several guys were engaged in a tense match. The smell of cheese dip and sandwiches hung in the air, and a few people already had plates of food.

"This is cool," Heather commented.

"Yep. Not exactly what I wanted for our first official date, but maybe we'll enjoy ourselves. There's supposed to be a mini concert at seven featuring Mike's band." He pointed at a portable platform in the corner. "There'll be plenty of free food too." He nodded toward the young woman with the sandwiches walking toward the kitchen with Mike close behind. "Thought you might enjoy it and like getting to know a few of my friends."

"Sure," Heather said. *I want to know everything I can find out about you, Duke Fieldman.*

He tugged her through the crowd toward a long table that held several open coolers. "Let's get something to drink first. Will it be water as usual?" he asked and pulled a bottle out of the ice.

"How'd you know?"

"All you ever drink, right?" he queried.

"How'd you guess?"

"I'm a very observant person," he said. "A health nut, are we?" he gently mocked. "No red meat or nasty carbonated beverages." He pulled a can of RC Cola from the ice and tilted it back and forth.

"Well, yes," Heather replied, "but don't ever get between me and chocolate. That's my vice."

"Maybe I can be your next vice," Duke commented, and his eyes slowly widened with an "I can't believe I just said that" horror.

For a split second Heather teetered between giving into the hot embarrassment that flushed her face or offering a flippant come-back. She went for flippant. "You'd have to smear chocolate in your hair before I would even consider putting you on my list."

"That can be arranged!" Duke exclaimed and roughed up his hair.

Heather gave into embarrassment and looked down. She gripped her water bottle's cap so tightly the grooves ate into her fingers.

"So what about your castle anyway?" Duke asked and popped the top on his soda.

She cut a glance at him and wondered if he felt like the room was spinning too. His eyes danced with a devilry that increased the spin. Duke was very convincing with his lines, and Heather figured that's what made him such a good writer. She just hoped he meant everything he was saying.

"My mom and I went to Scotland about ten years ago," Heather explained as she twisted the lid off her water. "She went into a serious castle mode after that and told Dad she wanted one. So, he had one built for her." Heather downed a swallow of the cold liquid and then wiped at the few droplets on the front of her jacket.

"Okaaaaay," Duke said, "so that's the whole story?"

"Yep." She nodded. "What were you expecting?"

"I don't know." Duke shrugged. "Dragons maybe."

"Dragons?" Heather laughed again and couldn't remember laughing so much with a guy—not even Tyler. "How did you figure that?"

"Well, it is a castle. I was expecting something a little more exciting," he huffed.

"That's about as exciting as it gets around our house," she said. "We don't even have a moat."

"Now that's a huge disappointment." Duke flattened his hand against his chest and gazed toward the rafters.

Heather's cell phone belched out *Bonanza* from the folds of her handbag. She considered not taking the call, but curiosity won out.

"Do you mind?" she asked.

"No, go ahead," Duke said and nudged her toward an empty table.

Heather set her bag on the table and noticed a few envious glances from the females in a neighboring klatch. Fleetingly she wondered if Duke had dated any of the women here...and hoped he hadn't. She checked the phone's screen display. Her mother's name appeared. Heather thought again about not taking the call, but didn't want to be that disrespectful. She flipped open the phone.

"Hello, dear," her mother crooned over the line.

"Hi, Mom," Heather replied and weakly smiled at Duke.

"I noticed you're not home, and I just wanted to remind you of our meeting at seven."

"What meeting?" Heather asked, straining for recollection.

"The Country Club Committee, remember?"

"No, I don't," Heather said and checked her watch. The meeting was only thirty minutes away. Heather would have to leave in ten to get home in time.

"We're planning next year's social calendar. You promised you'd be here. Do you remember now? It's here at our place. Lorna and Brittan are supposed to be here too."

Heather sighed and rubbed her forehead as an inkling of a conversation trickled through her mind. She did recall resigning herself once again to the annual ordeal a couple of weeks ago. Only the elite were allowed to join this country club, and the wives and daughters of some of the oldest money in the state met once a year to plan what they were going to sit around and do for the next year. Heather had been part of this event since she was fifteen. When she first sat on the council board it had been a point of mother-daughter bonding. And Heather did love her mother, even though she could be difficult.

Heather looked up at Duke. Hands in his front pockets, he gazed around the room. She thought about bringing him with her but decided that would only inflame her mom and make for a dreadful evening for everyone. Besides, Brittan was going to be there, and she didn't want Duke finding out she was friends with the family who owned the *Houston Star*.

Her brain went into fast forward. Duke was already cutting their evening short. The actual planning didn't start until eight, after the ladies had some social time and stuffed themselves on hors d'oeuvres. If Heather left in an hour, she could get home in time to make the actual meeting.

"Heather?" her mother questioned. "Did I lose you?"

"No, I'm here," she answered. "Just thinking."

"Where are you anyway?" Marilyn asked. "I hear music."

Heather hesitated and then decided to just tell her mother the absolute truth. "I'm out with Duke," she stated. "At his church."

Silence. "Well," Marilyn finally snapped. "I guess that means I'm stood up."

"No. I do remember promising. I just forgot. I'll be there by eight when the planning starts," she said and caught Duke's gaze.

"I'd prefer seven, as you promised," Marilyn insisted.

"I know," Heather sighed, "but I've double booked myself. The best I can do is eight."

"Heather, if you know what's good for you, you'll drop him!" Marilyn declared. "For all you know, he's probably been married twice and has kids by both women and a girlfriend too."

"Mother!"

"Besides that, haven't you listened to any of my warnings? When you're as rich as we are, the have-nots come after you for your money—not for you. Look at your Uncle Ray! That penniless floozy took him for a ride. He never knew what hit him! And didn't you learn your lesson with Tyler Madison? You need to be with your own kind!"

Heather's face went cold, and she stared across the room as her mother continued her lecture. Four years ago she'd been deeply in love with Tyler, and she thought he loved her too. She'd been all of nineteen, and they planned to marry once they finished college. Tyler had been about to transfer to Princeton with Heather and had already been accepted.

One day Heather overheard his mother talking at a family baby shower about how much money Heather's family had and how Tyler was so excited to have gotten a girl so rich. Even though Tyler's family were the successful owners of three restaurants, they held nowhere near the Winslow's resources.

Heather had immediately confronted Tyler. He denied the whole thing and swore he loved her, money or no. Heather was ready to believe him, but her mother was entirely too convincing. Even though Heather and Tyler split up and he didn't transfer from the University of Texas to Princeton, he continued writing her. Eventually Heather fully understood that his mother had spoken *her* thoughts only and that Tyler truly loved her.

Then he'd been killed in a convenience store robbery. Heather had gotten the call from his mother. An innocent bystander, Tyler had been in the wrong place at the wrong time. Even now Heather wondered if she might be partly to blame. If they hadn't broken up, Tyler would have been at Princeton, and maybe…just maybe…the shooting would never have happened.

"Heather! Heather!" Marilyn's sharp voice pierced her memories. "Are you still there?"

"Yes," Heather choked out. "I'll see you at eight." She flipped the phone shut and then blinked at the device. "Whoops. I just hung up on my mom," she said with a stiff grin.

"Is everything okay?" Duke asked. "You look a little pale."

"Uh, yeah," Heather said. "Just my mom. I promised her I'd be at a meeting. It's at seven."

Duke looked at his watch and lifted his brows.

"I told her I'd be there by eight. That means I need to leave here by about twenty till, so it looks like I'm cutting the date shorter than you were planning to."

"Ah, well." Duke rubbed his chin. "That just means we'll have to do this again really soon."

Her phone's ringing again cut off her reply. She scowled at the screen. This time Lorna's name appeared. Heather gazed a silent apology toward Duke.

"I'll allow one more than the police. You can have *two* calls," he teased.

"Thanks," Heather said and took the call.

"Are you with Duke yet?" Lorna asked.

"Yes," Heather answered and kept her face impassive.

"Found out anything about you know what?"

Heather fiercely focused on her pointed-toed pumps. "No."

"Is he listening?" Lorna pressed.

"Yes."

"Okay. Just let us know as soon as you hear anything."

"I will, but, um, I don't think…" She trailed off and then said, "Did you remember the meeting tonight?"

"Yes. I'm heading to your place now. Wait! Are you going to make it?"

"Yes. I'll see you at eight." Heather casually glanced across the crowd.

"Good. And find out anything you can. Brittan and I are, like, dying to hear."

"I feel your pain, believe me," Heather said and forced herself not to look at Duke. This time she remembered to say goodbye before hanging up. At least Lorna's call had given Heather a breather after the memories of Tyler.

"Sorry, Duke," she said and pressed the silent button on her phone. "See! I'm putting the ringer on silent."

"No problem. Like I said, it looks like this date is just going to have to be repeated. I'm still going to church with you in the morning, right?"

"Um…" Heather looked around at the room full of people and knew this was her opportunity to shift their church attendance to his. Mike appeared near the kitchen holding a plate full of food. The short, cute woman he'd followed in was at his side, and Heather wondered if they were a steady couple.

"I was actually wondering what you thought about me just coming here with you in the morning?" she asked.

Duke shrugged. "Sure. Whatever. That works for me."

"Okay, I'll count on it," she said and knew Brittan would be proud.

"Why don't we do lunch together and then drive down to the coast?" He shrugged. "You know, spend the day there just hanging out."

Heather nodded. "Sounds good." She recalled a sunset stroll on the beach with Tyler. Even though only four years had lapsed, Heather looked back at the person she'd been then and who she'd grown to be. She and Tyler had been painfully young, so she'd listened to her mom.

Her thoughts moved to Duke. Heather had to admit that it did make sense that a man might want to marry her for her money. She had watched plenty of young women chase older, wealthy men for those reasons.

Is Duke's interest colored by that motive? she wondered and wished the doubt had never entered her mind.

Heather dropped her cell phone into her purse and smiled into Duke's eyes. She'd known him nearly a week. Exactly how did a woman figure out something like that in such a short time?

Her mother's solution was simple—marry someone else with a lot of money. But wasn't that limiting God? What if the person He wanted her to marry didn't have a lot of money?

"Ready to eat something?" Duke asked and pointed toward the kitchen.

Heather nodded. "Sure." *Maybe tomorrow's time at the beach will answer my questions...and more.*

EIGHTEEN

The next morning Heather sipped her hot green tea while cruising the internet for the latest news. She didn't always take the time to read the paper during the week, so her Sunday routine included skimming through the headlines on a few local and national news sources to keep up with current events.

This morning Heather went straight to the *Houston Star* website and sneaked in a sip of hot liquid as the page loaded. Once the major headline was visible, she sputtered and splashed tea all over her computer monitor. "Arrests made in murder of Houston mayor," the headline read. And the byline underneath was Duke Fieldman.

"Go Duke!" Heather breathed and then hacked over a droplet of tea that slipped down the wrong way. Heather grabbed a tissue from the nearby box, mopped at the screen, and then dabbed her lips. She slipped the tissue into the pocket of her satin robe. Skimming the excerpt, Heather knew she'd have to read the paper to get the full article. Nevertheless, she pieced together the bits the website offered with the information she already had.

The city manager and his assistant had been involved in smuggling cocaine and laundering the money through a false corporation they'd set up called Drieb, Hines, and Associates. When Monroe

Longheed found out about their little operation, he threatened to turn them in unless they supported his political plans. The crooks sent in Eve Maloney, who seduced the mayor into being at the right place for an arranged assassination by a clever gunman who was able to slip out of the building without being seen. The only person still at large was the person who pulled the trigger.

"Shirley," Heather whispered and wondered if that was the first name of a woman or the last name of a man. She crossed her legs and leaned closer to the screen. Another article by Duke grabbed her attention: "Serial sleuth. Who is The Rose?"

She smiled as she read the excerpt. Duke made The Rose sound like the Wonder Woman of crime stoppers. The piece ended with a message for The Rose: "Whoever you are, this reporter is committed to uncovering your true identity."

Heather laughed and clapped. This was getting more fun by the case. And as much as she wanted to tell Duke that she and her friends were The Rose, Heather enjoyed the cat and mouse game even more. She couldn't wait until this afternoon with Duke. Now that the mayor's death case had broken, she hoped he would freely talk about his experience.

She grabbed her cell phone and punched in Brittan's speed dial number. When her friend groggily answered, she chirped, "Wake up and smell the *Houston Star*, girlfriend."

"Don't you mean smell the coffee?" Brittan complained. "You're starting to sound like Lorna."

Snickering, Heather said, "No. I mean read your paper. The mayor's murder has been blown wide open."

"No way," Brittan said, her voice going brighter.

"Way!" Heather replied. "There's an article by Duke. It's the lead story. He took our clues to the police, and they've already nabbed the whole crew—everybody except the gunman, that is."

"Wait until Lorna hears this," Brittan said. "She's going to just *die!*"

"She'll really die when she reads the other article by Duke. It's titled, 'Serial sleuth. Who is The Rose?' And his final line is actually a message to us: 'Whoever you are, this reporter is committed to uncovering your true identity.'"

"I love it!" Brittan exclaimed. "Whatever you do, Heather, you can't let him know it's us! That would ruin everything!"

"Don't worry," Heather said. "I'm being very careful." She crossed her fingers and hoped he never connected Lorna's Steam Monster blowout with Eve Maloney.

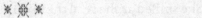

The Gulf of Mexico was in good spirits today, and Duke was glad. Nothing like an ocean in a bad mood to ruin a peaceful stroll. Duke had driven Heather to a stretch of beach he'd found wasn't too densely populated. Not by people anyway. The seagulls were another story. A few sunbathers lazed in their chairs while the gulls bombed the gray-blue water and squawked for someone to throw them a crumb or two.

Duke held his shoes in one hand and Heather's hand in the other. He nudged her to the edge of the water where cold wavelets lapped at their feet. Church had been good. They'd grabbed a bite of lunch at a deli and then on the drive down talked some and listened to the radio. The day had been as comforting and refreshing as the wonderful scent of ocean wafting into forever.

He hadn't said anything about the headlines because he didn't want to sound like he was bragging. But Duke was disappointed Heather hadn't brought the stories up. Even though she'd had a paper the other day when they went to lunch, he wondered if she bothered to read the news very often.

"I saw your article this morning," she said. "Congratulations."

"You must be reading my mind." Duke stopped and faced her.

She wore sunglasses so he couldn't see just how interested she really was. "I was just wondering if you'd noticed it."

"I guess I failed to tell you," Heather said. "Mind reading is my number one hobby."

Duke laughed. He liked the way the wind tossed her hair here and there, and he had to stop himself from touching it. After laying that kiss on her last night, he didn't want to crowd her. But then she hadn't acted like she minded a little crowding.

"Don't read too deep," Duke shot back and tapped his temple. "You might get lost."

Heather snickered.

He liked her laugh. A lot.

"Oh, I don't think so." She crossed her arms. "The article on the mayor's death was excellent."

"Thanks." Duke gazed past her and didn't mention that he agreed. He'd put everything he had into that piece, and his gut still told him it was his best writing yet. Mr. Gude hadn't been disappointed either. Not in the least. He'd asked Duke if he'd be willing to stay in Lifestyle until he got a replacement. Duke agreed as long as the replacement came within a couple of weeks.

"Actually, I found out the police were already on the tail of the city manager and his assistant. They'd been investigating their corporation before the murder even." Duke dug his toes against the sand and recalled the meeting with the police chief, who'd been as impressed as Duke with The Rose's envelope contents.

"The thing that cooked their livers was a digital recording of Victor McIntosh talking to the hired gunman—or gunwoman. They still don't have that one pegged."

"Yes, I noticed that's what the article said." Heather gazed toward the horizon, and Duke suspected her interest might be waning. "That Rose business is different, isn't it?" she asked, her voice growing a bit more intense—but not as much as Duke hoped.

He studied Heather's profile. He'd wanted a little more enthusiasm than this.

"So..." she darted him a sideways glance, "does any of this mean you get to leave Lifestyle?"

"Yes, actually. I bargained with my boss before I took the info to the police. He agreed to move me to investigative reporting if I did a good job."

She nodded and smiled a bit. "Good."

What Duke didn't tell her was that after turning in the articles at midnight, he'd lain awake until two eaten up by curiosity. He'd even dreamed The Rose was close enough to touch...that she was looking for a man exactly like him. Duke jolted awake at seven. The dream had been so real he felt as if she were in the room watching him. But the only watching eyes had been Jake's, who'd also put his cold nose in Duke's hand and woofed for his breakfast.

"Do you have any idea who The Rose might be?" Heather asked.

"Honestly, right now, none," Duke admitted. "But I'm going to find out or go crazy trying." He pulled the sunglasses from the top of his head and slid them on. No telling what his eyes might say, and he didn't want Heather or anyone else to suspect the allure The Rose held for him.

His rational side recognized the futility of being slowly mesmerized by an unseen woman who might be too young or too old or even married. Duke's imaginative side loved the whole idea of a delightful mystery woman...just like he'd loved taking shots of that unique tornado those many years ago. The Rose was the unusual... the unseen...yet a growing presence in his psyche.

"There's no evidence of her entering the newspaper office," he said, "and that makes me think she's got a key. She also somehow turned off the alarm system and the surveillance cameras. Mr. Gude and I both think she's close."

"Maybe," Heather mused.

Duke stared out to sea and contemplated all the women he knew who worked at the *Star*. The only person who kept coming to mind was Tisha McVey. As Mr. Shay's niece, she was family and a logical choice for someone who might have a key. He toyed with the idea of taking Tisha on a date, but didn't know if he could make it through without covering his ears and screaming, "Shut up!" And if he *did* go out with her just to investigate the possibility of her being The Rose, she might think they were an item. Then he'd have a different problem altogether.

And Duke didn't like the idea of going into a date with an ulterior motive. That would be using her. Even if she did turn out to be The Rose, Duke wouldn't be interested. He decided to keep his eyes and ears wide open when he was around Tisha. Couldn't hurt. No harm done. Despite the logic, Tisha didn't look or act like the sleuth type. Not at all.

Duke envisioned a lady who was tall, had dark hair, and possessed mysterious eyes...brilliant...captivating. *Exactly* what he was looking for in a wife.

He glanced toward Heather, who'd bent down and was scratching the sand from around a shell. She looked as much like a knockout in the walking shorts and blouse she'd changed into as she had in her Sunday morning suit.

Duke gave himself a hard shake. The Rose wasn't in his life. Heather was. And she was the most decent lady he'd met in a long, long time. How she'd kept her easy manner and carefree spirit in the middle of all that oil money mystified Duke.

She looked straight up at him and smiled. Duke wanted to kiss her again. He squatted beside her. "Whatcha got there, little girl?" he asked.

"It's a shell." She pressed her lips together, dropped her sandals, and dug hard with both hands. "A *big* one."

Chuckling, Duke set his sandals near hers and helped her pull the shell out of the sand. "This one's a beaut!" he said.

"Look!" Heather exclaimed and held it up to the sunlight. "The inside looks like a mother-of-pearl masterpiece."

Duke zeroed in on the shell and totally missed the looming wave until it swept on shore, soaked his shorts, and sucked up their sandals.

Gasping, Heather squealed and then plopped onto her bottom. "My sandals!" she yelled and dropped the shell.

Duke lunged into the chilling water toward the shoes that bobbed and were on the brink of disappearing. He pounced toward the shoes and somehow came up with one of each. He was struck by another wave. Moisture dripped from his hair and stung his eyes. Duke sputtered against the salty taste.

A wild giggle neared from behind, and Duke swiveled to spot Heather a few feet away. "I got one of yours," she yelled and held it up like a trophy. The ends of her hair hung limp, and water dotted her sunglasses.

"I got one of each," Duke responded and lifted the shoes, both in one hand.

Another wave swished and slapped past him, and Duke spotted the final sandal zooming toward the beach. He raced toward it and didn't see Heather doing the same until they collided and crashed into the water. More salt tinged his lips while the shoe dangled in the shallows. Laughter bonded them as Duke grabbed at the sandal like a bear going for a salmon.

"Got it!" he hollered and struggled to his feet. He extended his hand toward Heather, and she took it when yet another wave knocked him sideways. After staggering to keep his footing, Duke crashed back into the Gulf, sputtering all the way down.

Heather's laughter escalated to a new level and consumed Duke. She struggled to her knees and finally to her feet. Duke was close behind.

"You're a crazy woman!" he teased.

She pointed toward the ocean and blurted, "Run!"

Duke turned widened eyes toward a tower of water, this one bigger than its predecessors. By the time he shifted toward shore, Heather was six feet ahead of him. He scrambled to her side, swept her up in both arms, and hauled her to dry land seconds before the wave hit land.

While he struggled to keep his balance, Heather shrieked, "Don't drop me! Don't drop me!"

Duke dropped her anyway, right along with himself. The two crashed into the sand amid laughter and breathlessness. He rolled away from Heather to keep from bumping her. Duke stopped with an "umph" and sand burns on his knees.

"Are you okay?" Heather asked.

He sat up, brushed at his stinging knees, and crawled toward her. Heather's sunglasses were crooked. Her hair drenched. A piece of seaweed clung to her shirt sleeve.

He plopped beside her and removed his sunglasses. "Funny *you* should ask that," he said and straightened the glasses on her nose.

Smiling, Heather removed them. Duke was once again stricken with those baby blues, so enchanting.

"You've got seaweed in your hair," she gurgled out.

She might be saying seaweed, but she's not thinking seaweed, he thought and bent his head toward her. She pulled the stuff out while he removed the piece from her shirt.

When Duke lifted his head and looked into her eyes again, the laughter stopped. His wild night chasing The Rose through his sleep vanished. All he knew was that he was here with Heather. Now. And that she was real. Very real. So was the moment.

Duke ran his thumb along the length of her jaw. "I don't know when I've had so much fun."

"Me too," she whispered, and he didn't have to think twice to know she'd enjoy a kiss as much as he.

Not one to disappoint, Duke leaned closer. But just as his lips were touching hers, Heather burst into a laugh that was contagious. Duke backed away and laughed with her.

"I'm so sorry," she wheezed and covered her face. "I can't—can't stop."

"You're a crazy woman," he repeated and gently punched her shoulder. Duke placed his hand on the sand and enjoyed the rumbling chuckles that coursed through him.

"Where are our sandals anyway?" she asked and lowered her hands.

"I have no idea," Duke admitted and looked around to find all four scattered hither and yon.

"We're a *mess*," Heather said, looking down at her clothing and then his.

Duke glanced over his shorts and T-shirt. "I guess you could call me Mr. Sandman," he quipped and brushed at the grayish particles covering his clothing.

"More seaweed," Heather said and picked the stuff out of his hair. She dropped the seaweed and ran her index finger down Duke's cheek. "I really like you, Duke Fieldman," she said with no trace of humor.

"Mmmm," Duke responded and relished the trail of fire that followed her finger. "Ditto," he said. And this time when his lips touched hers there was nothing to laugh about.

Duke had known last night that if a first real kiss could leave him almost speechless, a second would take his breath away. He'd not been wrong. The pounding of the waves were rivaled by his heartbeat. Her nearness played havoc with his mind even more than the wind ravaged his hair. Duke realized he needed to put some serious boundaries on this little rendezvous...and quickly. He pulled away. The power of attraction left him longing for more...and shaking down to his toes.

"Whoa," he gasped.

Heather's wide-eyed appraisal assured him she might be moving faster on the relationship end of this deal than he was. Not only did he not want the physical side of things to get out of hand, he didn't want to promise more to this woman than he was ready to commit to. To say they both held a physical attraction for the other was a serious understatement. To say Duke was ready for a long-term commitment was another thing altogether.

Heather scared him. She scared him a lot. She'd captivated him when she wrote her number on that notepad and then sashayed back into the castle. That was the *last* thing he'd been expecting that night. And while Duke enjoyed everything about her, he still wasn't sure she was the type he needed to be pursuing. They came from two different worlds. She was a princess; he was a frog. And Mommy-O was very much like the Wicked Witch of the South. Duke shuddered to think what being her son-in-law might be like. He had yet to meet Heather's father. The guy must be gone more often than not. So that left her mother to reign through terror. Duke wasn't so certain he wanted in the "subject pool."

He shifted his weight, dusted off his hands, and gazed toward a young couple walking arm-in-arm along the shore. Fleetingly he wondered where The Rose was...who she was with...what she was doing.

NINETEEN

Once again Heather felt like she'd been dazed and dropped. Duke swiveled to face the ocean, rested his elbow on his knee, and remained silent.

She hadn't thought the kiss from yesterday could be bested. It just had been. Even though his verdict of "nice" had been replaced by "whoa," Duke had withdrawn…again. She realized she hadn't been imagining the effect yesterday either. At times the guy seemed mesmerized by her. But when they kissed, he immediately backed off—way off.

Either he's scared or he doesn't know if I'm his type, Heather deduced and flipped at the sand with her toe. *Or maybe he just doesn't like me,* she worried. *But then why would he keep asking me to do things with him?* Heather bit her lip, observed his profile, and fought for control of her hair, now whipping at her face in the increasing wind.

A new thought crashed through her mind. If Duke was after her money, he wouldn't be withdrawing like this. He'd do to her what that young floozy had done to Uncle Ray. Her uncle was a smart guy—the founder of First Bank of Houston—who'd taken his inheritance and made a ton of money making wise investments. But when it came to his swivel-hipped secretary, all his brain cells went into a coma. He was old enough to be her father and blind enough to think their whirlwind courtship had been all about love rather than his pocketbook. After a year of "wedded bliss," she'd divorced him and taken quite a chunk of everything he owned. His wife of twenty-five years, whom he'd left for the floozy, had taken her half at their divorce. So Uncle Ray had lost more than half of his fortune in eighteen months.

If Duke's motives were money-driven he'd probably be acting like the floozy and moving in fast with no intent to stop until they said "I do."

Heather examined her sand-crusted toes and decided she'd rather him be a little cool here and there than too interested all the time. At least this way her worries about the money business were put to rest. If he was tempering their relationship with logic, that meant Duke was cautious.

Cautious is good, Heather decided. She wondered how he'd react if she blurted, "I'm The Rose!" Her lips twitched as she imagined his shocked stare, but all humor vanished when she considered Lorna and Brittan's glares. By telling Duke, she'd be violating her word to her best friends and ending their "fun and games" sleuthing. Duke did say in the article that he was determined to find The Rose, and once he found her, he'd expose her. Heather figured Houston residents were cheering him on, and that heightened the thrill of the adventure. No, she couldn't tell Duke. And she prayed every day that he'd never recognize her and Lorna's connection to Eve Maloney's apartment.

Heather pulled her knees to her chest, wrapped her arms around her legs, and pondered the impact she and her friends made on Duke's career. He was going to have the job he'd wanted. The knowledge brought warmth to Heather's soul. She was glad to help and thrilled to make a positive impact on his life.

Idly Heather wondered if Duke had this effect on other women as well. Her arms tightened around her legs as she speculated about the women in Duke's past. She guessed him to be around thirty.

Like Brittan said, he wasn't hard on the eyes. And Heather suspected she and Brittan weren't the first ones to think that.

*Maybe Mom is right. He might have even been married before and
has kids.* Heather blinked. She imagined herself with custody of
a ten-year-old or two and nearly choked. She stared at the back
of Duke's head, wishing she really could read his mind. When he
turned to face her, she jumped.

"What are you doing?" he asked through a grin the size of the
moon. "Were you staring at me...or somebody else?" He glanced
behind him.

"Uh..." Heather swallowed.

"I always feel it when somebody's watching me."

"It was me," she admitted. "I didn't know you had a deal with
it."

"No deal. Just felt it." He scooted back and looked her in the eyes.
"So why the staring?"

"Just wondering..." Heather cleared her throat, "if you'd..." She
looked toward a sailboat floating out to sea. Brittan told her she
said what she thought too much. Maybe it was too early in their
relationship to ask about previous marriages. But then maybe his
kissing her into a tailspin gave her the right.

"I was just wandering if you'd ever been married," she rushed.

Duke's eyes rounded. "Who me?"

"No." Heather shook her head. "That guy sitting next to you."
She whacked at his arm. "Yes, you."

"Not on your life. Nobody would have me," he said, and a trace
of a memory flitting through his gaze suggested that might be
closer to the truth than his glib smile suggested.

"You?" he asked.

"No." Heather shook her head.

"Didn't think so. Too young."

"Oh, I wanted to at one point," Heather admitted. "But I was
very young then."

"Yeah, me too," Duke admitted. "She dumped me."

"I was the one who did the dumping. My mother…" Heather pressed her lips together.

"Doesn't surprise me," Duke mumbled.

"Yes. She's worried sick somebody's going to be after me for money." Heather peered squarely into Duke's eyes.

He didn't look away. "Truth is, your money makes me nervous as all get out." Duke never blinked. "I think I'd be doing better if you were broke." The sincerity spilling from his soul couldn't be fabricated.

"Good," Heather said and smiled.

"My parents aren't poor by any means, but we're still just ordinary folks." He eyed the increasing waves. "We own one ranch in West Texas. Whoopee!" He twirled his index finger in a circle. "And you live in a castle. It's like you're a princess and I'm a frog. And lady, no matter how many times you kiss me, I'm still going to be a frog." A smirk sneaked to the corners of his mouth. "Ribbit. Ribbit."

"I *like* frogs," Heather said and curled fingers around his arm. "Especially when they're covered in chocolate."

Duke laughed. "You and that chocolate," he teased. "I guess I *am* gonna have to put it in my hair."

Heather dared to gently scrape her fingers through his damp hair, and she enjoyed the gesture as much as his eyes said he did. "Maybe not," she said and rested her head on his shoulder.

"I take it you have a habit of going out with men your mother doesn't approve of," Duke mused.

"Hmmm."

"Is that why you gave me your phone number…because you knew your mom wouldn't approve?" The question was loaded with underlying vibes.

Heather lifted her head and held his gaze. "I gave you my phone number because… Okay, my mother *did* tell me to not see you— but then after I got to know you I didn't care. And I still don't."

Duke blinked. "Am I a rebellious fling for you? Are you using me to make your mom mad?"

Heather's face tightened. "No. Not at all. I'm my own woman. I'm twenty-three. I guess I just…" Heather sighed and pulled at her damp shirt. "Maybe at first…a little," she admitted, "but not any more."

Duke laughed.

"You don't believe me?" Heather demanded.

"No. It's just that we're both worried, I guess. You're worried that I'm after your money—"

"But I'm not—"

Duke held up his hand. "And I've started worrying that you're using me as some sort of a weapon against your mother."

Heather sighed. "Why does life have to be so complicated?"

"Maybe because we're people," Duke said with a sage nod. "And people are complicated. It also sounds like we've both been burned—or at least had bad experiences. Maybe we're both a little scared. Or maybe that's just me." He offered a sheepish grin. "I haven't done well since I was dumped."

"How long ago was that, anyway?"

"I'm embarrassed to tell you."

"That long huh?"

"Yeah. But it really hurt. I've been cautious ever since. My sister says I'm going to die an old maid."

"That's a weird image," Heather teased.

"All I need is some curlers and a worn-out dress and I'm good to go." He cut her a sly smile.

Heather tilted back her head and laughed out loud. "Now who's the crazy one?"

"You are." He softly punched her arm.

Heather shoved at him. He tossed sand on her leg. She kicked sand back while saying, "Hey you!"

Duke brushed at the fresh sand on his shorts. "I give! You win!"

Heather hugged her knees, savored the smells of sand and sea, and wished the day could last forever. Even though she'd only known Duke a week, she suspected her heart could be permanently snared. If things kept moving forward, she could fall madly in love very soon.

A cloud moved across the sunshine, and Heather gazed toward the horizon. More clouds were on their way, and the rain they held was the cause of the increasing wind and waves. "Looks like it might rain in an hour or so," she mused and glanced toward Duke.

His expression had gone from carefree to troubled. Heather strained to understand his differing signals. Duke peered toward the clouds and then directly into Heather's eyes.

"I think I need to be totally honest before we get any cozier," he said.

Heather's stomach did a flip-flop and then knotted. "Okay," she agreed, but dreaded the words that would match his expression.

"Like I already said, I'm a little scared here," Duke admitted.

"That's fine...understandable," Heather affirmed. Her shoulders stiffened.

"Let's see," he squinted toward the sky, "you're twenty-three. That means I've got eight years on you."

"That's about what I thought," Heather said.

"I've been single my whole adult life. I've never been married or lived with a woman, for that matter."

Heather's respect for him multiplied tenfold. "That means a lot," she said.

"It means nothing. I'm no good on my own," Duke admitted. "If not for God in my life, I'd have lived with several by now, I'm sure. I've had plenty of offers."

"What guy like you hasn't?" Heather blurted and then covered her mouth.

Duke's brows quirked. He snickered and dryly said, "Thanks, I guess." He traced a squiggly line in the sand before continuing. "I said all that to say I don't want to hurt you. Don't get your hopes up on my account, okay?" He held her gaze, and the sincerity in his brown eyes denied any hint of dishonesty.

"I'd like for us to see each other a while and see if maybe..." he pointed to her and back to himself, "maybe we have enough in common to make it. But I do have some reservations."

Her mouth dry, Heather nodded. "Is it my family—my mom?"

"A little, I guess." Duke shrugged. "Just being honest here."

Heather nodded.

"But if we're meant to be, I'd be willing to tangle with your mom." He grinned. "It's not just your mom though. It's me too. Which brings me to another point. Like I said, I'm eight years older than you, and I'm not interested in any kind of a multiple-girlfriend setup right now. Will you hang with me for a while and see where it leads?"

She dug her toes into the sand.

"And," he looked down, "I'm also telling you not to haul off and fall all the way in love. I can't promise anything right now—except I do like you *a lot*." His gaze trailed to her lips. "And I enjoy kissing you."

Heather swallowed and nodded.

"The deal is, I'm getting older now, and I'm seriously starting to think toward one day getting married. I won't stay in a relationship just for the sake of having a girlfriend. If it looks like it isn't going to work, why stay with it?"

"Who would?" Heather asked and felt beyond naive the minute the words left her mouth. She knew lots of people who did exactly that.

Duke observed her. "The Mike," he said without ever blinking.

"Actually, The Mike five years ago would have. And a few others like he used to be."

"I know," she answered. "It's just that I'm not like that."

He touched her cheek. "I want to move ahead here, but I also want you to know exactly where I stand. I'm as *infatuated* as all get out." He winked.

Her stomach flipped again.

"But I don't want to take advantage of you, okay?"

She nodded.

"Or lead you on. I'm not into hurting women. But I'm not promising a thing either. Just asking if you'd like us to spend a little time getting to know each other and maybe see if we can discover God's will along the way."

"Yes." Heather's breathless response whispered on the breeze.

He smiled, leaned closer, and said "Good" against her lips before sealing the deal with another kiss.

As Heather lost herself in his nearness, she wondered exactly how to stop herself from falling all the way in love...or graciously accept God's will if it didn't line up with her own.

TWENTY

🌹 How Lorna got talked into taking Heather's cat to the vet was still a source of great mystery. One minute she'd been sitting around Heather's place, looking through the paper for something that might warrant The Rose's efforts. The next minute Heather had been fluttering around her suite, squawking about lunch with Duke and having a vet appointment at the same time.

Next thing Lorna knew, she was putting a cat carrier in her Jeep. The prisoner was named Lucky. The orange menace glared at Lorna through the carrier screen, hissed, and growled. When Lorna suggested Heather get one of the household employees to manage the demon, Heather said she wouldn't trust the cat with anyone but friends or family.

"You'd think the beast was royalty," Lorna groused and slowed for a stoplight. The way he acted, Lorna wasn't certain who Heather was protecting from whom: the cat from the employees or the employees from the cat.

She wheeled the Jeep to the right and pulled into the veterinarian's parking lot on the outskirts of The Woods, north of Houston.

"Okay, fur ball," she mumbled toward the cat before rolling to a stop, "it's time for your checkup. Just five more minutes and we're no longer an item." Lorna had agreed to drop Lucky off. Heather was going to come by after her date to pick him up.

Her cell phone bleeped out a Caribbean-flair tune. Lorna put the Jeep into park and pulled the phone from her jogging pants pocket. The screen indicated Brittan. Lorna placed the phone to her ear and said, "Whazzup?"

"Where are you?"

"Taking one of Heather's cats to the vet," Lorna drawled, "and thinking how I'd rather be eating snake."

Brittan chuckled. "How'd you get stuck doing that?"

"I have no idea. It's all a big blur. One minute I was hanging out with Heather. The next I was hauling Lucky to the vet and Heather was going off to lunch with Duke."

"Again?"

"Yes again." Lorna turned off the engine.

"Man."

"He is one. You got that right."

Brittan laughed. "Seriously, it looks like they're getting thick."

"I don't know if *they* are, but *she* sure is," Lorna responded and squinted against the September sunshine blasting through the window despite the chill in the air.

"Yes, I know," Brittan said. "And after she told us how he warned her off falling in love, it really worries me."

"Me too," Lorna agreed. Heather had mentioned the conversation she and Duke had at the beach a few days ago. The anguished hope in her eyes had intensified Lorna's doubts. "I tried to warn her, but it's like beating your head against a dead horse."

"I think that's 'There's no sense kicking a dead horse' or 'It's like beating your head against a brick wall,'" Brittan corrected, her voice thick with a smile.

"*Whatever!*" Lorna huffed and waved her hand. "The whole

point is, I'm thinking he's got, like, some serious commitment issues going."

"All the way," Brittan agreed. "And have you seen the way she looks at him? She's got it bad, and I think he's really holding back."

Lorna sighed. "Heather said he was hurt once, but who hasn't been?" She wasn't even in the mood to think about her own failed romances. After the last heartbreak, Lorna decided to act like Brittan and swear off men until God drop-kicked the right one into her lap and sky-wrote "He's the one" while the Angel Gabriel played "Yankee Doodle Dandy" on a trumpet. And she didn't even want to measure the irony of that decision next to her parents pushing her toward her official debutante gala.

When I'm forty and still single, I might be the oldest debutante in the South, she mused.

"Do you think he's got someone else back home?" Brittan's question reflected Lorna's concern.

"I've wondered, but I don't know." She shrugged and toyed with the zipper on her jacket.

"All I know is, if he hurts her, I think I'm going to kill him," Brittan said.

"Yep, I know. I mean, Heather's the one who wanted to put the rose on his desk last time. And from what I understand, that landed him the job he wanted. He owes her, but he doesn't know it."

"You bet," Brittan said.

"I wish he could somehow know we're The Rose and we could keep our cover at the same time," Lorna pined.

"Let's just have our cake and eat it too, why don't we?" Brittan drawled. "If he finds out about us, we can kiss our fun goodbye."

"I know. I know." Lorna nodded. "I'm not going to tell him, and I'm sure Heather won't either."

Neither Lorna nor Heather had told Brittan that Duke had been with them in Eve Maloney's apartment, and so far the guy had missed the connection. Lorna had almost stopped worrying that he'd make that leap.

"Still, if Duke dumps Heather, he'll be eating my tennis racquet!" Lorna stated.

"Okay, but I get to kill him first," Brittan asserted. "Hey, have you heard the latest news report?"

"No." Lorna sat up straighter. She and Brittan had been closely monitoring current events the last week to see what kind of mischief they could get into. The Rose preferred high-profile cases but they were so ready for action they were thinking about jumping into something less prominent. "What gives?" she prompted.

"First Bank of Houston was robbed this morning at ten," Brittan stated.

"No way!" Lorna exclaimed.

"Way, girlfriend."

"That's great!"

Silence penetrated the line for several seconds, and then the friends burst into mutual laughter.

"Okay, maybe it's *not* great," Lorna rescinded. "But—"

"Maybe we ought to see what we can see. Can't hurt," Brittan suggested.

"Sounds like a winner to me," Lorna agreed.

"Wait!" Brittan said. Silence penetrated the line. "Wait a minute!" she repeated. "Isn't First Bank the one Heather's uncle is president of?"

Lorna's eyes widened. She gripped the steering wheel. "Yes! I think so." She doubled her fist and tapped the wheel. "What's his name? Oh…"

"Ray. It's Ray…uh… What's her mother's maiden name?"

"Morris," Lorna blurted.

"Oh my word!" Brittan rushed. "I wonder if Heather might have some connections we can use?"

Lorna snorted. "You're going to have to pry Heather away from

Duke. I don't know if she even remembers we're The Rose at this point."

Brittan sighed. "I'll pry her. Don't worry. I think a break from him will do her some good."

A long, low yowl swelled from the cat carrier, and Lorna eyed her companion.

"What was *that?*" Brittan asked.

"Lucky the Terrible," Lorna said. "I promise, this cat needs an exorcist. I don't know why Heather puts up with him."

Brittan chuckled.

"And would somebody please tell me why she named him Lucky? I mean, he's been neutered and declawed and his name is *Lucky?*"

Fresh laughter burst over the line before Brittan said, "Why not come back home and we'll start turning some stones. I'll see if I can catch up with Heather. Okay?"

Lorna checked her watch. "Works," she agreed. "I have an appointment with my accountant at three, but I'm free until then."

※ ※ ※

Duke and Heather paused near her Porsche in the parking lot of the Cracker Barrel restaurant in the suburbs of Houston. They'd met here for lunch because Duke enjoyed homestyle cooking more than anything else. Once Heather learned this, she'd insisted they eat at such places often.

A few times during the last month she'd dragged him to upscale restaurants that had more silverware than Duke knew what to do with. Once it had been for a benefit for some charity. Both her father and mother attended, and Duke found that Heather's dad was every bit as nice as his daughter, which explained a lot about Heather. Her father had paid for their meals, and Duke had been afraid to even ask how much it cost.

Probably more than I make in a week, he conjectured and couldn't ignore how much Heather was totally in her element during the benefit…and how out of place he felt.

Nevertheless, Duke was enjoying getting to know Ms. Winslow… although they talked more about him than her. She had her vague moments and didn't mention her friends much. Duke hadn't gone to church with her yet either. He was beginning to think she just wasn't that complicated of a gal and didn't really have much of a life. In some ways her winsomeness was refreshing. In other ways it made Duke restless.

He pressed his lips against her forehead, lowered his head, and smiled into her eyes. They'd just enjoyed a great lunch…again. And he had to admit Heather was nice to have around. Even though he was still not allowing himself to get lost in their relationship, the last month had been way less lonely.

"So what's the rest of your day like?" Duke asked.

"Partly cloudy with a slight chance of rain," Heather quipped.

Duke looked up. The dark bank of clouds that kicked off the morning had invaded Houston with a vengeance. The cool breeze that swooped down from the sky insisted they were on the first edge of autumn. Duke expected a flood any minute—or at least a gully washer.

"Might need to fire your weatherman and get another one," he said. "Looks like he forgot to look out the window."

Heather followed his gaze as several fat raindrops plummeted from the sky. One hit her smack between the eyes, and she squealed.

Duke was reminded of the day they'd spent at the beach. After their little talk he'd relaxed and enjoyed himself more than ever… more than he had with anyone since Sarah. The more accustomed he became to Heather's presence, the more he looked forward to seeing her. The weekend after next he was going to visit his folks in Lubbock. He was thinking he might even miss this woman. Looking back, Duke didn't remember mentioning the trip to her.

"Did I tell you I'm going to visit my parents in Lubbock the weekend after next?" Duke asked. "Several homes have been robbed in the area, and they're worried." Duke paused. "I feel like I need to go home. Not like I can *do* anything, but still…I'm overdue a visit anyway. My plane leaves Friday morning. I'll be back home Sunday night. Just thought you might want to know you won't have me in your hair that weekend."

"Oh you." She playfully slapped at his arm. "You're not in my hair, and you know it."

"Just wishful thinking, I guess." Duke glanced skyward. The dark clouds had stopped spitting at them, but the downpour was a given.

"Well," she tilted her head, "maybe I'll just come with you."

Duke blinked as his mind processed Heather's statement. His first instinct was to blurt "No!" He understood the implications of bringing a woman home to meet the folks. He hadn't asked Heather for the simple reason that he didn't want anyone to think he was getting serious about her—not his parents or sister or even Heather.

Because I'm not getting serious, he reminded himself.

Once his parents found out he was bringing home a woman, they'd immediately call Duke's sister, who'd have to come home to meet Heather. He imagined all three at the airport with a band playing "Here Comes the Bride."

"You've met *my* parents," she said. "And I've been dying to meet your parents. I'd love to see their ranch."

"I'd have to check to see if there are any seats left on the plane," Duke hedged and brainstormed for a way of graciously hinting he wasn't ready to take Heather home with him.

"I don't mind paying for my own ticket," Heather added. "And if there are no seats left on your flight, I'm sure we could find seats on some flight." Her expression said she'd give her life's savings to spend the weekend with him, and that was probably enough coins to fill up the Grand Canyon. That expression made him feel pretty doggone special and drove him to do all sorts of rash things, such as telling her he'd pay for her ticket.

"That's okay," Duke heard himself say. "I'll pay for your ticket. These shuttle flights aren't that expensive. And what kind of a guy would I be to invite you and then not cover your ticket?" *But wait!* he thought. *I didn't invite her, did I?*

"Oh Duke!" Heather hugged him tight. "Thank you! Thank you! Thank you! This is going to be so much fun!"

"Sure," Duke said and wrapped his arms around her. He enjoyed the smell of her hair, the way she fit into his arms just right. As the idea of her flying to Lubbock with him sank in, part of him really started looking forward to showing her the family ranch and his hometown. But the more cautious side whispered he'd made a mistake. A *big* mistake.

Flying a woman home to meet the parents was a significant milestone. And Duke was a long way from proposing. They'd only been together a month. *I'm not even getting serious about her,* he repeated and closed his eyes to savor her warmth.

Even though The Rose hadn't made another appearance, the mystery woman began dancing on the edge of his mind, an elusive phantom beckoning him to an exhilarating chase.

But Heather's real, he reminded himself. *The Rose—whoever she is—is just a dream woman.* And maybe his dream woman didn't exist. At least his sister didn't think so.

A few more raindrops crashed to earth, and rumbling thunder mingled with the honk and rev of traffic. A splattering of hard drops slammed into his scalp.

"Yikes!" Heather looked skyward, pulled up the hood on her sweater, and pressed her car's remote. The sports coupe chirped, and she popped open the door to crawl inside.

Duke rested his arm along the top of the vehicle, leaned inside a bit, and reached for the seat belt. The increasing raindrops soaked through the back of his sweatshirt as he pulled the strap around Heather, snapped it into place, and said, "You need to drive safe, Little Pink Riding Hood." He touched the side of her hood.

"I will," she promised and her expression said she was reliving their first kiss as much as he was. He'd leaned into her car just like now, and Heather had tasted just as sweet then as she promised to now.

He reminded himself they were in a public place and that serious restraint warranted. Duke inched away. "I'll call you later tonight, okay?"

Duke watched her drive away and tried to imagine himself married to Heather. Right now he couldn't. The realization made part of him feel safe. Very safe. But a restless part of him wasn't so sure he still wanted to be safe.

TWENTY-ONE

After rescuing Lucky from the vet's office and taking him home, Heather decided to swing by Brittan and Lorna's place. When she arrived, she knocked and Brittan answered the door. Heather stepped inside, lowered her sweater's hood, fluffed her hair, and looked for a place to set her wet umbrella.

"Here, I'll take that," Brittan offered. "We were just having some coffee." She pointed toward a small breakfast nook. "Lorna's at the table."

"Hey, girl," Lorna called.

Heather strode around the corner to see Lorna sitting at the tall table. She held a mug of coffee in one hand and several pieces of paper in the other. The wall-to-wall windows allowed the rain-soaked light to muddle its way into the room while wet pellets splattered the glass.

"Hey back," Heather replied, walking toward one of the chairs. She dropped her purse on the floor, stepped on the chair's bottom rung, and crawled onto the elevated seat.

"Have you had your radio on?" Lorna asked.

"No." Heather shook her head. "Just the CD player."

"Well, there's been a major bank robbery!" Lorna wiggled her brows and took a sip of her coffee.

"That's the good news," Brittan drawled from the doorway. "The bad news is it was First Bank of Houston."

"Uncle Ray's bank?" Heather gasped.

"We thought so," Lorna said.

"Isn't his last name Morris?" Brittan questioned.

"Yes. He's my mother's brother."

"They got away with a quarter million," Lorna said and waved some papers she held.

"I can't believe Mom hasn't called about it." Heather scrambled from the chair and retrieved her cell phone from the bag. "Oh man," she mumbled as she changed her settings. "I forgot I put it on silent before Duke and I met for lunch. There are some messages." She checked her recent callers list and noted a call from Brittan and one from her mother.

"I had Tilley buy some green tea just for you, Heather," Brittan cut in. "Want some?"

"Sure." Heather nodded and began retrieving the messages. The last one was from her mother. Uncle Ray and her mother never had been close, and when he left his wife for the floozy and Marilyn took her sister-in-law's side, that pretty much ended the brother–sister relationship. Nevertheless, her mother sounded disturbed. And even though Heather's opinion of her uncle had been marred by the way he treated Grandpa Morris, she hated that his bank was robbed. She turned off the phone.

Lorna passed several pages to Heather. "I downloaded this from the Channel 2 website. They've already got it plastered all over the internet. Look." She pointed at a series of photos of a man wearing a hat pulled low. He held a briefcase and was exiting the bank while a couple other guys behind him pointed weapons at bank employees and customers.

"There's an all-out search party on for these guys," Lorna explained and pulled up the zipper on her open jogging jacket, only to slide it back down.

Heather wondered what The Rose could do in this case. Tracking down the internet hacker had been a matter of using the computer to outsmart the guy. The mayor's murder had been all about snooping here and there. But hunting down armed bank robbers left Heather uneasy. She looked squarely into Lorna's eyes and saw her own apprehension mirrored back.

"For some reason this one's scarier to me," Lorna acknowledged.

"I feel the same way," Heather admitted. "Maybe because it's so close to home. And if we somehow get caught or mess it up, I'm fried."

Brittan appeared with a tray laden with thermal dispensers, a mug, and some cookies. "Tilley fixed this for us," Brittan explained. "I don't know what I'd do without her." She set the tray on the café table and laid her hand on one of the stainless steel dispensers. "This one's coffee and this one's hot water. Tea's here." She pointed toward a dish holding tea bags.

Heather retrieved a tea bag and a mug and filled it with steaming water.

"We're turning into two big, fat chickens," she admitted. "This bank robbery business bothers us."

"At first it did me a little too. But then I realized it's no worse than tracking down a murderer," Brittan explained. She plopped into her chair and pushed up the sleeves of her sweatshirt that bore the name Princeton University.

"Good point," Heather said. "But if we botch it and blow our cover, I'm sure it's going to make the next family get-together a little awkward."

"Yes, and besides that," Lorna jumped in, "those gunmen look serious, and I'm not in the mood to get shot this week."

"So do we let this one pass?" Brittan asked. "We don't *have* to take it on, you know." Yet her hungry gaze lowered to the internet printouts like this was the best find of the century.

"I just feel like we really need to be careful," Lorna qualified.

"This time me too," Heather replied and wondered how Duke would take it if she got wounded. *Probably pretty hard. After all, he invited me to meet his parents, so that must mean he's getting attached.*

"Duke asked me to fly home with him to meet his parents," Heather mentioned and couldn't stop a smile that felt as goofy as she was excited.

Lorna stopped in mid-sip and gazed at Heather over the rim of her cup. "Are you going?" Lorna lowered her mug.

"What do you think?" Heather said, her grin increasing.

"When do you leave?" Brittan asked.

"A week from Friday. He's checking into getting me a ticket on the same flight he's on."

"So this is a weekend trip," Brittan continued and pushed up her glasses. "You'll be gone two nights?"

"Yes," Heather replied.

A silent question hung in the air, and Heather glanced from one friend to the other.

"Are you staying at a hotel or at his parents'?" Brittan continued.

"In other words, is the guy pressuring you to sleep with him?" Lorna blurted.

Heather's mouth fell open. "Would you two just *stop* it!" She set down her tea. "Duke Fieldman is a Christian man—and I mean the real deal. He's been nothing but very, very..." Heather grappled for the right word. "Cool" sounded like he didn't really like her, but at times he did seem cool. "Cautious" sounded like he was afraid of her, and he'd already admitted he was a little afraid. "Firm" sounded like he was some stodgy old geezer, but he had been firm about their boundaries.

"He's never been married and never lived with anybody either," Heather said. "And that's saying a lot for a guy his age. Even several guys in our church's singles' group say they've messed up. But I don't think Duke has. As a matter of fact, if you want the truth, I wish he'd be a little warmer sometimes."

Like today when I left the restaurant, Heather added to herself. She really thought he was going to kiss her, but he hadn't.

"Okay, okay." Brittan held up her hand. "You don't have to go and get all huffed. We're just concerned, that's all."

"Well, we haven't talked about where we'll spend the night... and I don't mean together. I assumed we'd be staying at his parents' place, and I *don't* mean in the same room."

Lorna chuckled. "All right, girlfriend. All right." She patted Heather's hand.

Heather jerked it away and balled her fists in her lap.

"I wish you guys would be more supportive and have faith in me, for cryin' out loud."

The two exchanged meaningful glances. "It's not *you* we're worried about," Brittan admitted.

"It's him," Lorna said. "He is a male, after all. And when it comes to long-term relationships, we think he's as scared as a short-tailed cat at a rocking chair convention."

Brittan sputtered over her sip of coffee and hacked through a round of laughter.

Heather covered her face, shook her head, and smiled. "It's a *long*-tailed cat at a rocking chair convention."

"Whatever!" Lorna rolled her eyes. "Don't be so picky. You get my drift."

"I think he's got commitment issues." Brittan released a final cough and leveled her gaze straight at Heather. "And we're afraid he's going to rip your heart out."

"But he's asked me to go visit his parents," Heather defended.

"Just do what the guy told you to do and don't haul off and fall in love with him, deary," Lorna reminded.

"And exactly how do you stop yourself from falling in love?" Heather asked. She picked up her napkin and curled an edge into a tight roll. What Heather *didn't* tell them was that she was well on her way and was enjoying the journey so much she didn't want to slow down.

"Stop spending so much time with him," Brittan suggested. "Focus on something else for a change." She picked up the internet printouts. "Like a bank robbery, for instance."

"The one thing I've got to give Luke—"

"It's D—"

"I know," Lorna interrupted. "I'm just being ornery."

"Stop acting normal, will ya?" Brittan teased.

Lorna narrowed her eyes at her friend. "As I was saying, the thing that I will give the guy is that he has been honest with you from the start. I'm just not sure you really *heard* him or *understand* what he said." Even though Lorna had some dingbat moments, her green eyes sometimes took on an intensity that could rattle stone.

Heather wadded her napkin.

"I don't think his asking you to go home with him means as much to him as it does to you," Lorna asserted.

"I don't either. Not really," Brittan agreed.

Heather gazed downward. Duke had yet to hint of any deeper commitment, although she longed for exactly that. She knew her friends cared. She also knew their concern would quadruple if they understood just how much she was longing for a deeper relationship with Duke...or that she'd actually been the one to introduce the idea of going to Lubbock with him. *Duke did readily agree and invite me,* she justified.

But would he have if I hadn't brought it up? Heather gazed at the printouts sprawled across the table and decided maybe her friends' warnings were wise. Even though she adored spending time with Duke, he *had* told her up front not to fall madly in love with him. When she looked into his eyes, Heather saw a lot of interest, some serious attraction, and then indulgence. But she couldn't honestly say she thought Duke was falling in love with her.

"I need to get a grip, don't I?" Heather admitted.

"A serious one." Brittan nodded and chomped into a white-chocolate cookie.

Heather eyed the cookies, picked one up, and nibbled at it. Brittan ate like a horse and stayed as skinny as a rail. She said it was her Chinese genes. While Heather was a size 6, she worked hard to keep it that way. She glanced toward the "food disposal," who'd already downed two cookies and was working on a third.

"I remember you guys trying to talk to me when I was on the tennis pro tour," Lorna stated. "But would I listen? No!" She pointed at Heather. "Now we're trying to talk to *you*. And you need to take the same advice you gave me."

Heather swallowed hard. Lorna had gone on the pro tour for a couple of years and had fallen hard for another tennis pro who was ten years older and known for womanizing. Before the nasty mess was over, Lorna came close to being raped. She'd escaped only because Heather heard her screams and had promptly given the jerk a dose of black belt he probably hadn't forgotten yet. Lorna quit the pro tour. When she pressed charges against the creep, three other women stepped forward. None of them had been as fortunate as Lorna. He'd been forced to retire and was now taking a nice little vacation in prison.

The whole time Lorna had been infatuated with him, Heather and Brittan had tried to tell her he was no good but she refused to listen.

Now Heather's friends were telling her some of the same stuff she'd told Lorna. Except Heather knew for certain that Duke wasn't a womanizer. He was just not ready to commit. Well, to her anyway.

Nevertheless, except for the Tyler business, Heather had always gotten everything she wanted. And she would have had Tyler if not for his getting killed. But now... Even though she heard her friends and even recognized she was tottering on the brink of falling in love with a man who'd told her not to fall in love with him, Heather found it hard to accept that she wouldn't get her guy in the end. He'd been hooked from that first night they met. He admitted that. Now it was just a matter of getting him to swallow the whole hook. Maybe her backing off a little would make that happen…and at the same time help her friends chill out.

"So what do you think we should do first?" Heather asked and lifted one of the bank robbery photos.

Brittan spoke up. "We were wondering if you might have some connections we could um…"

"Exploit," Lorna said through a giggle.

TWENTY-TWO

Nine days later Lorna pulled the hat lower over her eyes and tried not to scratch at the fake beard. This was the first time she'd ever dressed as a man, and she didn't think she'd like to repeat the beard. When she'd told her friends she'd rather dress up like a guy and deliver the rose in broad daylight than go in at night again, they took her seriously. Lorna hadn't minded. *Anything* was better than running from a security guard and police backup.

She strode down the sidewalk toward the entry to the *Houston Star*. Arriving at the door at the same time as a short-skirted young woman, Lorna decided she should be a "gentleman" and open the door for the gal. When the girl offered a simpering smile, Lorna wondered if she were an "attractive man." She considered glaring, but realized her sunglasses would block the effect, so she looked down and the woman scurried away.

Lorna caught sight of herself in the glass door's reflection as she stepped into the building. The oversized trench coat with extra shoulder padding gave her added masculinity. The pads had been Heather's idea. Brittan said that with her larger frame, beard, and hat she really did look like a man. Lorna shifted the box from under her arm into her gloved hands and was glad the unpredictable September weather had blessed them with a cool day. Even though the gloves were probably too much for fifty degree weather, she could wear them and hide her feminine hands without raising too many eyebrows.

The buxom receptionist looked up from her desk as Lorna approached. Her lips were as red as the rose inside the box, her hair too blonde to be natural.

"May I help you?" she asked.

"Yes," Lorna rumbled and even impressed herself with how manly she sounded. "I have a delivery for..." Lorna pretended to examine the label, "for Duke Fieldman."

"Of course." The receptionist took the box and suspiciously eyed Lorna.

Lorna held back a snicker.

"I'll make sure he gets it," the blonde said and stood.

"Thanks." Lorna turned and strolled out of the building and back onto the busy sidewalk. Once she crossed the intersection, she pulled her cell phone out of her coat pocket. First she checked the time. Eight fifteen. Heather and Brittan had dropped her off at this exact spot. She'd made her delivery and gotten back in only ten minutes. Lorna smiled and pressed Heather's speed dial number.

"I'm through," she said as soon as Heather answered. "I'm waiting."

"Okay. We're only a block away."

Within two minutes a black Taurus pulled to the curb. The back door opened. Lorna crawled into the smell of new leather and slammed the door.

Brittan shared the backseat with her.

Heather sat at the wheel. She glanced toward Lorna. "Everything okay?" she asked.

"Yep. No problem."

With the scarf over her hair and a pair of black, narrow sunglasses, Heather looked like she belonged in a 1950s murder mystery. She glanced to her left and eased into traffic.

Brittan hunched down in the seat and gazed out every window like an on-duty police dog. Her floppy straw hat drooped down to cover her profile. She looked like an Asian peasant.

"I think the coast is clear," Lorna said. "Nobody suspected a thing. I just got in and got out."

The farther they drove from the paper, the more the tension drained from the atmosphere. Once again The Rose had used her connections to pull together clues and implicate a criminal. Lorna just hated that this time the criminal had been Heather's uncle.

※ ❋ ※

At ten after ten Duke came off his break early because he itched to get back to the article he was working on. The robbery of First Bank of Houston had been hot news for days now, and he'd covered every angle of the story. He hustled through the cubicles in the "real news" department and plopped at his desk. Even though he'd given up a regular office and was starting over in another department, Duke was prouder of his new desk than he'd been of his real office in the Lifestyle Department. His framed photos were crowded onto the cubicle walls, but his tornado looked better in here.

He eyed his computer and was eager to finish the article he'd begun. But his cell phone lying on his desk bleeped at him. Duke looked at the screen and saw he had a voice mail. A glimpse of his recent callers indicated Heather was the last one to call.

He'd left three voice mails the last few days, and she hadn't responded. At first Duke had been exasperated. They were supposed to be leaving for Lubbock in two days. At the very least, he needed to talk with her about the plans.

But this morning he began to wonder if something was wrong. So he'd placed a fourth call and told her if she didn't respond he was going to be at her place by six to see if she were still alive.

"That got her," he mumbled under his breath and wondered if Heather was playing the hard-to-get game. Whatever she was up to, Duke was not amused. On top of that, he'd missed her. As he'd told Mike this morning, Duke wasn't serious about her. Not at all. But still, when you get used to palling around with someone and then they aren't there for a few days and don't return your calls, there you are. Alone. And as of last night—worried.

Duke's finger was on her speed-dial number when a female voice from behind said, "Mail." He looked over his shoulder and saw the box first, the grim-faced secretary next. Martha Baskin was Mr. Gude's right-hand woman and didn't look thrilled to be Duke's mailperson.

"Thanks," he said and took the box. The secretary left.

Frowning, Duke placed the phone back on his desk and examined the upper left-hand corner of the package. No return address. Duke pulled his dad's old knife from his pocket and slit the tape. The first thing he saw when he opened the flaps was a single rose as red as blood.

Duke closed the flaps and glanced behind him. No one gave him a glance. He inched out of his seat and searched for Martha. The straight-backed lioness was walking down the hallway, back toward her den. Duke fully stood. He folded his knife, slipped it into his pocket, and placed the box under his arm.

He wanted privacy. The cubicle was about as private as a circus. No telling who might walk by and see him holding that flower. The next thing he knew, Mr. Gude would be toting off his prize. Duke grabbed his jacket, shoved his cell phone into his pants pocket, and hurried toward the short hallway that led to the back exit. His trusty Chevy called his name. Duke slipped out the door to his truck and couldn't wait to find out exactly what The Rose had been up to this time.

※ ※ ※

Heather hung up from leaving Duke a voice mail and put her cell phone on top of her handbag. She stepped to her couch, picked up Tigger from his usual spot near the pillows, and sat down. A striped tabby, Tigger was her prettiest cat and her sweetest one. Heather found him in the woods behind the castle over a year ago. He had a compound fracture in his right back leg and was in dire straits. Heather immediately took him to the vet, and he was rushed into surgery. Now the feline loved her with a devotion that Heather returned. She scratched his ears and enjoyed his purring while her mind wandered back to Duke.

When he'd called and left the first voice mail she'd been with Lorna and Brittan at First Bank. Her ringer had been off. Once Heather got the voice mail, she'd used every ounce of willpower not to return his call right away. The second one was harder. After last night's voice mail, she'd decided to call Duke this morning.

Then he called and the voice mail message essentially said he was ready to hunt her down. The blatant concern in his voice made Heather feel a bit guilty, but it was guilt mingled with warmth. Maybe Lorna and Brittan were wrong and Duke cared for her more than anyone realized.

Heather couldn't wait until this weekend. She rubbed her cheek against Tigger's soft head and imagined what Duke's boyhood home looked like. She worried about letting him know just how much her heart was set on the trip. And she sure wasn't going to let Brittan and Lorna in on the truth. Heather had no clue if absence had made Duke's heart grow fonder, but it had the opposite effect on her than Brittan had predicted. Heather was closer to being in love than ever.

The very knowledge that Duke received their box today heightened her desire to talk with him. But Heather could do nothing but wait for him to be available…or read the headlines when the paper came out.

She'd left Duke a message apologizing for not having returned his calls. She made a vague reference to having a very busy week. Duke seemed to think she lived a fairly uncomplicated life, which was exactly what Heather wanted him to believe at this point. The truth was, The Rose women had been exceptionally sneaky, and that ate up a lot of time and mental energy. They'd uncovered some interesting information that Heather knew the police...and the tabloids...would enjoy having.

Smiling, Heather curled her feet beneath her, rested her head on the pillows, and drowsily yawned. She, Lorna, and Brittan had been up until two finishing the final details of their investigation. Then she'd gotten up at six-thirty to get Lorna to the paper by eight. The most awkward thing in the whole ordeal was that Heather's uncle was involved. Heather knew she couldn't obstruct justice, even when the criminal was her mother's brother.

Her thoughts wandered back in time. Uncle Ray had never been that respectful to Grandpa Morris. Even two days before his death she'd walked in on them fighting. Grandpa Morris had called his son a crook that day. Heather hadn't known what was going on and didn't pry for details. But Grandpa Morris told Heather Ray had swindled him out of a chunk of money. At the funeral she'd been as aggravated at her uncle as she was grieved over her grandfather's death. Now Heather could add embezzlement to Uncle Ray's list of "virtues."

❋ ❋ ❋

Duke scrambled into his truck's cab, placed the box on the seat, and opened the flaps. He looked at the rose with an awe that bordered on reverence. Whoever she was, she'd pinpointed him...again. The skin on Duke's back prickled, and he felt The Rose must know him...was watching him. He gazed around the parking lot to see if a mysterious woman was spying on him. He saw no one except Mr. Young, the janitor who had been at the paper since before Moses' time. He was rolling a trash barrel toward the dumpster.

Lifting the flower, Duke pressed it to his nose and inhaled. He imagined that the woman who placed the flower inside the box smelled as good as the rose...only more exotic. Yes, *more* exotic. Her eyes would be as captivating as her perfume. Dark, sultry, entrancing. There was no end to her many facets. He could live a lifetime and never fully discover everything about her. The rose trembled.

Duke set it on the seat and began pulling out documents. Glancing through them, he realized they pointed to a surprising truth. Ray Morris embezzled money from his bank and staged the bank robbery to cover his crime. The money taken was counterfeit.

Duke crammed the documents back into the box and pressed down the flaps. Only then did he notice no postage on the box's upper-right corner. His eyes widened. "That means it must have been hand delivered!" he exclaimed.

Duke stared at the brick building. He dug his cell out of his pocket and pressed speed dial for the paper. When the receptionist answered, Duke grappled for her name. She hung out with Tisha some, and Duke had made a point of *not* knowing her name.

"Hello," he said and tried to sound polite. "This is Duke Fieldman."

"Yes?" she cooed.

"Martha Baskin brought a box to my desk a few minutes ago," he explained.

"Yes," the blonde repeated.

"Do you know anything about it? Did you see who delivered it?"

"Yes," she said again and then paused.

Duke wondered if that was the only word the woman knew.

"Well?" he prompted. "What did she look like?"

"It was a man," the blonde replied.

"A man?" Duke's forehead wrinkled.

"Uh huh. He had a beard and wore a long coat and a hat and… uh…gloves too, I think."

"Gloves? In this weather?" Duke asked.

"Yes. Gloves. I remember because… I just remember, that's all. When he handed me the box, there were gloves."

"What about his eyes. What color—"

"He had on sunglasses."

"Sunglasses," Duke repeated and narrowed his eyes. This was starting to sound like the mafia. "And what about Martha Baskin? Did she see him too?"

"No. Not that I know of. She was walking through a couple hours later and I gave her the box to take to you."

"A couple of—"

"Just a minute. There's another call coming in." The line clicked.

Duke shut his phone and stared at it. "A couple of hours!" he exclaimed. "You let the box sit up there for *two hours?*" That was a lifetime for a breaking story.

He slammed his fist against the steering wheel and dialed the direct number to Martha Baskin. When her lifeless voice came over the line, Duke snapped, "Martha. It's Duke Fieldman. I need to talk to Mr. Gude."

"He's not taking any calls right—"

"Put Gude on the phone now!" he demanded. "It's an emergency!"

Silence. Finally she snipped, "I'll not have you talking that way to me."

Duke imagined her lips in a hard-line pucker. "Never mind then!" Duke blasted. "I'll let *you* explain why the police found out about The Rose delivery before he did this time."

More silence.

"Just a minute," she finally snapped. "I'll put you through."

TWENTY-THREE

Heather stood near the Continental Airlines boarding gate for the shuttle flight to Lubbock. She checked her watch for the third time and looked up one length of the airport terminal and then the next. She and Duke had played phone tag for two days. Heather had known that receiving the box from The Rose would absorb his time, so she completely understood his sporadic attempts to return her calls. In the call late last night he'd told her to meet him at the gate. He had emailed her the electronic ticket.

Spotting a businessman poring over the front page of the *Houston Star*, Heather smiled. He wasn't the only one interested in the lead story. It was brilliant, and the photo of her shocked uncle vindicated Heather's grandfather. The companion article on The Rose poured fuel on everyone's flaming curiosity. Duke quoted the receptionist's description of the man who delivered the box and asked for anyone who had any information on him to step forward.

The previous article had assumed The Rose was female, but this last one seemed more ambiguous on the serial sleuth's gender. Heather chuckled. Each case grew more and more adventurous. She was already brainstorming about another creative way to deliver the rose to Duke the next round.

She glanced at her watch. Boarding started in five minutes. Heather had already left a voice mail for Duke fifteen minutes ago, but she decided to try him again. She was pulling her phone from her purse when his voice interrupted her.

"Hello, gorgeous."

Heather's head popped up, and she stared into a huge bouquet of ruby-red roses. She stiffened and stared as horror slowly washed through her mind. Duke had deduced she was The Rose, and he'd brought her roses as a symbol of his discovery. Her widened gaze shifted to his face.

"Are you okay?" he asked, his eyes full of concern…and nothing more. "What gives? Are you allergic to roses or something?" He lowered the bouquet. "Do they give you hives or—"

"N–no! No, oh—oh no!" Heather stammered. She'd assumed the worst, that was all. She was paranoid—a paranoid serial sleuth. Heather giggled and Duke eyed her like she was *really* strange.

"I'm sorry. You just shocked me. That's all. I wasn't expecting…" She accepted the gift, buried her face in the roses, absorbed the luscious smell. "Wow! They're fantastic."

Duke's face relaxed into a smile the size of Canada. "I'm glad you like them," he said, his gaze traveling over her features. "Wow! You look great! I think I've missed you."

"I *know* I've missed you," Heather replied and snuggled in closer as he wrapped his arm around her. He wore a sweatshirt, jeans, and the usual boots. Heather was glad she'd chosen a simple jogging suit.

"Sorry to run up at the last minute like this." He checked his watch. "I wrote way late and had to rush around like crazy this morning. And the traffic!" He pressed his fingertips against his temple. "On the way here I was wondering if I was crazy to even think of going to Lubbock now. But Mom and Dad have been so nervous about the robberies, and I feel like they need me home. One of their neighbors was shot last week."

"My word!" Heather gasped.

Duke nodded. "Yep. Shot, but not killed. The bullet shattered his thigh bone. They're starting a Neighborhood Crime Watch this weekend."

"Well, maybe that will help."

"I hope so. Problem is, their 'neighborhood,'" Duke drew invisible quote marks in the air, "is about a ten-mile radius and involves several ranches outside Lubbock. It's kinda hard to look out for each other when you have to use binoculars to see your neighbor."

"Maybe they can take turns patrolling during the night or something."

"Yes, they're talking about all sorts of things. And the local authorities are beefing up their patrolling too."

"Good." Heather nodded. "Listen, I saw your article this morning."

The attendant announced their flight.

"Great!" Duke's expression brightened. "I was wondering if you'd noticed it."

"Noticed it?" Heather chuckled. "Ray Morris is my *uncle*."

Duke's eyes rounded, and he went stone silent. "You're kidding," he finally rasped.

"Nope." Heather lifted her chin. "I've never been close to him. My mom was until he ditched his wife for his secretary. She's been mad at him ever since for that one. And, really, the way the article read, I think Uncle Ray is probably going to get what he deserved."

His face relaxing, Duke adjusted his carry-on and stepped toward the flight clerk. Heather fell in beside him, and they presented their tickets.

"He treated my grandfather like a dog," she continued as they entered the boarding tunnel. "Two days before Grandpa Morris died, he called Uncle Ray a crook. I was there. Then, when Uncle Ray left, Grandpa Morris told me he had swindled him out of money. No telling what else he's done that nobody knows about."

"The police are on it," Duke said. "As a matter of fact, they were already on to him."

"Good." Heather nodded.

"Glad to hear you're taking this so well," Duke said. "I had no idea he was your uncle."

"I'm all for justice being served," Heather said. "When my grandfather died, I was nearly as aggravated at Uncle Ray as I was upset that Grandpa Morris was gone."

They paused in the short line that formed at the plane's doorway.

"My mom's pretty upset about Uncle Ray," Heather continued. "I think she knows he needs to pay for what he's done, but she hates that he's done something so despicable."

"Of course," Duke said. "But this is a pretty big family upheaval. I'm sure your mom doesn't want you to go right now."

"Oh well." Heather waved the roses and didn't let herself relive the argument she and her mother had over this trip. Her mom would have used anything as an excuse to get Heather to stay, and this robbery business was the most convenient. "She'll just have to deal with it," Heather said, repeating what she'd told her mom.

"Are you sure you should be going out of town?" Duke worried. "You don't have to—even now."

Heather beamed up at Duke. "The only thing that would stop me from this trip is my own death," she confessed...and immediately wondered if she should be so transparent.

Duke glowed for a few seconds before the attendant said, "Move along, please."

Heather glanced at the smiling woman and then at the line forming behind them. She and Duke had stopped the flow of traffic. A line ten deep was waiting for them to board. Duke cleared his throat and stepped aside for Heather to enter the plane. Not even the jumble of finding their seats could minimize the delicious tremor that slowly assaulted Heather. Duke's enthusiastic welcome had been worth every phone call she didn't return. And once they stowed away his carry-on and the roses, settled into their seats, and buckled their seat belts, his taking Heather's hand didn't surprise her. She twined her fingers with his and smiled into his face.

"Grandpa Morris," he said. "I've heard you mention him before, haven't I?"

"Yes." Heather nodded. "He's the reason I have the theme song from *Bonanza* on my cell, remember?"

"Oh yeah." Duke nodded.

"Right. And did I tell you that your eyes remind me of his?" Heather tried to hold back the admiration oozing from her heart, but her voice sounded as enthralled as she was.

"Ah ha! So we've gotten to the bottom of it," Duke gloated. "You're after me because you have a grandfather fixation."

Heather slapped at his arm. "Not at all. I didn't mean it that way. It's just that he had brown eyes and he was really honest—a good man. I can see the same in you."

"So you *don't* have a fixation on me." Duke groaned. "*Now* she tells me—*after* I bought her plane ticket."

"Well, when you put it *that* way, maybe…"

"Look," Duke leaned within kissing distance and smiled into her eyes, "it really doesn't matter why you have an asphyxiation. Just as long as there *is* one."

Heather laughed out loud. "So now you want me suffocated?"

He moved toward her ear and growled, "No, I want you kissed." Duke lingered near, and Heather's pulse raced as if he *had* kissed her.

The attendant's voice scratched over the intercom. The plane started rolling. Duke inched back, and his dark gaze melted the last traces of Heather's resolve. She was in love, and she couldn't do one thing to stop it.

Still holding Heather's hand, Duke rested his head against the seat and closed his eyes while the plane taxied down the runway. Heather looked good. She smelled good. She felt great next to him. He had missed her. A lot. Too much. He'd missed her more than he realized.

You're getting carried away, he told himself. *Cool it.*

Heather's eyes told him she was getting more eager with every meeting. While the adoration did wonders for his ego, Duke didn't want to hurt her. His initial worries that Heather might be a rich, fickle female who'd toss him aside when she became bored with him now seemed ridiculous. She was just the opposite, and he was the one hedging on commitment.

Nevertheless, he still wanted to kiss her like crazy. But this was a public place and kissing was off limits. *Probably for the best,* he admonished himself and recalled the strict limits he and Mike had set for each other. Despite Mike's jesting, the guy had been very good for him, and he hoped he'd been just as good for his bud.

The plane lurched into the air. Duke shifted against his seat. He turned his head toward Heather and opened his eyes. She was staring out the window, watching the runway slip away while they floated into the blue sky. She shifted in her seat, glanced toward him, smiled.

"Penny for your thoughts," Duke said.

"I was just thinking about that other article you had in the paper this morning."

He lifted his head. "You mean about The Rose?"

"Yes." She glanced down.

"Let's talk about a fixation," Duke admitted. "That mystery is driving me nuts."

"Sounds like it's driving most of Houston nuts, too. I remember reading several letters to the editor about it."

"And those were just the ones printed," Duke revealed. "We started getting immediate emails again this morning when the paper hit. Our subscriptions have gone way up. So have our direct sales. And Mr. Gude thinks I'm the fair-haired boy. He told me to take Monday off if I wanted it. He's even talking about giving me a real office again."

"So this has been good for your career?"

"Beyond good. I don't know why she's singled me out, but it looks like I'm da man now."

"And you're sure it's a woman?" Heather stroked the back of his hand.

"Well, the receptionist *did* say the person who delivered the box was a man, but I'm wondering…" Duke gazed out the window and went into the brain file marked "The Rose."

"Chances are very high," he thought aloud, "that she wouldn't deliver her own box. And if she did, she wouldn't show up in broad daylight looking like herself, ya know. Also, he was dressed like a gangster or something—even wore sunglasses and gloves. Maybe it was a woman disguised as a man. I don't know. Whoever it is, I think she's someone I've met or who is known in the community. She's *got* to be."

He focused back on Heather and said, "Thanks for asking, by the way. I'm glad you're interested."

"Interested?" Heather responded. "It's fascinating."

"Well, you didn't act like you were into it much when we were at the beach."

"Maybe I was distracted." Heather's smile held myriad underlying messages, and Duke relived that wild chase with the waves. Of all the times he'd spent with Heather, that day was his favorite. They'd been drenched and sandy and his knees burned like the dickens. But there'd been something magical in the sun and sea. They'd absorbed the wonder and gotten a little high.

"Actually, I can't believe The Rose story hasn't been syndicated by now," Heather continued. "I figure the whole state's going to be on its ear before this is over. Who knows! *20/20* might call."

"Oh, now why don't we just dream big." Duke rubbed his chin but couldn't push away the pleased grin.

"Your article today sounded like maybe you aren't so sure she's a woman anymore."

"Did it?"

Heather nodded.

"Didn't really mean to have that effect. I do still believe it's a woman." Duke narrowed his eyes and gazed past her. "My gut says she's female. And really clever and crafty."

Just my kind of woman, Duke thought and tried to rein in his wandering mind. He'd lectured himself this morning about giving Heather a chance. She was real. The Rose was a fantasy, nothing more. For all he knew the person who delivered the package might have been a man. Maybe the guy was married to The Rose, and they were working together. So technically that would make them *both* The Rose. Who knew?

Rose or no, this weekend with Heather was happening whether Duke meant for it to or not. He'd have to be blind not to see this lady was enamored with him. And he would be a lying dog if he didn't admit that what he saw in her eyes made him feel like one special guy.

Duke glanced toward Heather. She was once again looking out the window. He allowed his gaze to linger on her profile, on her hair. He recalled the first night they met and how he'd been jolted into the awareness that Heather wasn't average by any measure of the word.

Eyeing the seat in front of him, Duke weighed the whole situation. Did he know himself well enough to determine whether his caution in the relationship was stemming from the old scars with Sarah? Or was it logical awareness that Heather wasn't the type of woman he needed for a lifetime commitment? A marriage couldn't be based only on how special she made him feel or whether or not they had chemistry. It had to be based on mutual love, respect, and long-term compatibility.

As his eyes lazed shut, his sister's annoying voice barged into his thoughts. *Listen, Duke, you over-analyze everything. And if you don't stop, you're going to analyze yourself right into a nursing home and die alone!* Duke frowned. That woman had a way with words. And most the time Duke wished she'd keep her way with words to herself. Shauna had been opinionated their whole childhood, and she didn't seem to think she should stop now. Duke wouldn't be surprised if she met him at the airport with a sermon ready to be delivered smack on top of his head.

Just leave me alone, will ya? he thought and slammed the door on his sister's voice. Shauna's warnings aside, Duke decided this weekend would be a good time for him to do some serious praying and searching his heart to see if maybe...just maybe...

TWENTY-FOUR

Duke hadn't been wrong about Shauna. When he and Heather neared the luggage area, she stood waiting for them like a tall, skinny army sergeant. She was dressed in a navy trench coat with gold buttons on the shoulders. That plus her short, dark hair added to her military look. Duke decided that Shauna and Heather's mother would get along really well. *Either that or they'd rip out each other's eyeballs like the vampire cat tried to do to Jake,* he thought.

Arms crossed, Shauna gazed across the baggage claim area bustling with people, luggage, and more people. She chewed a piece of gum like she was mad at it and appeared to have no idea Duke was feet away. He looked at Heather, winked, and carefully approached his sister from behind. When he was a couple feet from her, he leaned in and said, "Boo!"

Shauna flailed her arms, jumped, and whirled around. "Duke!" she yelled and punched him hard below the shoulder. "Why do you always do that!"

"I have no idea," he admitted and reached for Heather's hand. "Just something I have to do."

She gazed at Heather. "You must be Heather." Shauna extended her hand. Heather shifted the roses to her left hand, and the two shook. "I hope my brother treats you better than he does me."

Heather grinned.

"It's really great to meet you," Shauna continued. "We've heard *so much* about you."

"Oh really?" Heather asked and glanced toward Duke.

He didn't comment. He'd called his parents last week and told them he was bringing Heather with him. When his mom pressed for details, he'd just said she was a new friend. Duke filled in the rest of what probably happened. His mother and sister most likely kept the phone lines hot since they'd learned the news. Hence the claim of hearing a lot about Heather. Shauna had "heard" herself talking to her mom. Since bringing home a woman was a first for him, he could only imagine what they'd said. He was sure he saw wedding bells in Shauna's eyes.

This weekend might be a long one, he determined and rubbed his forehead. *Why can't my family take everything at face value and not read more into this than there is?*

"So, Shauna, what brings you home?" Duke asked and spotted his sole piece of luggage gliding along the baggage claim belt. He hustled past a couple and moved toward the belt while quickly eyeing his sister over his shoulder.

"I flew in yesterday," she explained and crossed her arms. "I wanted to meet Heather." Shauna smiled at Heather again.

Duke figured Heather was going to glow in the dark before all this was over. He reached for his bag and didn't bother to respond to Shauna.

"That's mine coming now." Heather stepped beside Duke and pointed to a hot pink number that was the size of a small elephant.

"Egads, woman!" Duke teased as he picked it up. "Did you bring your entire wardrobe?"

"No, just a few extras—just in case." Heather giggled.

"I'll pull yours, Duke," Shauna said, "and you pull Heather's. She's got her hands full with her roses and purse." She peered at Heather. "Where *did* you get those roses anyway? Surely not from—"

"*I* bought them for her," Duke bragged.

"What's this world coming to?" Shauna drawled. "I didn't even know you knew what a rose was."

Heather giggled again.

"I know all about roses," Duke boasted. "We've got one on the loose in Houston. Have you heard?"

"Actually, yes. Mom faxed me your last article and then called me this morning after you called her. I went online and saw your new stories." Shauna nodded as tinges of respect and affection filtered through the big sister persona. "Not bad for a West Texas boy."

"Not bad?" Duke bellowed. "Not bad!"

"I thought it was brilliant," Heather chimed in.

"Okay." Shauna lifted her hand. "I'll admit it may have been br–rrill–lient." She stumbled over the last word.

Duke threw back his head and laughed. "I heard you! You said 'brilliant.' This is a historical moment!"

"Let's not get carried away," Shauna warned.

Nearing his sister, Duke grabbed her hand and pressed his lips against the back of it.

"What was *that* for?" she asked.

"Just thought you might enjoy being kissed by someone brilliant," Duke flirted.

Shauna directed a fake glare at him and then walked toward the glass doorway. "Come on, Heather. I found a parking place in the garage. It's not far." Her smile was encouraging. "You can sit up front with me, okay?"

※ ※ ※

When Shauna steered the Ford down the ranch's long drive,

Heather was taken with the quaint, frame home in the middle of acres and acres of flatland Texas. Once the car stopped, she stepped out and stood beside the open door while she absorbed the essence of Duke's childhood home. A few oaks clustered near the house and some patches of grass were the only foliage. A lone swing hung on the porch and swayed in the wind. Two coon hounds whacked the porch with their tails, but didn't bother to drag their lazy bones up. The wind whipped a dust devil into a frenzy in the pasture. And in that pasture, Texas longhorns mingled with ordinary-looking cows. Heather couldn't remember the other breed's name, and it was making her crazy. The cool breeze carried smells of dust and livestock and a whiff of home cooking.

Already she loved this place. Heather could see how the area had shaped the man she was falling in love with. It was an unapologetic land that wasn't in the mood to change for anyone. She caught at her flying hair and smiled. This was going to be a really good weekend.

An older woman, every bit as tall and thin as Shauna, stepped out onto the porch. "You're already here!" she called and hurried down the steps. She wore a sweat suit and walking shoes. Her gray hair was cut in a chic, chin-length style that pleasantly surprised Heather.

Duke dragged the pink bag to the front of the car, released it, and met his mother with open arms. He swayed back and forth and then pulled away and planted a firm kiss on the center of her forehead.

"Look at you!" Mrs. Fieldman said and placed her hands on either side of her son's face. "Just look at you! You're getting thinner and thinner. It's a good thing I've cooked all day. You need every bite of everything I've made."

"Ah, Mom," Duke said. He motioned toward Heather.

Heather stepped around the car door toward Duke while Shauna dragged his bag out of the trunk.

"And this must be Heather," Mrs. Fieldman said with a welcoming smile that put Heather at ease. Even though Shauna and Duke had verbally sparred all the way from the airport, Shauna had pleasantly chatted with Heather between rounds. And that had made Heather hope the mother was as open and friendly as the daughter. Her wish was fulfilled.

"Hello, Mrs. Fieldman," Heather said. "It's so nice to meet you."

"Call me Fran," the woman insisted and shook Heather's hand. Her brown eyes were as warm as Duke's, and Heather decided right then that if she couldn't have Fran Fieldman for a mother-in-law, she wanted her clone. Grandpa Morris would have liked these people.

No, he would have loved them, Heather corrected as she detected the aroma of apple pie clinging to Fran.

"Where's Dad?" Duke asked and gazed across the pasture.

"He's down at the Trentons'." She pointed south. "He's at the community crime watch meeting. I'd have gone, but I wanted to wait for you."

"How is all that?" Duke worriedly gazed toward the house. "Have any other houses been broken into?"

"No." Fran shook her head. "Just what I told you—the Trentons' three nights ago and the Jones' the week before that."

"Oh man," Heather gasped.

"Looks like they're after what they can sell at a pawnshop. You know, computers, guns, TVs. We figure it's probably for drug money." Fran nodded and crossed her arms.

Sighing, Duke shook his head and gazed up the road. "I guess you're not safe anywhere these days."

"It'll be okay. We're talking about installing an alarm system, and then there's the community crime watch." She waved her hand as if dismissing any anxiety, but her eyes hinted that she wasn't as at ease as her words indicated.

"Well, Super Duke is here!" he claimed and stuck out his chest.

"Oh brother," Shauna snorted from behind.

Fran patted Duke's shoulder. "You're a good son," she said and smiled a silent message toward Heather: *And some lucky woman is going to get a good husband.*

Heather glanced down.

"Did Dad take his truck or the Jeep?" Duke asked.

"His truck," Fran said. "The Jeep's 'round back."

Duke grinned at Heather. "Wanta go for a ride?" he asked. "We can drive down to the Trentons' place and check out the meeting. Then I can show you the little house I lived in when I came back home from college." He gestured to the east, and Heather spotted a tiny frame home a hundred yards away.

"Sure," she said.

"I've got the extra house all fixed up and ready for you this weekend," Fran said. "Since Heather and Shauna have our two guest rooms, I didn't figure you'd mind."

"Not at all," Duke agreed.

"Well, let's at least get your luggage in before you go drag the poor girl into a dust storm," Shauna complained.

Looking skyward, Duke placed his hand on his chest and said, "I've gotta be a saint to put up with this."

"Dream on," Shauna drawled and dimpled at Heather. "Come on." She jerked her head toward the house. "Mom's got some apple pie ready. Maybe Duke will at least let you get a piece before he makes you start feeding the cows."

"Okay," Heather said. "I just need to get my purse and the roses." She glanced back while moving toward the vehicle.

"Mom," Duke said, draping his arm across his mother's shoulders, "wanta go with us to the meeting? That way you won't miss anything important."

"Sure," Fran agreed.

Purse and roses in one hand, Heather snapped the car door closed.

"You're always so thoughtful Duke," Fran continued, just loud enough to ensure Heather's hearing.

Smiling, Heather stepped beside Duke, took his hand, and wondered if he was as ready to get married as his family was ready to marry him off.

TWENTY-FIVE

Saturday after dinner Duke sat in the shadows in the sunroom at the back of the house. The sun had long ago dipped below the horizon, and a full moon rose from the east. Duke gazed across the acres of cattle country that stretched as far as the moonlight's silvery beams and relished the familiar comfort of being back at his roots.

His stomach was full.

His mind was at ease.

He was comfortably drowsy.

He stretched. The wooden chair rocked with his movement. He rested his sock-clad feet on the table and yawned.

Over dinner the conversation had centered on Duke's photography. By the time the meal was finished, his mother was ushering Heather to the hallway she'd turned into a photo gallery.

Then Heather had promised his dad another game of checkers. Last Duke saw, the two were locked in battle for their third game of the weekend. Yesterday after the neighborhood meeting, Heather had soundly beaten his father the first round. He'd returned the favor the second. Tonight they were going for the tie breaker.

Earlier that day Duke took Heather to the place where he'd photographed the rope tornado. He'd been pleased that Heather was as fascinated as if she'd seen the phenomena in person.

This afternoon the whole family went to a matinee performance of *The Sound of Music* at the community theater. Heather said the place was quaint. Duke figured she and her family had probably been invited backstage for many opening nights on Broadway, yet her enjoyment of the local production seemed genuine enough.

Tomorrow they'd do church, lunch, and then catch the afternoon flight home.

Duke rested his head against the back of the rocking chair and closed his eyes. So far no one had proposed for him or made any embarrassing remarks. He was beginning to think they weren't going to push it. *This has been an easy weekend after all,* he thought as footsteps tapped through the tile kitchen and neared the sunroom.

The light came on. Duke lifted his head, squinted against the invasion, and gazed up at his sister. "Turn that light off, will ya?" he complained.

She obeyed. "Sorry. We were just wondering what happened to you."

"I'm getting sleepy and grouchy." He yawned again. "Came out here to check out the moon."

Shauna plopped into a chair near him and softly whistled. "Not bad."

"You don't see this in downtown Houston," Duke admitted.

"Not in Nashville either," Shauna said.

Duke appreciated the moon all over again...along with the million or so stars and the black-indigo sky. He had a hunch Shauna had hunted him down for a reason and discreetly glanced toward her.

She caught him in the act. Even in the shadows, the woman was like the control room of a warship. She never missed a thing. Duke wouldn't be surprised if X-ray laser beams shot from her eyes every second.

"Heather is beating the socks off dad again," she said through a smile.

"Good." Duke chuckled. "He's had it coming for a long time. I finally quit playing him."

"You're a sore loser."

"Nope. I just know when I'm whipped." Duke placed his feet on the floor, rested his elbows on his knees, and laughed. "I don't see *you* standing in line to get beat."

"Are you kidding?" Shauna said. "I'm as sore a loser as you are."

"I think he's been king long enough," Duke said.

"She says her Grandpa Morris taught her." Shauna slipped her feet out of her loafers and rested them on the table.

"She is crazy about that guy. He died a few years ago. I would have liked to meet him. I think he was a big influence on Heather. He and her father, anyway. Her dad is a really nice guy too. Her mother..." Duke hesitated and hunted for a delicate way to describe her. Then he decided to just do what had always worked for him in the past—tell it like it is. "Her mother's the Wicked Witch of the South."

"Ooo," Shauna said.

"I'd like to see her try to tear into you though," Duke said through a laugh.

"What's *that* supposed to mean?"

"Oh, I don't know. You figure it out." Duke leaned back, crossed his arms, rested his head on the back of the chair, and observed his spunky sister. The moonlight offered enough illumination for Duke to see her narrow her eyes. He laughed. "I just think you'd do a good job of handling her, that's all," he offered. "It's a compliment, big sister."

Shauna gazed toward the stars and finally said, "So her granddad was an oil man?"

"Yep. He hit it big during the Kilgore, Texas, oil boom. That's East Texas. Ever heard of it?"

"No. You?"

"Uh uh. I guess we need to go to *East* Texas and get some culture." Duke rubbed the sides of his mouth.

"I don't know if *you* can get any culture. Heather's about as close as you've come. I take it she's rich then?"

"Stinkin'," Duke responded. "You heard of Shelby Oil?"

"Yes." Shauna shifted.

Duke nodded.

"That's them?" she gasped.

"Yep. Her parents are it. Her father's family had oil too. From what Heather's said, I figured they merged what her mother inherited with what her father inherited. I'd say we're talkin' billions. She lives in a castle, for cryin' out loud."

"You mean a real one?"

"Well, as real as a replica can get. It looks like it was picked up from Scotland and dropped outside Houston."

"What is she doing with *you* then?"

"She likes me." Duke shrugged and extended his hands. "What can I say?"

"Humph."

"At first I thought she was just having a rich girl fling, and she'd get rid of me when she got bored."

"I don't think so." Shauna shook her head.

"Me neither," Duke admitted. "Not now." *Now I've got the opposite problem*, he thought but didn't verbalize it. "Anyway, I told her she's a princess and I'm a frog, and no matter how many times she kisses me, I'll still be a frog."

"So you *have* kissed her?" Shauna asked. "Mom and I wondered."

"That's none of your business," Duke countered good-naturedly.

"Well, there *is* something I'm going to make my business."

Shauna placed her feet on the floor, leaned closer, and pointed at him. "If you let her get away, I think I'm going to strangle you."

"Well, I love you too." Straightening, Duke observed his sister and waited for her X-ray laser beams to strike him dead.

"Seriously, Duke, she's nuts about you. I can see it all over her."

"We've only been seeing each other about six weeks." Duke made sure every word was measured and tempered with plenty of reserve.

"Well, I knew by then that Keith was the right one."

His back stiffened. "Yes, but you didn't marry him for two years."

"I'm not suggesting you should elope right now! I just think she's the best thing that's ever happened to you. Forget the money. She's really sweet."

"Truth is, I wish she weren't so rich. But even if she were broke, I'm just not sure, Shauna. I'm going slow." Duke hoped she had the sense to hear the warning in his voice.

"You've got commitment issues. You know that, don't you?" Shauna leaned toward him again.

Duke looked back at the moon and didn't bother to answer.

"If you're going so slowly, why'd you bring her home?" she challenged.

He eyed his sister in the moonlight. Her ivory skin held a translucent appeal that Duke figured many men would find attractive. His brother-in-law sure thought she was a babe. Duke just wished she'd *have* a babe…or maybe six. That would get her focused elsewhere…and it would be great to have some nieces and nephews.

"She sort of invited herself," Duke explained in a low voice and glanced toward the doorway to make sure no one was listening. "I didn't have what it takes to tell her no."

Shauna's volume matched his when she replied, "Well, if she

did invite herself, you should count yourself lucky." She crossed her arms.

"And when are you and Keith planning on having kids?" Duke questioned.

"What does that have to do with—"

"I think it's high time. It'll give you something to do besides harass me."

She looked toward the moon. "If I'm harassing you, it's because I love you," she asserted, her voice firm. "And I want to see you find a good wife. And I think maybe Heather would be perfect."

"I'm just not sure," Duke repeated.

"At some point you've got to let go of what Sarah did to you."

"Who said anything about Sarah?"

"*I* did," Shauna insisted. "God can help you finish working through all that if you'll let Him."

Hesitant footsteps entered the kitchen. Duke gazed through the darkness and detected the pale outline of a petite frame.

"Out here, Heather," he called. "Let's drop this," he mumbled to Shauna.

"Of course," she whispered back. "But I *will* be praying for you." And the promise sounded more like a threat.

Duke would have retorted, but Heather was too close. He stood, turned toward her, and smiled. "Hello there, Little Pink Riding Hood," he said because she wore her pink sweater with the hood. "We were just out here watching the moon. Wanta join us?" He pointed to the chair nearest him.

"Sure," Heather agreed and paused near to Duke's chair.

He squeezed her hand and enjoyed the way it felt in his. *I'm not getting serious about her,* he reminded himself. *Just warming up a little, that's all.*

"So what happened with the checkers?" Shauna asked. "When I left you were on the verge of beating Dad's socks off."

"His socks are *gone!*" Heather dashed her free hand through the air.

"I hear you out there!" Daniel Fieldman bellowed from the kitchen. The kitchen light clicked on. The porch light was next.

The towering cattleman stood in the doorway. Hands on hips, he observed all three of them. "And I'll have you know I'm still wearing my socks." He lifted a bootless foot. A white sock extended from beneath his jeans.

Duke chuckled.

"She may *look* innocent," his eyes sparkling with mirth, Daniel pointed toward Heather, "but she's a checker demon."

"I learned from the best," Heather bragged with a smug grin.

"I was just telling Duke it's high time you got whipped," Shauna said. "It's time you got a dose of your own medicine."

"I'm not going to talk about it anymore," Daniel said with a grin. "Fran's bringing us apple pie and decaf." He crossed his arms. "Do you bunch of renegades want ice cream with it?"

Lifting his brows, Duke eyed Heather.

"Sure," she said. "Why not?"

"I'll tell her to put an extra helping of arsenic on yours, lil' lady," Daniel said with an exaggerated wink.

"Are you sure you don't want to rent a hotel room tonight, Heather?" Duke asked. "You might just wake up dead in the morning."

"I'll take my chances." Heather observed Daniel and playfully squinted. "He doesn't scare me."

"Come on, sweetie," Shauna said and tugged on Heather's arm. "Let's go help Mom and let these big boys sit out here and commiserate."

Duke released Heather's hand and watched her walk into the kitchen with his sister. A slow realization dawned on him. Heather was single-handedly stealing his family's hearts.

And maybe mine too, he admitted.

With a jolt Duke realized The Rose hadn't crossed his mind since yesterday. His eyes widened. Duke felt his father's gaze. He stared into his dad's dark eyes a few seconds. What he saw there was a man-to-man awareness that transcended his sister's nosy threats. He looked down.

Part of the reason Duke had come out to the sunroom was to get some distance between him and Heather. The weekend had been creating one memorable experience after another. Everything was getting too cozy too fast. Nevertheless, Duke found himself swept ever closer to Heather like a canoer fighting white water and heading straight toward a waterfall.

TWENTY-SIX

As much as Heather enjoyed sitting in the sunroom, chatting through the evening with Duke's folks, she was ready for bed. The day had been one pleasing oasis after another. Heather had gathered up special moments and memories and stored them in her heart to savor. After a giant yawn, she snuggled under the covers and reached to click off the lamp. A languid smile tugged at her lips. Some of the savoring would start now.

"Goodnight, dolls," she said to the collection in the corner. They reminded her of the dolls that had been in Grandpa Morris' guestroom. They had belonged to her grandmother, who'd died when Heather was eight. The room's Victorian decor also resembled her grandparents' furnishings. This place felt as much like home as the welcoming light in Daniel and Fran Fieldman's eyes.

Before turning off the light, Heather admired the vase full of Duke's roses now perched on the Queen Anne dressing table. Even though they were wilting around the edges, they were still the most beautiful flowers Heather had ever seen. Before she and Duke left for their flight tomorrow, Heather planned to move them to the dining table as a gift for his mother. The cut crystal vase they were in came from Tiffany's. Heather had brought it as a hostess gift. When she left the roses, she'd leave the vase too.

She clicked off the light. Her mind flowed around her ranch experiences. Yesterday afternoon, after the crime watch meeting, Fran had asked to go back home. Duke had obliged and then taken Heather to the little house he'd lived in before moving to Houston. Before driving away to explore more of the ranch, Duke told Heather she was beautiful and laid a lazy kiss on her that curled her toes even now.

He'd repeated the event today when he showed her the path that wild tornado had taken...except today's kiss was far from lazy... more like an unpredictable twister. Duke had kept a respectable distance after that one. Heather sensed his restraint and respected him for it.

Later everyone went to town. The play hadn't been half as smooth as the Broadway encores her family attended, but she enjoyed it. Duke held her hand the whole time. Heather crumpled the sheet under her chin and tried to remember what the actors looked like, but nothing came...except the delicious memory of Duke next to her.

Her cell phone bleeped from across the room. Heather's fingers relaxed around the covers. *That's a text message,* she thought and wondered if it were from her mom, or Brittan, or Lorna.

Heather tossed aside the covers, switched the lamp back on, and crawled out of bed. Once she left the cotton throw rug, Heather enjoyed the cool hardwood floor against her feet. She grabbed her cell phone from her purse, flipped it open, and read a message from Brittan.

> *Breaking news. Houston girl nabbed at Neiman Marcus. Promi-*
> *nent family. Kidnapper asking ransom. We're on it. Come home*
> *soon. B & L*

Heather eyed the message with disbelief. After the bank robbery she'd expected a break for The Rose. But it looked like Brittan and

Lorna hadn't shared her thoughts. A young girl being kidnapped did drive Heather's sympathy, and if that wasn't a worthy project, nothing was.

Here we go again! Heather pressed Brittan's speed-dial number. Her friend answered on the first ring.

"Can you get to a computer?" Brittan asked without saying hello.

"Well, the Fieldmans have one in their family room," Heather hedged. "I didn't bring my laptop. Duke said it wouldn't do any good. There's no wireless service here."

"The kidnapping is featured on the Channel 2 website," Brittan explained. "Three customers saw her walking across the parking lot crying. A man was close behind. They thought she was just arguing with her father, but now the authorities are saying the guy probably had a gun to her back."

"Wow!" Heather gasped. "And he's asking for a ransom?"

"Yep. The mother and father are a husband–wife surgeon team. This guy didn't just randomly strike. He wanted someone who could fork over dough."

"How much—"

"One million," Brittan stated.

Heather whistled. Her taking karate had been her father's idea for this very reason. He told her when she was eleven that she could either enroll and excel or he'd hire a full-time bodyguard like he did for her mother. Heather chose enrolling and excelling. Her mother preferred the bodyguard and had assigned Lars to her on occasion. Heather had permanently shed Lars when she won the national karate championship her senior year of high school. She'd repeated the honor two years ago.

"Like I said," Brittan continued, "we're all over it. When are you due home?"

"The plane lands at six," Heather replied and was torn by a poignant desire to extend the weekend while also itching to be with her friends in the middle of another case.

"Call us when you get home, okay?" Brittan asked.

"You bet," Heather said before the two disconnected the call.

The wedding march plodded through Duke's mind like a dirge. He dragged himself toward the minister and stopped and waited while Heather glided down the aisle in the halting gait of brides everywhere. Her face was covered in a white veil, but Duke caught a gauzy glimpse of pink lips and blue, blue eyes. She was beautiful... so beautiful. But Duke felt like he was stepping into a cage. And every inch she progressed, the larger the box loomed.

Heather stopped at his side. Duke took her hands. His heart's hammering drowned the minister's droning. Finally he told them to put on their wedding bands. Heather tried to put his ring on his finger. She pushed and shoved. Duke wanted to stop trying, but Heather kept on until the ring was forced into place. The tight band felt like it was around his throat. And with the "I dos" said, the knot was tied as tight as death.

The minister's final words closed the door on the cage. "I now pronounce you husband and wife. You may kiss the bride."

Duke lifted Heather's veil and bent to kiss her. Before their lips touched, an anguished cry of "Noooooooo!" erupted from the back of the church.

Jolted, Duke turned toward a tall woman dressed in black and holding a single-stemmed red rose.

Joy took his breath away. Panting, he rushed toward The Rose's open arms, but after two steps he hit the cage walls. Like a crazed ape, Duke shook the bars and bellowed. The Rose faded away, an anguished ghost never to return. *Never*.

His opportunity passed.

He'd sealed his doom.

He was now Mr. Heather Winslow.

Duke opened his eyes, sat straight up in bed, gasped for air, and shoved aside the covers that bound his legs. Cold sweat dampened his body. He shifted and stared at the space beside him. No one was there. He rubbed his face as reality chased away the dream's hazy terror.

"Only a dream," he whispered. "Just a dream." *An insane dream, that's all it was.*

Duke scrambled out of bed and checked the digital clock on the nightstand. "One forty-five," he mumbled. He was wide awake. He made a necessary trip to the bathroom and then found the remote in the tiny living room and turned on the tube. Nothing was on except *Bonanza* reruns, and that was the last song Duke wanted to listen to right now.

His stomach rumbled, and he understood exactly what it was saying: "Apple pie." Duke's mouth watered. Apple pie was his mother's cure for every ailment known to mankind. And it usually worked. Duke figured after that dream he was due a slab the size of South Dakota. He also knew he needed to make a decision about Heather.

As he pulled on his jeans and shirt and got ready to walk to his folks' home, Duke told himself he either needed to forget The Rose or forget Heather. Both were going to be hard to give up.

He opened the door of his old house, stepped into the cool Texas night, shut the door, and struck out down the lane. The moon, now high, illuminated the way like a dim streetlight. Duke figured he'd have pie in his gut in five minutes flat.

Heather is real, he asserted. *Dreams are crazy. They don't mean anything. And if you ever did marry Heather, you'd be so far gone you wouldn't even give The Rose a second look.*

A coyote's howl made the back of his neck crawl. Duke hastened his step. What he hadn't told his sister was that after that kiss this afternoon, he was seriously slipping on the edges of a cliff marked "Caution! Falling-in-Love Zone."

Shauna said he had commitment issues. Duke couldn't disagree, but he didn't quite know what to do about it. He picked up his gait to a jog to release some tension. By the time he arrived on the front porch he was puffing for air, but the release felt good.

Quietly he unlocked the front door and was in the kitchen before he sensed someone's presence. Something wasn't right. Someone was watching him. He knew it. Duke pivoted to look behind him. A bump from the direction of the sunroom snared his attention. Certain the noise must be one of the dogs outside, Duke went toward the room, reached inside, and flipped on the light. But the dogs he saw weren't the variety with pointed ears and fur. This breed was human—and one of them held his parents' computer.

Heather couldn't sleep no matter how many times she turned over, punched her pillow, and counted animals. She'd started with sheep and went on to longhorns. Finally she'd tried a round of here-fords. That's what Duke said those ordinary-looking cows were called. She looked at the digital clock and sighed. Two o'clock was swiftly approaching.

She sat up and snapped on the lamp. The soft glow illuminated the dolls and roses and antiques. Heather swung out her legs, stood on the cotton rug, and found her slippers. Brittan said there were already drawings of the kidnapper and photos of the girl on the Channel 2 website. She and Duke both had checked their emails earlier on the family's computer. Heather didn't think his parents would mind if she used it again tonight.

She picked up her raw silk robe from the end of the bed, slipped it on, and opened the door. A hard thump, a muffled cry, and Duke's bellowing, "You jerk!" stopped Heather in her tracks. Immediately, her mind flashed to the crime watch meeting she'd attended with Duke and his mother and twelve other farm and ranch owners in the area.

Heather grabbed her cell phone, plunged it into her robe pocket, and dashed down the short hallway that opened into the kitchen. More yelling. More bumps. A crash. Shattering glass. All came from the sunroom. Heather turned left and raced through the kitchen.

The sunroom's light blazed into the dark kitchen, and shadows cavorted in the glare. The first thing Heather saw was Duke sprawled on the floor. He struggled in a sea of glass below the light switch while blood dripped from a gash on his cheek. One burly man wearing a knit cap hunkered by him as another, holding a computer, kicked open the sunroom door.

"Come on!" he barked.

"But he's seen us!" the big guy protested. "We gotta get rid of him."

"Let's just get outta here!" the man with the computer urged. "I'm *not* a murderer."

That did nothing to deter the man now looming over Duke. He reached into his hip pocket and pulled out a small handgun.

His eyes wide, Duke stared at the gun and started shaking his head.

Heather wondered if this was the way Tyler had looked before he'd been murdered. Half a nation away, she'd been helpless to stop his death. But she wasn't helpless now. She was here for Duke in a way she couldn't be for Tyler.

Heather shed her house shoes, charged forward, and screamed, "Stop!"

"Heather! No! Are you crazy?" Duke hollered.

The man with the computer laughed, his thin lips stretching against yellow teeth. The husky guy twisted toward Heather and lifted the gun. Years of training took over, and Heather's body went into fight mode.

Her foot a swift blur, she kicked the gun out of the criminal's hand just as it fired. The sunroom's north wall shattered. His eyes huge, the criminal gripped his wrist. The weapon hit the floor and spun across the boards until it hit a settee's leg.

"Heather?" Duke croaked.

"You little…" the man roared and lunged forward with the swing of a beefy fist.

Heather buried the ball of her foot into his solar plexus.

"Uuuumph!" he grunted. His eyes bulged and then rolled back. He crashed to the floor like Goliath.

"Watch out!" Duke yelled.

The other guy dropped the computer and charged her. A step and a swift twist to the right put Heather in position to slam her fist against his nose. He grabbed his face, flopped to his knees, and wailed while blood stained the front of his overalls.

"What's going on in here?" Daniel Fieldman's voice boomed from the kitchen.

"Call the police!" Heather said and pitched her cell phone toward Daniel.

The clunk and clatter against tile attested that he missed the catch, but Heather figured he'd waste no time retrieving it.

She turned back to the bleeding man who'd stopped bellowing. A wild look in his eyes, he was attempting to stand.

"Don't even think it!" Heather commanded. "Sit down!"

He stood anyway. His arms flailing, he ran for Heather.

She jumped into the air and gave him another taste of the Goliath treatment. He crashed near his partner in crime.

"Hello, this is Daniel Fieldman," Duke's father said into the cell phone. He gave the necessary information and hung up.

"What happened?" Fran rasped.

Heather swiveled to face Duke's parents and his groggy sister, all rumpled and dressed in night clothes.

"She just beat the stuffin' out of the neighborhood robbers," Duke eked out and stared up at Heather like she was Godzilla.

"Well, I guess that cat's out of the bag," Heather mumbled under her breath while slipping her house shoes back on.

"Oh, Duke!" Fran ran to her son. "You're bleeding."

"Be careful!" Duke admonished. "There's glass everywhere. I'm afraid I broke your mirror." He pointed to the wall where the mirror had been hanging. "And it looks like we lost a wall too." He nodded toward the gap in the windows through which the arid autumn air flooded the room with the fragrance of the plains.

"I don't care about that!" Fran exclaimed. "But you... I'll get you a damp cloth."

Heather picked her way through the glass and neared the handgun. She had limited experience with guns. Brittan was the weapon guru of the bunch. But Heather figured the bad boys didn't know that. She stood about five feet from both and waited, gun in hand, in case they regained consciousness and tried to escape.

Duke crunched through the glass and stopped at Heather's side. He held the damp cloth to his cheek and observed Heather with a new level of respect. "What *was* all that?"

"Karate," Heather said on a sigh. "I hold a black belt. National champ two years ago...and three years before that too." Then she decided to totally come clean. "Remember when we were at your church and I'd pulled a muscle?"

"Yes."

"Well, I teach karate during PE to those girls at that Christian school, and I pulled a muscle sparring with one."

"Why didn't you tell me?" Duke asked.

"Because some men don't like dating women who can beat them to a pulp." Her smile was as weak as her knees. Even though she'd trained for years to remain calm and focused in these sorts of encounters, the aftermath of the adrenaline rush always affected her.

"Well, I won't cross you, that's for sure," Duke asserted.

Heather shook her head. "Please don't. I'm not going to—"

"It's okay." Duke gently punched her upper arm. "I'm joshing you. I'm cool with it all."

One of the criminals moaned.

Heather lifted the gun. "Do you know how to use this?" she whispered toward Duke.

"After all that you can't shoot?"

"Well, I could if I had to," Heather explained. "But I don't have any formal training."

"Who needs a gun when you can kick the mean out of somebody or break his nose, right?" He pointed toward the man unfortunate enough to taste Heather's knuckles. A slow trickle of blood dripped from his nose to the floor.

"Well…" Heather's shoulders drooped. The mild tingling in her foot and fist testified to her victory.

The larger man sat up, and Duke took the weapon. "Don't try anything stupid!" he barked.

The guy looked into the end of his own gun and slowly lifted his hands. "Don't shoot! Don't shoot!" he begged.

"I hear the police!" Shauna shouted from the front of the house. "And I see their lights too."

Daniel stepped into the sunroom behind his wife, who brought a fresh cloth to Duke.

As the distant siren became more pronounced, Duke's dad placed his hand on Heather's shoulder. "Now this is my kinda woman, Duke. You can bring her back any time."

TWENTY-SEVEN

The plane eased off the runway and drifted into the air like a giant eagle floating toward the sun. Duke glanced toward Heather, seated next to the window. She gazed at the puffy white clouds that resembled huge wads of popcorn suspended in a sea of blue. Her face was as wan now as it had been all morning. Dark circles smudged her eyes. While Heather had been responsive and polite, she hadn't said much today.

She's probably tired, Duke told himself and rested his head against the seat. After the criminals had been taken away, the police asked for full statements from him and Heather. Duke's parents investigated the house to see if anything else was missing, but found nothing gone. Once the police left, they all pitched in to clean up the glass, patch the sunroom with some plywood, and see if the computer still worked. Fortunately there was nothing wrong that a technician couldn't fix.

Even though the Fieldmans were sticklers about attending Sunday services, Duke's folks decided this was one Sunday morning they wouldn't make it. The clock in Duke's old house read four o'clock when he crawled back into bed. He hadn't gotten to sleep until six. The whole family resurrected for a late brunch. Then it was time for Heather and Duke to get packed and catch their flight.

After all that Duke didn't doubt that Heather must be drained. He was. Nevertheless, he couldn't shake the impression that her preoccupation involved more than just being tired.

"You okay?" he asked her.

Her eyes haunted, she turned toward him. "I'm exhausted," she admitted. Closing her eyes, Heather rested her head against the seat. "I was so wired after I went back to bed that I didn't go back to sleep until seven. And even then I just dozed off and on."

Duke took her hand and rubbed the back of it with his thumb. "I didn't get to sleep until nearly six." He was thankful he didn't have another wild dream about weddings and cages. He didn't share that part with Heather.

"We had a rough night."

"Yep." She kept her eyes closed.

"You've had a few hard days," he continued through a smile. "Let's see, you beat the pants off the checker king. You charmed my mom and sister so much they're ready to build a monument to you in the town square. And then you kicked the rears off the neighborhood robbers. Maybe we should change your name to Wonder Woman. I never imagined you were a deadly weapon waiting to happen. What other mysteries are you hiding from me?"

Heather's fingers flexed against his hand. She lifted her head and looked straight at him like she hadn't registered a word he said. Then her eyes filled with tears. Heather sniffed and fumbled through her pants pocket for a tissue. The search moved to her purse until she found one. Dabbing at her eyes, Heather turned her head back toward the window.

Duke stared at her. He never knew what to do when a woman cried. He was at such a loss he wished crying women could be outlawed—at least when he was around. Duke wondered if he'd done something wrong, but he couldn't imagine what that might have been.

"What's the matter, Heather?" he gently asked, and figured that was the most clichéd question on the planet.

"Oh…" she whispered, her voice quivering. After a sob, she continued, "I might as well tell you. Remember that guy I told you about…that I wanted to marry?"

"Yes," Duke said, scenarios flying through his mind. *Maybe the guy phoned Heather this morning and wanted to get back together. Maybe she never broke up with him. He's probably older and filthy rich and owns a fleet of ships or jets. He's been touring Europe. Now he's back, and Heather is going to sail off with him.*

Slow heat crept up Duke's back, spread to his neck, and warmed his cheeks. He didn't appreciate being used and then dumped. He groaned softly. Gripping the armrest, he gritted his teeth. Heather was doing exactly what he'd feared from the start. She'd used him as a rich girl's plaything, charmed his family, and now that she had the "big boy" back in her life, she was dumping him. *Just like Sarah did.*

Heather sniffled a while and wiped at her eyes.

Duke twisted into a whirlwind of mixed emotions. *If she's about to dump me, I'll never have to worry about that nightmare again. I won't have to make a decision about this relationship. And if The Rose ever does come into my life, I'm free to pursue her.*

"Well," Heather finally wobbled out, "he died."

"He died?" Duke released the hand rest. "Like, over the weekend?"

"No. He died four years ago."

"Oh," Duke said. *So much for being dumped,* he thought as cold dread was replaced by warm relief. *There is no filthy rich boyfriend. No ships or jets. Heather is as guileless as she's been from the beginning. Except she did hide that whole karate business from me.*

Is she keeping anything else from me? Like, who were those three text messages from that came through right before we boarded the plane? She'd

briefly excused herself for the ladies' room after that. Was that trip nec-
essary or an excuse to deal with the messages? And what were they about
anyway? Maybe she's really a secret spy for the CIA, Duke thought and
then nearly laughed out loud. When he was tired, his imagination
went wacky. Today he diagnosed himself as officially wacked out.
Not only was Heather not dumping him for a yacht prince, but
there was no way she could be any kind of spy.

"Anyway, we broke up, like I told you," she continued. "My
mom." She waved the tissue and let the gesture once again be
explanation enough. "And then I went on to Princeton. He stayed
at UT. Later we decided to get back together. And then..." she
gulped for air, "and then he was killed in a convenience store
robbery."

"Oh man," Duke said. "I'm so sorry."

Heather nodded. "Last night when I saw you on the floor with
those guys over you and the one pulling out his gun, I thought of
Tyler and how his murder must have gone down. Everything came
crashing back. Except this time it was *you*." She rested her head on
his shoulder, and Duke wrapped his arm around her.

The woman isn't about to dump me, Duke thought. *She's falling in*
love with me for real. The reality hit him smack between the eyes.
Shauna saw it. Mom saw it. And Dad saw it too. Sighing, he rested
his cheek on her head. *What next?*

His mind wandered to the fact that, strangely, he'd still only
met one of her friends—that gal who was the Steam Monster
flunky. And that whole apartment mess was beyond odd. Why
would the heiress to the Shelby Oil empire be running around
with someone who cleaned carpets?

Well, she's running around with me, he conceded. *And I'm just a*
newspaper reporter. But that logic didn't stop more questions from
barging in. *If that Lorna person really is cleaning carpets to make money,*
why doesn't she know what she's doing? And why did Heather tell me not
to ask questions? Duke wrinkled his brow. *Maybe there's something*

I'm missing here, he mused and wondered whose apartment that had been anyway.

Heather lifted her head, mopped at her cheeks, and took a deep breath. "I guess I was so focused last night that the situation didn't sink in until I tried to go to sleep. And now…" Heather shook her head. "I'm going to be okay. Really. I'll be fine." She batted her long, wet lashes at him.

Duke brushed at a tear trickling to the corner of her mouth. "You were phenomenal," he said and couldn't have meant it more. "I don't know many guys with a bodyguard who looks like you."

A tiny smile tugged at the corners of her mouth. "And you're not intimidated?"

"No way." Duke shook his head and fingered the scratch on his cheek. "Why should I be?"

Heather shrugged.

"At least this way I don't ever have to worry about you while you're out alone." He chuckled. "Maybe I need to worry about anybody who tries to attack you."

A soft laugh tottered from Heather.

Duke wrapped his hand around hers, lifted it to his lips, and kissed the backs of her fingers. "I guess this is one weekend we won't forget!"

"I'll never forget it," Heather replied, and the adoration spilling from her soul forced Duke to admit that he couldn't put off his decision much longer. He was either going to have to get over his terror of commitment or get over Heather.

I need a break to sort this out, Duke decided. He was noticing a pattern. When he was with Heather he lost the ability to think logically. He got tangled in her charisma. No human being could make a rational decision in that state. And if ever a man needed to make a rational decision, it was he. Hopefully Heather would understand…and Shauna would leave him alone. She'd been on his tail about this commitment business for six months.

His heavy eyelids sliding shut, Duke tilted his seat back as far as it would go and relaxed. Heather settled her head on his shoulder once more. The hum of the jet's engines lulled Duke closer and closer to the brink of slumber. Hovering between consciousness and the dream-scene, his exhausted mind wandered and rambled and fabricated. Finally he slipped into the depths of relaxation. Awareness of his surroundings faded.

He and Heather were married now. The wedding was over. So was the honeymoon. They were lying in bed, Heather's head on his shoulder. Her hair's light floral scent filled his senses but did nothing to kindle appreciation. Midnight had long passed. He was awake...wide awake. And he heard her once again, as he'd heard many nights before.

The Rose.

She called to him with a silky cadence that stirred his heart with longing. Though her voice wove through his psyche like satin, he couldn't see her. She was trapped in another reality where he couldn't go. The bonds of marriage confined him in his world... a world forever forbidden to The Rose. She was the woman he'd never met but had been yearning for. And her voice...her voice was like warm, dripping honey that satisfied his heart and promised a lifetime of joyful discovery.

Heather stirred against his shoulder, and Duke was reminded that he'd promised to love, honor, respect, and cherish her unto death. Terror crept up his legs and gnawed his soul. Hard sweat washed his body. Duke flung aside the covers and tried to scramble from the bed, but a tight strap held him down, an unrelenting chain forcing him to stay. No matter how he tried, he couldn't break the bond.

"No...no...no..." he mumbled, thrashing for his freedom.

"Duke?" Heather's urgent voice invaded his struggle.

His eyes opened. He attempted to make sense of what he saw. He wasn't in a bedroom...he was somewhere else. Somewhere familiar yet so hard to grasp.

"Duke?" Heather repeated, shaking his arm.

He snapped his attention toward her. She looked groggy-eyed and seemed worried or scared or both. Duke's attention flicked to the window. Blue sky dotted with popcorn clouds stretched into infinity.

He and Heather weren't married. He'd been dreaming. Nothing in the dream was reality. Except The Rose was still calling him. Duke could hear her voice, sense her presence. And even if the actual woman leaving those roses in his office wasn't his dream woman, The Rose somehow represented her.

He rubbed his face until it stung.

"Are you okay?" Heather questioned.

"No." He shook his head. "No, I'm not. We need to talk. I…we just need to talk." He propped his elbow on the armrest and placed his forehead in his hand.

"Okay," Heather agreed as the flight attendant's voice came over the intercom. According to her, they'd be landing in five minutes.

Duke's dry mouth testified that he had slept through the complimentary refreshments. He glanced to the left and caught a gray-haired matron watching him. She jerked her gaze downward and fumbled with her magazine.

"I think we have an audience," Duke whispered to Heather.

"Probably because you were really wild," Heather replied. "Did you have a nightmare?"

"Yes." Duke nodded. "Like I said, we need to talk. Let's wait until we get to your car, okay?"

Heather's puffy eyes took on an anxious glint. She nodded.

Duke hoped he could be suave enough to ask for some space without hurting her. But that would probably take a miracle. Of all the things Duke had been called, suave was not one of them.

TWENTY-EIGHT

🌹 Duke hadn't said much while they left the plane and claimed their luggage. Heather would have attributed his silence to exhaustion, except he'd said they needed to talk. His voice had been laced with something that affected Heather like a cold douse of water.

Once Duke had wrestled her bag into the trunk of her Porsche, Heather waited by the door. Like Duke, she'd taken a nap on the plane, but she still felt like she'd been banged over the head. Yawning, she thought the nap might have made her feel worse. She pulled a roll of mints from her pants pocket, popped one in her mouth, and extended the roll toward Duke. He'd left his bag near the back of her car and stopped a few feet away.

"No thanks," he said. "I've got a peppermint. Found it in my jacket pocket." He patted the front pocket of his leather jacket. "It's probably been there since 1970." He bit down on it and grimaced. "It's way too chewy."

Heather tried to smile but couldn't. The anguish over what Duke might want to say smothered her.

"Heather..." Duke rubbed his face. He looked every bit as haggard as Heather felt. "I don't know exactly how to say this, but..." He gazed past her as a plane's roar pierced the autumn breeze.

Heather's heart began a slow shrivel, and she fully sensed what was coming. Duke had warned her on the beach not to get too attached to him. Both Lorna and Brittan had told her he wasn't playing for keeps. And now, after a weekend when he'd made her feel so special, a weekend Heather would never forget, Duke was about to break off their relationship.

"But why?" she whispered, shaking her head.

When he lifted his brows and looked at her, Heather realized he hadn't actually verbalized his thoughts.

After seconds of gazing into her soul he said, "Because I'm just not sure. And I need some space to sort it all out."

"Some space?" she repeated and bit her mint in half.

"Yes." He gently gripped her upper arms. "That's all I'm asking for. Okay? Just a little time."

"Time?" Heather's fist relaxed, and her burning palm attested that she'd been grinding her fingernails into her skin.

"Yes. I've got to make a decision. Either I'm going to jump in head first or walk away. And I can't decide when I'm all tangled up in you. I don't seem to be able to think straight when you're around."

"So you aren't breaking up with me?" she asked, and her eyes misted despite her determination to stop the tears.

"No, not exactly. Maybe just temporarily, I guess." He shrugged and looked at his feet. "I guess you could technically say it's a breakup. But I won't leave you hanging."

He raised his head, looked her in the eyes, and Heather was stricken by the presence of something she couldn't define. Or maybe it was the presence of *someone*. "There's someone else, isn't there?" Heather croaked and picked at the onyx beads on the arm of her jacket. Both Lorna and Brittan had hinted they thought he had another lady. But Heather had been too certain of his integrity to entertain such nonsense.

"No." He shook his head. Then he stared into space. "Not literally," he qualified.

Heather crossed her arms. "Either there is or there isn't."

"It's not a real person," he explained and held his palms upward. "It's just—just— Well, I... This is going to sound weird, but I've been looking for this woman who haunts my mind, and I'm not sure you're *her*. What if she's out there waiting for me, and then here I am promised to you?" He dropped his hands to his sides.

"Brittan and Lorna said you'd do this," Heather said and didn't bother to wipe the tear trickling beside her nose. She sniffed. "They both said you have commitment phobia, but I didn't want to believe them."

"Maybe I do." Duke raised his hands again and looked toward the heavens. "Somebody just strike me with lightning! I'm a human being. I have a few hang-ups."

"It's because of that girl who dumped you, isn't it?" Heather pressed and was too unnerved to stop herself.

"Maybe." Duke rested his hands on his hips. "All I know is that I keep having these nightmares, and—and—" He covered his eyes and stopped.

"Like the one you had on the plane?" Heather whacked at the tears.

"Yes. Exactly."

"So I'm giving you nightmares?" Her voice squeaked.

"I didn't say that. No, it's not like that. It's that other woman in my mind. I'm sorry. Really, this is my fault." Duke pounded his fingers against his chest.

Heather stepped to the front of her car, plunked her purse on the hood, and dug out another tissue. "Well, this d–day is turning into a nightmare for me," she said, sniffling. She'd talked herself into believing that the weekend had sealed something special for her and Duke, that his family would one day be her family. They certainly seemed to hope so.

"Look, Heather," he continued from behind. "Whether you realize it or not, we have more issues going than just mine."

She blew her nose and didn't bother to answer.

"Like, why haven't I met any of your friends? And why haven't we gone to *your* church?"

Heather's knees locked.

"The only thing we've done that's in your life is that cancer benefit. You've vaguely mentioned one friend a couple of times, and I did meet Lorna, but that was only a fluke—and a really weird one at that. What was the big secret with all that Steam Monster business anyway?"

She swallowed and fought for air.

"In some ways," Duke continued, "I feel like maybe...you...you aren't really in this relationship all the way. Like you're keeping me separate from your real life. And maybe that's part of the problem..." Duke trailed off.

The airport blurred. The roar of planes landing and taking off mingled with the cacophony in Heather's mind. Never had she so desperately wanted to tell Duke that she and Lorna and Brittan were The Rose. But in telling him, she'd break her word to her best friends. She'd promised. A promise was a promise. And Heather was a woman of integrity. Grandpa Morris told her over and over again that if you didn't have anything else, you had your word— and your word should be as good as gold.

If only I hadn't dragged him up to Eve Maloney's apartment, Heather fretted. For if she hadn't, it wouldn't have been as risky if he found out Brittan was Leon Shay's daughter. But with all the questions Duke was asking, that knowledge very likely could be the final piece of information that would catapult him into a series of discoveries, ending with the identity of The Rose.

"Wait a minute!" Duke announced. "I see it now! You're keeping me separate from everyone because I'm not in their league. I'm just a newspaper reporter, and you run with jet-setters."

"No!" Heather whirled to face him. "No, Duke!" She hastened forward, gripped his hands, looked into his soul, and prayed he saw her sincerity. "My mom's that way, but I'm not—and I never will be. I don't even *like* most of the rich guys my mom keeps throwing at me."

The disenchantment in Duke's eyes faded. His face softened. His gaze settled on her lips.

"You've got to believe me," Heather insisted. "I think you're wonderful just the way you are. And I'm not ashamed for my friends to meet you. Not at all. It's just that…" Heather pinched her lips together and prayed for the right thing to say.

"So what is it then?" Duke asked.

"I can't tell you," Heather admitted. *My friends would never forgive me,* she added to herself. Telling Duke would be like proclaiming the news to all of Houston. He'd already told his readers that once he learned who The Rose was, he was going to publicize it. Then the serial sleuth and adventure would be history.

He narrowed his eyes.

Heather could see the man's brain whirling in thirty different directions. Finally, the revolving stopped. Resolve took its place. Duke backed away.

"Well," he said, "it really doesn't matter anyway. Even if you tell all and parade me in front of your whole world, I'm still just not sure. And I want to make sure before I fall all the way in love."

"All the way?" Heather questioned and prayed that he'd already begun falling.

"It is possible to fall in love with the wrong person," Duke added as if Heather had never spoken. "I need to make sure you're the right woman for me. And I need you to make sure I'm somebody you can share your *whole* life with. If we get back together, Heather, you can't keep me separated from the rest of your life."

He shrugged and his voice took on a gentleness that usually accompanied a kiss. "I guess I'm suggesting you need to do some soul searching too." Duke pressed his lips against her forehead.

"And if it doesn't work out, I'd rather hurt you a little now than rip your heart out later."

Heather closed her eyes and savored his warmth, his nearness, the smell of peppermint on his breath.

His voice firm, he said, "I'll be calling as soon as I get it sorted out, okay?" He inched away.

"So this is, 'Don't call me, I'll call you?' " Heather snapped and couldn't stop her cheeks from heating.

An apology cloaking his features, he grimaced. "I didn't mean it that way, but yes."

Heather leaned against her car as her heart shattered. She covered her face and mumbled against her palms, "Just go, Duke."

The September wind dipped down and tangled its fingers in Heather's hair while the growl of an engine testified to a bus nearing.

"The shuttle's coming," Duke said. "So I guess this is it."

His footsteps moved to the back of her car. "Goodbye, Heather." The soft words were like a caress, but they weren't enough to stop the pain.

The click of his bag's handle preceded the sound of luggage wheels on pavement. When Heather raised her face, Duke was stepping into the shuttle that would take him to where he'd parked his truck.

Heather retrieved her purse, unlocked the car door, flopped into the driver's seat, and wept. She had never failed at anything. She'd never questioned she'd win the national karate championship. She'd never doubted her family fortune would provide for all her wants and needs. And she'd assumed that since she wanted a permanent relationship with Duke, he'd feel the same.

She pulled another tissue from her purse and mopped at her face. The evening sun descended behind a bank of dark clouds that blocked the warm rays from her windshield. A hard shiver wracked Heather's soul.

What if Duke never feels the same? she worried. *What if it simply isn't God's will?* Heather rested her head against the seat and closed her eyes. The smell of new interior increased the nausea beginning a slow spin in her stomach. A few months ago her pastor had started a sermon series on understanding God's will, and Heather was still trying to embrace the concept. What she'd realized during the last couple of sessions was that sometimes a person might want something, but that didn't always mean God wanted the same for that person. According to Pastor Thom, God knows what's best for everyone. And He doesn't grant every wish for that very reason.

Following God's will had sounded so reasonable, especially since she'd pretty much gotten everything she wanted. But now with her relationship with Duke in the balance, panic seized her soul.

What if God doesn't want Duke and me together? Am I willing to accept that? She gripped the steering wheel and rested her forehead against it.

How many times have I prayed, "Your kingdom come. Your will be done" like I meant it? I've been for God's will as long as it lined up with my will, she realized.

Heather knew in that instant that God was asking her to release her relationship with Duke into His hands to do with as He deemed best...but she didn't want to.

※ ※ ※

Duke plunked his suitcase onto the shuttle's luggage shelf and dropped onto the bench seat. A couple of women sat across from him. They carried briefcases and wore designer suits. One reminded him a little of the photo of Eve Maloney. She was dark, striking; her eyes, sharp. And Duke wondered if she looked anything like The Rose.

He focused out the window before she caught him watching her.

His gaze rested on Heather's Porsche. He thought about the week ahead. He'd be back to only Jake and Mike for company. His heart begged him to jump off the bus, race back to Heather, and tell her to forget everything he said. He'd just had a bad case of cold feet. He'd beg her to stay in his life.

The chilling terror from those nightmares wormed its way into his mind. Duke clamped his teeth together. The shuttle doors squeaked shut. The vehicle rolled forward.

I made the right decision for now, he told himself. *I was honest with her from the start. If we don't make a go of it, she'll hurt a lot less now than she would if we broke up in a few months.*

Duke pulled his cell phone from his jacket pocket and pressed the on button. He'd turned it off last night before he went to bed and never bothered to turn it back on. He noticed a message waiting and dialed his voice mail. Solomon Gude's voice boomed over the line.

"Fieldman. Leon Shay wants to see us first thing in the morning. I know I told you to take tomorrow off, but that ain't gonna work anymore. Meet me here at eight sharp. The meeting's at eight-thirty." The call ended.

Duke squinted and wondered if he'd imagined the message. *What would Leon Shay want with me?* He listened to the voice mail again and accepted it as true. The owner of the *Houston Star* had summoned him to the holy of holies. This was either really good or really, really bad.

TWENTY-NINE

Heather didn't bother to go to her place. She drove straight to downtown Houston and marched up to Brittan and Lorna's penthouse. They'd sent her three text messages before the plane departed from Lubbock, and Heather went to the airport ladies' room to call them. Brittan meant it when she said they were on the missing girl case. The police had released photos of the alleged kidnapper, a former family employee, and Lorna and Brittan were making plans to hunt him down.

She stepped off the skyscraper's elevator and pressed a tissue against her burning eyes. There was no way she was going to be able to hide the fact she'd been crying. She planned to tell her friends everything and be done with it. As she knocked, Heather could almost hear Brittan saying, "I told you so," while Lorna nodded in agreement.

"Here goes." Heather sighed as the door opened.

Brittan took one look at Heather and said, "He dumped you, didn't he?" But "I told you so" never crossed her lips. Instead, her face drooped into a sympathetic wilt.

Heather bit her lips and blinked hard. She refused to cry anymore. All that weeping on top of jet lag was wearing her out. She stepped past Brittan and dropped her purse on the end table.

The door closed behind her. Lorna looked up from the couch. Her eyes widened. Then she glanced toward Brittan. She set aside the papers she'd been scrutinizing and stood.

"You guys were right," Heather said and lifted her hands. "He *does* have commitment issues." From there, she spilled the whole horrid story, right down to her taking on the robbers.

"I'd like to beat the pulp out of Duke Fieldman," Brittan threatened. She brought Heather a new box of tissue, then shoved up the sleeves of her fleece shirt with a vengeance.

"Sounds like a plan to me." Lorna settled on the floor near Heather, crossed her legs, and tucked her sock-clad feet beneath them.

"I'm not going to really beat him up," Brittan corrected. "It's just the way I *feel*. I knew he'd do this. I just knew it. And it makes me furious that he waited until after such a great weekend." She turned to Heather and settled into the chair next to hers. "It's like he invited you to meet his family just so he could get your hopes up and then drop you."

Despite Heather's commitment not to cry, she'd added a dozen tissues to the trash can at her feet. She slammed another tissue into the can and pulled out a fresh one.

"Really, I don't think he planned it," Heather said and rubbed her damp palm along the front of her slacks. "I really don't. And in all honesty, I guess I was the one who first brought up the idea of going to Lubbock with him. That's when he offered to buy me a ticket."

"Oh..." the two friends said in unison.

Heather leaned forward and hugged herself. "I thought we were really going to make it. He's been so good to me and seemed to really care."

"He just told you it was over, and that's it?" Lorna asked.

"Not exactly," Heather confessed. "He said he needs a break to see if I'm 'the one.' But...but...but..." She looked from one friend to the other and debated whether to tell them The Rose was part of the problem.

If she and Duke did get back together, Heather would be faced with letting him all the way into her life. That meant he'd find out she was best friends with Leon Shay's daughter and that Lorna's family was as wealthy as hers. From there, Duke would wonder why an heiress to a merchant monopoly was cleaning carpets. And if he took his questions one more level, he'd eventually find answers. Then Brittan and Lorna would never forgive her for being the weak link. She'd have her man, but she'd lose The Rose...and maybe her two best friends.

Duke was right. Heather needed to search her heart as well. If he *did* want to reunite, then she would share her whole life with him...whatever the sacrifice. If he backed away, that took the pressure off Heather's revealing The Rose, but she'd lose the man she was falling in love with.

I'm between a rock and a fireplace, she thought.

A hysterical giggle teetered forth, then a wail swelled from Heather's soul. She covered her face and rocked back and forth. "I can't talk about this anymore," she garbled out. "I've got to get a grip."

"Okay...okay..." Brittan soothed. "We understand. Look, why don't you go into the bathroom and wash your face with cold water. When you come out, we won't talk about this any more. We've got some info on Debbie Miller, the missing girl. On a hunch, we followed the girl's nanny this morning. Looking back, we think there might be something we overlooked. Maybe talking about the case will take your mind off everything else."

Heather nodded and lowered her hands. "You guys are the best!" she proclaimed.

✳ ✳ ✳

Duke thumped into his townhouse, slung his bag onto the sofa, ripped off his jacket, and tossed it. He didn't bother to look where it landed. Jake was with Mike, so the apartment was as empty as Duke's heart. He walked into the kitchen and pulled out a can of RC. Supper was a bag of microwave popcorn and a salami sandwich. He didn't taste either one. Once he crashed into bed with the remote in one hand and a second can of RC in the other, he pronounced himself a miserable wretch who was going to do exactly what Shauna said—die alone in a nursing home.

His telephone's ringing pierced through *ESPN* and his thoughts. Duke retrieved the cordless from the nightstand.

"I just talked to Heather," Shauna said without bothering to say hello.

Bolting up, Duke swung his legs off the bed and slammed his soda onto the nightstand. "You did what?" he barked.

"I talked to Heather," Shauna repeated. "I asked for her cell number while she was here, and she gave it to me. She told me you backed off."

"Did she tell you everything?" Duke boomed.

"Yes," Shauna said.

"Everything? Even the fact that I know almost no one in her life? No one?"

"Uh…"

"It's not all one-sided, Shauna. There's something she's hiding, and I don't know what it is. I didn't even know about the karate. She purposefully hid that from me. Why? What else is she hiding?"

"Maybe she's not hiding anything. Maybe you just haven't spent enough time together," Shauna reasoned, "and eventually she'll get around to all of it. Look, I've talked to Mom. We both think you're making a big mistake, Duke. You really need to get over this fear of commitment. If you don't, it's going to cost you the best woman you'll ever find. And if you don't commit to Heather, I'm sure there's a line of men a mile long who will be glad to."

"This is none of your business!" Duke roared.

"You know what, Duke? It's high time somebody seriously confronted you."

"High time? You've been on me for six months!"

"Right. I know. And I'm staying on your trail until you work through this. I wouldn't be able to live with myself if I didn't tell it like it is one more time."

Duke sighed. "Shauna, there are two sides to this. And if you refuse to see that then…" He rested his elbow on his leg and placed his forehead in his hand. "Look, it's been a long weekend," he continued. "I'm really tired. And right now I need to chill."

"All right," she agreed. Her voice softened. "I know you're tired. I'm tired too. And, well, maybe there are two sides."

"Thank you." Duke lifted his head. Shauna's admission fueled his determination to prove his side. "I'm telling you, Heather's hiding something on purpose. I don't know what it is. When I challenged her on it she told me she couldn't tell me."

Her tone curious, Shauna asked, "Do you have any clues?"

"Nope." Duke stood, yanked the covers back, and punched at a pillow.

"Surely it's not anything that would make a difference in your relationship."

"All I know is that if we're going to make it she's going to have to totally let me into her life. Anything less is a no-deal with me."

"Have you met her parents?"

"Yes. Remember, I told you her mother was—"

"The Wicked Witch of the South. Yes, I remember."

"But other than that, I have no idea who she hangs with, where she goes to church, anything personal. Most of the time we talk about me. She doesn't say much about herself at all. Up until this weekend I talked myself into believing she was a simple little rich girl who just happened to be able to charm the tusks off an elephant. But then she hauled off and beat the livin' daylights out of those robbers, and suddenly I'm seeing a whole new side of her. Did you know she holds a black belt and has been the national karate champ twice?"

"That's impressive," Shauna acknowledged.

"Well, yeah…it is," Duke admitted.

He sat on the bed, reached for the remote, snapped off the TV. "She gets text messages and phone calls from people quite a bit, but she never tells me who they are. We've been going out six weeks, and I've only met one of her friends. And that was a fluke…and beyond weird."

"What happened?"

Duke briefed her on the Steam Monster story.

Shauna fell silent.

"I always did say I wanted a woman of mystery. I guess I've got one, don't I?" Duke joked before plopping back on the pillows and staring at the ceiling.

"Now you've got me intrigued," Shauna admitted.

"Join the club," Duke said and closed his eyes.

"Do you know whose apartment it was?" Shauna asked.

Duke's eyes popped open. "No. I've wondered but haven't checked into it."

"Hmmm…" He could almost see his sister snapping at her gum. "Maybe it's time you found out," she prompted.

"Maybe so," Duke agreed.

Silence permeated the line.

"Look, Duke, I'll be praying for you, okay?"

"You do that." Duke paused and then in a moment of unexplained softness he said, "I love you."

"I love you too, little bro." Shauna's voice was full of a fondness he seldom heard. "I just want to see you happy."

"I know." Duke sighed. "I know."

The doorbell's repeated ringing announced the presence of a regular in Duke's life: Mike Mendez. Duke had left him a voice

mail on the way home saying he could bring Jake over. Mike lived
on the other side of the townhouse complex, so the journey was
a short one.

"Look," Duke said, "The Mike's here with Jake. We'll talk
later."

"Count on it," Shauna warned.

He placed the phone back in its cradle and padded through the
living room to the front door. Yawning, Duke glanced down at
what he wore—a pair of running shorts, no shirt. *Ah well, it's just
The Mike.* He opened the door.

Mike delivered a welcoming punch to Duke's arm while Jake
jumped like a jackrabbit and barked about how much he'd missed
his owner. When Duke closed the door, Mike said, "Whoa, man!"
His eyes wide, he examined the gash on Duke's face. "What happened to your face?"

Duke reached to touch the wound. "I had a wild weekend," he
said, and told Mike everything.

THIRTY

After Mike left, Duke went online to check out the *Houston Star's* website, which prompted him to toss on a T-shirt and jog to the corner convenience store to buy a newspaper. He devoured the articles about the kidnapped girl and wondered if The Rose might respond to this case. He was beginning to notice that so far she'd chosen the high profile cases. This one would fit the bill.

Even though his body told him he was exhausted, Duke's gritty eyes refused to droop. Too much was going on; too much to think about. *Why did Shay summon me? What should I do about Heather? And if the police don't find the Miller girl, will I receive another rose next week?*

To chase away the wondering, Duke settled at his computer and toyed around with the mystery novel he'd already gotten twenty-three rejections on. Its predecessor had received fifty-one rejects. Duke figured this one was still young. He'd collected cryptic advice from more than half the rejects and had applied as much of it as he thought was valid. One publisher had even asked him to do some rewriting and resubmit. He was nearly through with the rewriting.

With Jake at his feet, Duke tapped away at the story of a

newspaper reporter who solved criminal cases. Concentrating on the story grew more and more difficult. What his mind had done in sleep, it was now doing while awake. Except instead of being trapped in a marriage, Duke was exactly where Shauna said he'd land—in a nursing home, president of the Lonely Hearts Club.

Duke rested his elbow on the desk, pressed his fingertips against his eyes, and couldn't stop the scenario from whipping up a storm of anxiety as daunting as the cage nightmares. He stayed in room number 103 at the nursing home and didn't even rank a roommate. In his mind's eye Duke saw himself bent over a cane, hobbling up the tiled hallway. Oddly, he wore the same running shorts and T-shirt he had on now. His lean legs had gone bony and shriveled with age. Furthermore, he'd gotten so grouchy, he snarled at everybody he saw.

A nurse passed. A young, good-looking redhead, no less. And Duke got aggravated at her for being so pretty. He smacked her with his cane. She grabbed him by the arm, marched his scrawny body into his room, threw him into his bed, and tied him down with something that resembled Jake's leash. Bin Laden didn't have anything on that dame.

Even worse than being tied up was the fact that Heather's wedding photos hung all over his room. She'd hauled off and said "I do" to some rich wimp who must have made Mommy-O happier than a cat eating salmon. The photos of Heather with her shrimpy kids couldn't have been more nauseating. Those kids were supposed to have been his! And if they had been, they wouldn't have been shrimpy, that's for sure.

So there Duke lay, tied up, no place to go, and no one to visit him. He wanted to go see Shauna and her kids, but Shauna had gotten old too, and she'd been too ornery to have any kids.

He could even hear her croaking from the next room, "I told you this would happen, you moron!"

Duke tilted in his chair, jumped, and caught himself before he fell smack on top of Jake. He rubbed his face, yawned, and gazed down at his dog. Jake's good eye was glazed, and Duke figured his eyes were probably just as glassy. He also realized he'd flirted with sleep for a few minutes.

Slumping back into his chair, Duke stared at the words on the screen. He pressed the save button and shut down his computer. Standing, he paced to the patio door and opened the blinds. His small backyard looked as dark as his heart felt. Even though he'd wrestled with the terror of committing to Heather, he was now overtaken with the fear of *not* committing to her.

What if I never meet the Rose?

What if my dream woman really doesn't exist?

What if Heather is my dream woman, and I don't have enough sense to see it because of what Sarah did?

He dug his bare toes into the doormat and snapped the horizontal blinds shut. They clapped out a protest.

"And if she is the right one and I break it off for good, is Shauna right about the nursing home?" Duke wondered aloud.

Turning from the window, he collapsed into a dining chair mere feet away. He rested his elbows on the glass top and crammed his fingers against his scalp. He recalled Heather's touching his hair that magical day at the beach. How sweet her lips tasted when he kissed her at the ranch. The shattered ache in her eyes at the airport.

Before Mike left, he'd told Duke he was crazy if he didn't try to make it work with Heather Winslow. Then Mike had the audacity to say *he'd* ask her out if Duke broke it off. A jealous sting pierced Duke's mind. He lifted his head. Shauna said there was probably a line of men a mile long waiting for Heather. He imagined Mike Mendez at the front and the sting turned to a burn.

What if she finds someone else while I flounder around making up my mind? Duke stared at the collection of signed baseballs on the corner shelf.

"Oh, God, please help me," Duke groaned. He shoved aside a

half-empty bag of corn chips and the newspaper, laid his arms on the table, and rested his forehead on his arms.

"God, help me," he repeated as he relived the tearing of his heart the day Sarah walked away with the jock she eventually married. At the time Duke had believed himself a fully grown man. Looking back he now understood he'd barely tasted manhood. But that hadn't stopped him from gorging himself on love—the kind that lasted. His parents had married when they were just eighteen, and so had many other now-senior couples Duke knew. Some, even younger. So nobody could convince Duke what he felt for Sarah was nothing but adolescent infatuation. It had been the real deal. And when she broke his heart, she broke it all the way.

Duke imagined how his life would have played out if he'd married his high school sweetheart. He'd still be in Lubbock. They'd move into the little house near his parents' home and probably have a couple babies within five years. He would have supported his family by working the ranch with his dad.

The natural talent for writing his high school English teacher had raved about would never grow into a dream for journalism. He'd never see that rope tornado because he would be with Sarah. Since the article wasn't ever written, it was never syndicated. He never experienced the thrill of knowing people all over the nation read his story. College probably wouldn't happen. Too busy making a living for Sarah and the kids.

Duke wouldn't have moved to Houston...wouldn't be working for *The Star*...wouldn't have started writing novels...wouldn't have ever received a rose...wouldn't be an investigative reporter... wouldn't have ever met Heather.

As the memories and realities unfolded, so the final traces of pain seeped from Duke's soul. So did the fear. What Sarah did had wounded him. And while that wound might leave a scar, he needed to let it once and for all heal. Otherwise the infectious pus would continue to rule his life...and his choices.

A slow realization dripped healing balm into the wound. *I love my life.* Duke raised his head. "I love my job," he rasped. "I like Houston. I've got great friends, a good church, and a girlfriend most guys would eat their hearts out over."

He'd not allowed himself to get close to a woman since Sarah. Duke always broke it off when he sensed himself getting too attached. His dream woman always blocked his chances at a commitment. Lately she'd taken on the identity of The Rose, but the truth was she'd been with him for many years.

He pinched his lower lip. *Maybe she's been a protective blanket that keeps me from getting too close to another woman.*

Duke repeated aloud what he'd told himself several times already. "My dream woman isn't real. Heather is real."

And I am falling in love with her. I really am.

He bolted up and struggled for air. A mixture of leftover terror and new exhilaration pulsed through his veins. Duke paced to the front door and back, and then repeated the steps.

"I'm falling in love," he repeated.

I went to that blasted party six weeks ago to get through a boring interview with a shallow debutante I thought would be condescending. But she wasn't shallow and boring and snobby. She hauled off and flirted with me. Next thing I knew, we were going out, chasing waves at the beach. And now my family's on the verge of beating me up if I don't marry her.

He stopped at the table, picked up the half-full bag of corn chips where they'd landed on the floor, and jammed his mouth full. Duke didn't stop eating until he finished the bag. Then he balled it into a tight knot and tossed it toward Jake. It landed in front of the dog's nose, and he woofed.

Duke laughed and stepped toward his friend. "Listen you," he said and roughed up Jake's ears. "I've got a girlfriend now."

Jake panted and playfully pawed at Duke.

"She's got six cats. If we get married, you're going to have to do some serious adjusting." Duke thought about the near miss with the next door neighbor's cat. Jake had ripped off half the poor guy's tail when he fell into Duke's backyard. Duke had paid the vet bill and didn't want another.

Duke believed dogs remembered their puppyhood. Jake had rabidly detested cats from the day Duke adopted him. Even as a ten-week-old pup he'd gone insane at the sight of one of those pointy-eared monsters. Duke figured it all boiled down to that vampire cat who took out his eye. Nobody could convince him that dogs didn't remember their puppyhood.

"Maybe I need to send you to House Cats Anonymous," he teased. "Hello, my name is Jake and I'm a cataholic. I can't stop eating them alive."

He sobered and mumbled, "If Heather and I do get married, we really will have to figure out what to do about the cat/dog business."

Duke scratched the dog's neck as a reality check crashed through his mind. *What if Heather won't have me now?* He had essentially laid out an ultimatum at the airport. If they did try to make it, he wanted to be involved in all aspects of her life. Yet there was something she couldn't tell him. He squinted. What if that something ended all chances of having a relationship?

I need to call her now! Duke checked his watch to see that it was just past one in the morning. Sighing, he knew now was impossible. Besides, he had that mystery meeting with Mr. Shay at eight-thirty. He needed to get to bed.

I'll call Heather first thing in the morning, he decided. *Whatever she thinks she can't tell me, maybe her knowing how I feel will make a difference. And if it's some huge obstacle, maybe we can work through it together.*

Duke grabbed his suitcase from the couch and wheeled it to his bedroom. He wouldn't bother unpacking tonight, but his toothbrush was inside. After flopping the case onto the end of his rumpled bed, Duke unzipped the top and flipped it open. A Ziploc bag lay on top of his clothes. Inside was a small velvet box and what looked like a note. He hadn't put the bag there. *Who's been in my suitcase?* he wondered.

He opened the bag and pulled out a handwritten note. It was in his mother's tell-tale scrawl. Before reading the message, Duke flipped open the box and stared at a gold filigree ring with a magnificent ruby.

"Wow! What's the deal?" Duke muttered and began reading the note.

> *Duke,*
>
> *This ring belonged to my mom. I've kept it all these years because I wanted you to have it as a gift from our family to the woman you'd one day marry. I'm passing this along to you for safe keeping until you think you might need it. No pressure, but I'm hoping you might need it soon.*
>
> *Much love,*
>
> *Mom*

"No pressure?" Duke said through a smile. "Yeah, sure, no pressure."

When he first met Heather, Duke had questions about whether or not she'd fit into his world. After this past weekend, he couldn't believe he'd ever entertained that worry. Now he possessed a new vein of concerns—like running away from his whole family if he *didn't* propose.

He laughed out loud, snapped the ring box shut, and wondered if he'd have to have it sized to fit Heather's finger.

✳ ✳ ✳

Heather lay in the guest bed at the penthouse and tried to go to sleep. True friends that they were, Lorna and Brittan had insisted she spend the night so she wouldn't have to be alone in her wing of the castle. Heather had gladly agreed, but only after she called the senior housekeeper to make sure her cats were taken care of.

Until ten o'clock the friends had plotted how they would hunt down the kidnapper. That included a trip to Goodwill for some worn-looking jogging gear for Heather. Brittan and Lorna had made their purchases yesterday. They went to bed with plans to get up early and spy on Debbie Miller's nanny. According to the paper, the kidnapper was her former boyfriend, Howie Prince. The nanny, Brenda Zapala, denied any knowledge of the kidnapping and the police hadn't found any evidence to prove otherwise. However, Lorna and Brittan weren't convinced.

But right now Heather wasn't thinking about kidnapping. Her mind was tangled in the man who'd stolen her heart. She hadn't felt this way since Tyler—and she suspected her love might run deeper with Duke than it ever had with Tyler. Sighing, she wondered what Duke was doing, if he was awake. The clock said one-fifteen.

"He's probably sleeping like a baby," Heather groused into the darkness, "and hasn't given me a thought since he rolled off in that shuttle bus."

Heather's eyes stung. She doubled her fists around the sheet and blinked back the tears. She'd cried enough. Losing Tyler had been beyond everyone's control. He hadn't chosen to die any more than Heather chose for him to die. But the prospect of losing Duke involved his purposeful rejection, and that hurt in a way she had never experienced.

Her earlier thoughts about God's will spun through her jumbled mind. She grabbed the spare pillow and crammed it over her head. *I don't want to think about all that!* But calm insistence in her soul suggested God wanted her to think about it.

"Oh, Lord," Heather responded, "please, please don't make me give up Duke. I don't think I have the strength to do that. If he does want to reconcile and then finds out I'm The Rose, that's a whole different stress."

Heather lay in the heart of the night and wrestled with relinquishing her will to the holy Creator. She stood on the precipice of doubt, clinging to her needs, desires, and goals while the Lord beckoned her to release...release and fling herself and her future wholly into His care. In her human weakness she struggled to comprehend that God was fully able to give her more in her release than He could in her clinging.

Finally, after tossing until her head spun, Heather fell to her knees beside the bed. Weeping, she extended her hands heavenward and whispered, "Father, take Duke. Take my future. Whether we split up or stay together, give me what it takes to deal with the situation."

THIRTY-ONE

It was seven when Duke's call came through. Heather knew the caller was Duke before she looked at the ID screen. Sitting in the rental car's passenger seat, she glanced up at Lorna, then Brittan.

"Is that Duke?" Brittan asked from the backseat.

Heather nodded.

"Don't answer," Lorna advised as she skillfully steered the sporty sedan along the Houston freeway.

Brittan shook her head. "Don't do it."

Rubbing the side of the cell phone with her thumb, Heather closed her puffy eyes and prayed for guidance on what to do.

This morning they were headed to Sam Houston Park, where the Miller nanny had walked the last two mornings. After renting the vehicle Saturday, Brittan and Lorna followed Brenda Zapala to the park yesterday. Not dressed in sports gear, they'd watched from the vehicle while the nanny walked. They'd kept their distance and simply waited for any clues. The woman had offered no leads whatsoever. She stopped and chatted with a few people who looked like they might be park regulars, and that made them think the morning walk was her normal routine. In retrospect, Brittan and Lorna decided it was odd that she exited the park at a different entrance than the one she parked at.

This morning they'd all changed their hair color, donned the faded running gear purchased at Goodwill, and put on sunglasses. None of the three wore makeup. The low-riding caps crested their disguise. They each carried latex gloves in their pockets "just in case" they encountered a situation where they didn't want to leave fingerprints. Today they planned to follow Brenda wherever she went.

The phone continued to blast out the *Bonanza* theme song. Heather had no idea whether Duke was calling to end it forever or to reconcile. Whichever it was, she didn't have time right now to deal with the inevitable emotions. Rooting Out a Kidnapper, Phase One, left little time for weeping over a lost boyfriend...or for hyperventilating over how to share her life with him if she had him back. Brittan and Lorna would *not* be impressed if they had to babysit her while the nanny got away. Even though she was still committed to trusting God's will in the situation, Heather knew she'd be affected no matter what the outcome of the phone call.

The phone finally stopped ringing. Heather released her breath.

"Good girl," Brittan encouraged and reached up to pat Heather on the shoulder.

Lorna snapped on the blinker and steered the sedan toward the exit. "No sense being too easy to get a hold of." She flashed Heather a smile. Now that her hair was black, her skin appeared much paler.

"Yeah, and it's high time you called a shot or two," Brittan advised. "He's set the rules of this relationship from the start. *You* need to have some say in it too, you know. Even if he's about to dump you, let him do it on *your* schedule, not his."

Heather eyed the cell phone screen and wondered if Duke left a message. Her heart begged him to beg her back. But her common sense knew there was wisdom in Brittan and Lorna's advice. If he was on the verge of dumping her, she didn't want to appear to be pining for his call. She'd wait to return it after their morning excursion…and then only if he'd left a message.

Duke stepped into the posh office that had "Leon Shay, Shay Publishing" on the door. The skyscraper office reminded him of the outer court of a five-star hotel. Windows lined one wall. Inlaid beveled mirrors lined the other. Plants that looked like they'd been imported from the Amazon filled the corners. The place smelled like a Colombian coffeehouse.

If he put the last two nights together, Duke might have gotten enough sleep for one night. His eyes hadn't been this heavy since college. He hadn't had time to make coffee this morning before he left, and his zombie brain was telling his taste buds he needed that Colombian stuff.

Behind a massive desk sat a woman with ivory skin, black hair, and the eyes of a goddess. She observed them with an interrogator's curiosity that would have made Duke squirm if he hadn't been so tired.

"Solomon Gude and Duke Fieldman here to see Mr. Shay," Gude said, his voice a mere wisp of its usual self.

Quirking his brow, Duke eyed his boss and enjoyed seeing the guy in discombobulated mode. The few hairs on the top of his head were smoothed down for a change. He even wore a tie and coat.

"I'll tell Mr. Shay you're here," the secretary said and eyed Duke like he'd been dragged from the bottom of a trash barrel.

Duke glanced down at his own attire. Too tired to think straight, he'd crawled into his usual jeans, boots, and sport shirt this morning. Only when he was ready to walk out the door did he think that maybe he should put on a sports coat. He'd grabbed the black one Shauna gave him last Christmas. Despite a few of her annoying habits, she had a way of bailing him out when he needed it most. Duke looked over his image in the mirrors. Aside from his boots being a bit scuffed, he thought he looked sharp…even if the secretary didn't.

Covering another yawn, Duke spotted the source of the aroma in the corner and meandered toward the coffeepot. He felt more like he was floating through one of those crazy dreams he'd been having lately. He wouldn't be surprised to see someone pop out from behind one of those plants to tie him on top of the desk.

Thankfully, once he got to sleep at two this morning, Duke's brain had been too tired to make up a cartoon strip. But stress had clanged him awake at six fifty-five with the announcement that it was time to call Heather. So Duke had.

He'd left her that voice mail an hour and a half ago and still hadn't heard from her. Duke already knew she sometimes slept late and figured she wasn't up yet. Still, he was more than antsy to hear from her. He'd simply left a message saying they needed to talk. While Duke had itched to say something like, "Oh, by the way, I'm in love with you," he'd held off. Voice mail wasn't exactly the place to lay that line on a lady.

He stifled another yawn and helped himself to a cup of coffee. It was every bit as good as the smell promised. Duke downed half the cup and was refilling it when the secretary slipped back into the outer chamber.

The giant door she left ajar made Gude look like a mouse. Duke hid his smile behind his cup. He had no idea what this meeting was about, but whether the outcome was good or bad it was well worth seeing Solomon Gude so intimidated. Despite his high ethics, the man enjoyed throwing his weight around far too much.

"Mr. Shay is ready for you," Ms. Secretary said. This time when she looked at Duke her black eyes held a tinge of respect. Duke figured he'd either gotten dramatically better dressed from the time she left to the time she arrived or Mr. Shay had said something to change her attitude. The last option seemed the most logical, even to a brain that had yet to recognize the coffee jolt.

Okay, he told himself, *maybe this meeting is a good thing.*

Ms. Secretary opened the door wider for them, and Duke followed Mr. Gude inside. The inner chamber was an extension of its outer counterpart...except it was bigger. And the two walls that weren't taken up with more windows and mirrors were lined with photos. One of those walls was behind Mr. Shay's desk, which was the size of Duke's kitchen.

A tall, lean man stood from behind the desk. His graying hair was slicked back from a broad forehead and straight nose. His smile revealed even teeth, and Duke figured his face might crack if he grinned any bigger. He wore a suit that probably cost more than Duke made in a month, and the sparkle from the diamond on his hand could put out an eye.

"Solomon!" Mr. Shay boomed. "It's great to see you!"

"Mr. Shay," Gude responded, his voice stronger than it had been minutes before.

Shay turned that smile onto Duke, and that's when he realized he still held the cup of coffee in his right hand. He switched hands and met the publishing guru's shake midway. By the time the pumping was over, Duke felt like he'd been on a seesaw. This guy was thrilled about something, and it appeared to involve him and Mr. Gude.

"I was going to offer you coffee," Shay said, pointing to Duke's steaming brew, "but I see you've already found it."

"Yes, and great stuff!" Duke lifted the cup. "I could jump in and swim around in it."

Shay threw back his head, and his laugh bounced around the office like he was one happy camper.

Gude joined in the laughter while cutting Duke a nervous glance.

Duke chuckled and didn't think the joke was *that* funny.

"Have a seat! Have a seat!" Shay commanded and motioned for the men to claim the leather chairs opposite his desk.

"Do you want some coffee, Solomon?" Mr. Shay asked.

"Yes, that would be nice," Gude said.

He pressed a button on his phone and said, "Kim, please bring us a tray of coffee. And while you're at it, throw on some of those pastries we got yesterday."

"Of course," Kim's voice sounded as enthused as an earthworm.

Duke's gaze wandered to what he assumed to be family photos. The center of attraction was what must be a family portrait of him with a petite, Chinese lady and a couple of adult offspring who resembled both mother and father. The son and daughter possessed the height of the father and the Asian features of their mother.

"You've noticed my family," Mr. Shay commented proudly.

"Yes, I assumed that," Duke replied and focused on Shay.

"That's my son Adam, my daughter, Brittan, and my wife. A good-looking bunch if I do say so myself," Shay said, and his grin was back. "I guess you're both wondering why I asked you here this morning." He beamed some more.

Mr. Gude shifted. "Well, the thought *had* crossed my mind," he admitted with a wry smile.

"Not mine," Duke said, his bottom lip protruding. "Haven't thought about it even once."

Mr. Shay went into another round of laughter. "You're just what I need this morning, Duke." He leaned forward, placed his flattened hands on the desk, and said, "And apparently, you're what Houston needs too."

"I am?" Duke blurted, his forehead wrinkling.

"Yes. Did you know that sales of *The Star* are at an all-time high?" He focused on Duke.

"They are?"

"Yes, they are."

"Your treatment of The Rose is brilliant. The first time it hit the paper we saw a small swell in sales, but you've handled it in a way that has Houston buzzing. I love that! Even more, I like what it's done for our revenue flow."

He shifted his attention to Mr. Gude, and Duke snuck in a sip of coffee. "And your moving him to investigative reporting was brilliant."

Duke sputtered against the warm liquid.

"Well I…" Mr. Gude's eyes shifted downward. Then he lifted his head and squared his shoulders. "Mr. Shay, I've got to be honest here, that was more Duke's idea than mine."

That's when Duke forgave his boss for all the bully tendencies.

"Yes, but Gude—I mean, Mr. Gude—agreed to my suggestion," Duke hurriedly added. In the middle of glancing from one boss to the other, his gaze snagged on an 8 x 10 to the right of Shay's shoulder.

Duke's eyes widened. The conversation diminished into a monotone of "blah, blah, blah" as he leaned forward to determine if his mind was playing tricks. Duke finally accepted that he really was seeing a photo of Heather Winslow with Steam Monster Lorna and Leon Shay's daughter. Duke wracked his foggy mind for her name and came up with Brittan. Yes. Brittan Shay.

So she hangs out with Mr. Shay's daughter and a carpet cleaner person? Duke pondered. *Uh uh. That Lorna is no carpet cleaner.* Logic insisted she was probably as rich as the Shays and the Winslows.

He tuned back into the conversation and found out he'd just been promoted to a big office next to Mr. Gude's. Duke sat a little straighter.

"I don't know how long this Rose business is going to last," Mr. Shay admitted. "But I like your style, Duke Fieldman. It's clever. Brilliant with an edge. And whatever happens with The Rose, I believe you've got more good stuff in you."

The Colombian brew was kicking in, and Duke felt like he was juggling three thought processes at once. The Heather, Lorna,

Brittan thing. His new promotion. And the sudden awareness that maybe this would be a good time to mention his novels. After all, as Duke understood it, the Shay empire included a couple of New York book publishers.

"Actually, Mr. Shay," Duke said and forced himself not to stare at the photo, "I'm also working on a novel or two."

"You are?" Shay said, his brows rising. "Well, why didn't you say so? I own two publishing houses in New York. Did you know that?"

"Well..." Duke hedged and felt Mr. Gude's gaping stare.

Kim's entrance with a silver tray saved Duke from answering. He downed a good portion of his coffee and welcomed more. While Mr. Gude declined the pastries, Duke accepted a couple. They were as flaky as coconut and filled with chocolate goo that made Duke want to howl. He decided howling would not be a good thing at this point and refrained. During the coffee exchange, Duke's gaze slid again to the photo of Heather and her friends.

When the office door snapped shut, Shay settled behind his desk again and commented, "Duke, you keep looking at one of the pictures. Which one?"

Duke shifted his attention back to Mr. Shay. "That one," he said, pointing toward it. "The one in the black frame."

"I should have known," Shay said through a grin. "Three good-looking women and you a single man. Of course your eye's going to wander there."

Duke ignored the implications and dared to ask the question that he already suspected the answer to. "Can you tell me...the brunette...who is she?"

"That's Lorna Leigh. The other one is Heather Winslow of Shelby Oil fame."

"Yes, I've been dating Heather," Duke admitted and glimpsed Gude again. The guy's teeth were going to fall out if his eyeballs didn't first.

"Well now," Shay said. He placed his elbows on the desk and made a tent of his fingers. "You certainly get around, don't you?"

"I was surprised to see your daughter and Heather are friends."

"Those three are inseparable." He pointed toward the photo. "They all went to Princeton together."

"And Lorna's family, what do they do?" Duke prompted.

"They own six national chains—cleaners, drugstores, flower shops, an import business or two. They've got a merchant monopoly."

And you're the publishing king, Duke thought. He shifted his attention back to Shay, but the publisher became a distant blur in the face of flaming curiosity centered on apartment 212.

I've got to find out whose apartment that is! He tossed the final bite of the chocolate heaven into his mouth and downed the rest of his coffee. Mr. Shay came into focus. He was looking at Duke like he suspected something important had just happened but had no clue what that might be.

Duke set his empty cup on the edge of the desk, stood, and glanced toward Solomon Gude. His desperate eyes sent Duke a silent message that went something like *Sit, boy! Sit!*

But Duke didn't sit, roll over, or play dead. He extended his hand toward Mr. Shay and said, "It's been really good meeting with you, sir. But I just realized an important key to a story I'm working on, and I've got to go. I'd love to talk with you more…and also discuss my novels," he continued, wondering if he was nuts to step out at such a time. But the lure of apartment 212 could be a big break in a story…although he wasn't sure what it was all about yet.

"Yes, of course," Shay said and fumbled around for a business card. "Here." He grabbed a pen and scribbled something on the back of the card. "That's my personal email address. Send me a proposal. I'll make sure it lands in the right hands. If it's half as good as your articles, maybe we can talk business."

Duke accepted the card, gazed at the scrawled email address, and then pointed at Shay. "You got it!" He smiled and hustled toward the door.

As he stepped into the outer chamber he heard Mr. Gude say, "I'm so sorry. I don't know what got into him."

Duke paused on the other side of the door.

"Not to worry, Solomon," Shay replied. "No telling *what* he's got up his sleeve. The brilliant ones are always unpredictable. But without them, we'd be sunk. I'm sure we'll all know what he's up to in a day or so. Just wait."

Humph, Duke thought as he exited the office. *I don't know how much all this has to do with brilliance and how much it has to do with just being at the right place at the right time...with the right person.* He shrugged and paused by the elevator. *If Shay wants to think I'm brilliant, far be it from me to disillusion him.*

THIRTY-TWO

The debutantes parked the rental car a block away from the city park and separated there. Heather was assigned to wait near the park's east entrance where the nanny left yesterday. Lorna was near the north entrance where Brenda Zapala had entered yesterday. And Brittan was at the west entrance just in case. All three had their cell phones on vibrate and planned to communicate via text messages or brief calls.

The September morning was kind to them. Lots of sunshine, no sign of clouds, a nice breeze. Heather went through a stretch routine while waiting for her phone to vibrate in her pocket. Each was supposed to alert the other if Brenda arrived at her entrance.

They'd been there for more than an hour and a half, and Heather was beginning to think Brenda wasn't going to come today. In a recent conversation with Brittan, they'd decided if she didn't show up in the next half hour they were going to snoop around the house she rented.

The phone vibrated. Heather pulled it out of her pocket, flipped it open, and pressed the text message icon. The lone note read, "She's here. North entrance. L" Heather eyed the voice mail indicator and knew the message waiting there was from Duke. As tempted as she was to listen to it, Heather exercised self-control again and resisted. She had to keep her senses until after the nanny business was over.

Heather jogged up the walkway a piece, turned around, and jogged back. She repeated the routine until she spotted Brenda rounding a curve in the walk. The dark sunglasses shielded Heather's eyes so Brenda wouldn't detect her scrutiny. She looked exactly as Brittan and Lorna had described her. Short, plump, bleach-blonde hair, and bright-pink lipstick. The tight knit jogging suit did as little for her figure as the clash of bleached hair with pink lips did to improve her looks. On her back Brenda carried a small pack with a bottle of water hanging lopsided in a side pocket.

Keeping her head down, Heather jogged past her. Lorna and Brittan said yesterday Brenda had walked a good forty-five minutes before leaving the park. Heather expected a repeat performance today. But just in case, she counted to ten before a quick glance over her shoulder. She was just in time to see Brenda ducking down the pathway for the east entrance. Apparently today wasn't going to be a repeat of yesterday. She was leaving as soon as she arrived, and that looked suspicious.

Heather turned around, jogged to the pathway, and caught a glimpse of the nanny hurrying across the parking lot. As planned, all three sleuths had composed several text messages and saved them for quick sending. Heather chose the one that read, "BZ left east exit. Following her. H" and hit the send button. Lorna and Brittan would be close behind.

Duke stood in the lobby of the Rockworth Plaza and allowed his breathing to slow to a normal rate. He'd jogged off and on from the Shay Complex to the plaza, which had taken him fifteen minutes. His body was used to a hard, 45-minute workout, so Duke recuperated within a couple of minutes as he watched the wealthy tenants rushing in and out, as if their agendas were the most important duties on the planet.

He pulled his cell phone from the pouch on his belt and flipped it open. He checked for messages. The screen was blank. Duke wondered if Heather was ever going to call him back. He sensed he was on the verge of a discovery that would reveal what she was up to. His mind had been racing ever since he saw the photo in Shay's office. For the first time he wondered if Heather knew who The Rose was.

He'd thought The Rose had to be close…someone who could get access to the company keys and the surveillance camera remotes. Who else besides the owner's daughter? Then a rose had been left in his office after he got to know Heather and she found out he wanted to be an investigative reporter. Furthermore, if his deductions were correct, someone involved in the mayor's murder lived in apartment 212. And he'd received clues to the murder and more on his desk shortly after he rescued Lorna from the Steam Monster.

Duke recalled Heather's reaction when he gave her the roses at the airport. At the time he'd passed it off as surprise. But now he decided she'd been stunned and wary.

Somewhere between Mr. Shay's office and Rockworth Plaza, Duke reasoned that The Rose was not one woman. The Rose was three women. All working together. Three women no one would suspect because they were rich, idle heiresses, and playing that up with great finesse. After seeing the way Heather took down those crooks at the ranch, he shuddered to think what Lorna and Brittan might be capable of.

But before Duke found out for sure, he wanted Heather to know he loved her. He loved her just the way she was, even before he knew she was one-third of The Rose. He eyed the concierge desk and decided before he approached the man wearing the black jacket that he would send Heather a text message.

As much as Duke didn't want to send his love by phone, he decided it was best to document the time for later reference. He found a seat on one of the posh couches and began tapping in the note. "Last night miserable. Falling in love with you. Can't stop it. Want to give us a try. Please call when you can." Duke checked his watch and typed, "It's 9:10, Monday morning." Even though he knew her cell phone would indicate the time, Duke wanted absolute proof. He hit the send button.

Heather lagged behind Brenda, but stayed close enough to watch her progress. The way she looked around like she was being hunted told Heather the woman was up to something. She walked to the ladies' room on the other side of the parking lot and went inside. Heather trotted toward the building, stood at the outside water fountain, and waited. When Brenda came out, Heather planned to pretend she was getting a drink while keeping an eye on the target.

Her cell phone vibrated in her shorts pocket, and Heather debated whether or not to check it. Brittan and Lorna should be close enough to see everything by now, so she couldn't imagine why they would text her. But just in case, Heather slipped the cell from her pocket and flipped it open.

When she opened the message window, Heather saw Duke's name instead of one of her friends. The subject line read "I love you." Her heart in her throat, Heather didn't try to keep from opening the message. She devoured every word, covered her mouth, and trembled through a wave of relief.

The snap of the ladies' room door jolted Heather back to the task at hand. As much as she wanted to savor Duke's love, now was not the time. Seizing control of her mind and emotions, Heather flipped the phone shut and slipped it back into her pocket. She bent over the water fountain and bathed her lips in the cold water while watching for Brenda out of the corner of her eyes.

But the woman she saw leaving had red hair and wore a loose-fitting jogging suit. She carried no backpack and aimlessly strolled toward the highway. Heather released the water lever and lifted her face. Either Brenda Zapala was still in the ladies' room or she'd changed clothes and put on a wig in order to hide her identity. The only resemblance from the back was that the woman in the black fleece was certainly as plump as Brenda. But many women were.

There was only one way to determine if this person was Brenda: Go into the bathroom and see if she was in there.

Footsteps neared from behind. Heather glanced over her shoulder and spotted Lorna close by. Heather skimmed the area for Brittan and saw her stepping behind a clump of trees.

"I'll keep an eye on her," Heather mumbled under her breath and nodded toward the woman in black. "Get a good look at her. Then you go into the bathroom and see if anyone else is in there. If there's not, see if you can find a backpack. Text me and let me know. I'm going to stay on this woman's trail. If she's not the one, Brenda's still in the bathroom. You and Brittan stay with her and text me."

Lorna nodded and casually strolled toward the ladies' room while Heather trailed the redhead, who was heading straight toward a shopping strip on the other side of a busy intersection.

In less than a minute Heather's phone vibrated against her leg. She retrieved it, and the text message read, "Bathroom empty. Lockers in here. Backpack probably in one."

Heather typed in a quick message to both her friends. "Redhead = BZ. I'm on it." Then Heather followed the lady through an inter-section to an Asian restaurant. Instead of going inside, Heather decided to check out the alley behind the restaurant. She walked around the back, ducked into the alley, and called Brittan. "She just went into the China Buffet," Heather reported. "You can't miss it.

I'm in the alley behind. Somebody track her inside." She closed the phone and waited.

✳ ✳ ✳

Duke neared the concierge and paused at the desk while the man dealt with a brunette with false eyelashes holding a high-strung toy poodle. He eyed the yapping mutt and decided it looked more like a stuffed animal. Jake could eat that puffball in one bite, except he wouldn't—unless it meowed. Duke thought about telling the eyelash queen she needed to get a *real* dog but decided to keep his thoughts to himself.

Once the dog and its slave left, Duke stepped forward and smiled at the young man whose name tag read "Maurice Townsend." "I was here a few weeks ago with a carpet cleaner," Duke began. "We worked on apartment 212. Can you tell me whose apartment that is?"

Maurice eyed him, and Duke wondered if he looked as suspicious as he felt. "I'm not allowed to give out that information," the clerk finally said and looked at the person standing behind Duke.

He thought about trying to push for the information but decided to blend into the scenery. "Okay, thanks," Duke said and smiled. There were other ways to find answers, but he wouldn't be able to if he got himself thrown out for being pushy.

Now, I need a notepad, Duke thought and reached for the trusty duffel bag he carried on every job. But this morning there was no bag...and no notepad. "Shoot!" he mumbled. He usually made a point of being armed and ready for any potential story. But today wasn't usual by a long shot. Duke had gone to bed way too late, and this morning all his groggy mind focused on was meeting with Shay. He'd had no idea he'd be chasing down The Rose.

He perused the lobby and spotted an upscale gift shop between a coffee bar and a black tie restaurant. *All this place needs is a mall and an airport,* Duke decided as he strolled toward the shop. The second he stepped through the door, he realized the place smelled like a candle factory. He spotted a trio of candles burning near a corner display and sneezed. His nose clogged up, and he wondered how the clerks could stand it.

He perused the racks of overpriced merchandise until he found a section of stationary. All Duke needed was a plain, lined notepad that usually was a couple of bucks at a department store. He had a pen in his pocket. After rifling through gold embossed this and lacy that, he found a blue pad at the bottom. No lines, but plainer than the rest. He turned it over and checked out the price.

"Six ninety-five," he muttered. *This place is an organized thief ring.* Frowning, Duke walked toward the checkout counter. He made his purchase, declined a bag, and bit his tongue. Upon exiting the shop, he gazed toward the concierge to find that Maurice was heading outside. Duke ambled across the marble floor toward the elevators and pressed the up button. In a few seconds an elevator hissed open. He stepped inside, mashed the button for the second floor, and drummed his index finger against the side of the notepad. Since the mild-mannered question trick failed, the direct approach was the next option.

Her heart thudding, Heather eased down the alley and into the smells of garbage mixed with fresh egg rolls. She wrinkled her nose and didn't think she'd be ordering any egg rolls for awhile. Her sunglasses deepened the alley's shadows, but Heather didn't dare take them off. She glanced over the restaurant's graffiti-scarred brick wall that stretched up two stories. A trash bin sat near a metal door on the ground floor that appeared to be the back entrance to the restaurant. A row of windows lined the top story. Another metal door opened onto a fire escape staircase. Heather wondered where the upstairs door led and if it was unlocked.

She pulled her cell from her pocket and pressed in a cryptic message, "Heading up fire escape to second floor. H" The sleuth tiptoed halfway up the metal stairs when her cell phone vibrated with a message from Brittan: "Inside. We got table. Watching BZ at table talking to manager. Wait. She's walking toward kitchen. Must go. B"

Heather continued the upward trek. Her gut told her the Debbie Miller girl was either in a room above the restaurant or someone in this place knew where she was. The restaurant's back door opened. Her eyes widening, Heather looked down between the stairs. A plump redhead stepped out. Heather plastered herself against the wall and prayed she didn't look up.

The woman hustled up the alley and disappeared around the corner. Heather released her breath then gasped when the upstairs knob rattled and the door began to open. Knowing she had no time to scurry back down the steps without being seen, Heather grabbed the handrail, hoisted herself over, and dropped with the faint plop of sneakers against gritty pavement. When a blue sedan turned up the alley from the direction Brenda had left, Heather crouched and crawled behind the trash bin. The smell of rotting fish added sushi to the list of things she wouldn't be ordering anytime soon. She looked down and saw that she'd hunkered over a mound of decaying food that had missed the bin.

"Okay, let's go!" a gruff voice commanded.

Heather gazed up and watched two pairs of feet start down the stairs. Soon the garbage bin blocked her view. She dared to peer around the edge and spotted a tall man with a shaved head shoving a blonde-haired girl toward the sedan. When she turned toward the car, her profile attested that this was the same girl whose photo was posted all over Houston.

Heather's blood ran cold. *She looks like me at her age,* she noted and knew she couldn't let these people drive off with the terrified child. If that fiend shoving at her didn't get what he wanted out of the Millers, he could easily sell her for big money to some high-powered, New York pimp.

Her stomach clenched. Her heart hammered in her temples. A primal roar erupted from her soul. She sprang forward. Hunching over, Heather ran toward the bald man. The closer she got, the more determined she became. She would rescue Debbie Miller or give her life trying.

THIRTY-THREE

Duke got off the elevator at the second floor landing. Four luxury apartments opened off this section of the hallway. He approached 212, pulled a pen out of his pocket, and rang the doorbell. Duke poised the pen over his tablet and waited for the resident to open the door. When no one came, he rang the bell again and accompanied it with a firm knock. Still no answer.

"Great." Duke pivoted to observe the door across the hallway. He strolled to that door and repeated the bell ringing. When no one answered there, he moved toward the third door.

The elevator dinged; the door opened. Duke halted.

The woman with the mile-long eyelashes and the puffball dog got off. She eyed him like he was a robber wanna be, but that didn't stop Duke from his mission.

"Excuse me," he said.

She flounced into the hallway, and her cotton pantsuit flopped with every step. When she didn't respond, Duke didn't stop.

"Excuse me, ma'am!"

She stopped in front of 214 and made a monumental task of sighing at Duke. The dog growled through a squirm.

Duke hid his irritation and smiled. "We recently cleaned the carpets in apartment 212," he explained, "and I wanted to talk to the owner. Can you tell me—"

"Ha!" she said and tossed her hand upward. "You won't talk to *that* woman for a long, long time."

"Oh?" Duke prompted.

The brunette fumbled through her bag and pulled out her keys. "She's in jail."

"Jail?" he blurted.

"Yes." The brunette paused before inserting her key into the doorknob. She eyed Duke like she was seeing him for the first time. Then she leaned forward and hissed, "She was involved in the mayor's murder."

"Oh really?" Duke sensed the woman's ego was getting a charge out of delivering the details. Duke feigned the most awestruck expression he could muster and said, "You sure know a lot."

The woman nodded and adjusted her toy poodle. "Everyone has been talking for weeks. No one here suspected a thing." She rolled her eyes toward the ceiling. "And the bail is set so high none of them are getting out until the trial."

"Wow!" Duke oozed and then carefully added, "Do you happen to know her name?"

"Of course. It's Eve Maloney."

Duke smiled as all his assumptions about Heather and her buds clicked into place. "Well, thanks for everything," he said and backed away.

The dog yapped, and the lady focused on shushing him while Duke pressed the elevator button. The door opened and he stepped in. As the door was closing, the lady trotted across the hallway.

"Didn't I see you downstairs?" she insisted. "Wait! I didn't get your name."

Duke offered a final smile and wave as the door closed. The last thing he saw was eyelashes batting at a worried rate. And he knew he needed to get out of this place before the concierge was alerted to his snooping.

Once he hit the pavement, Duke trotted back in the direction he'd come. As his boots pounded against concrete, he was stricken with the irony of the last few weeks. He'd been afraid to commit to Heather because The Rose represented his dream woman. Yet all the while The Rose was right under his nose. He paused at the intersection he and Heather had crossed the day they'd done lunch at the burger joint.

After a quick glance toward Rockworth Plaza, Duke hurried across. By the time he spanned the next strip of sidewalk, Duke deduced that the three friends must have a vow of silence written in blood. Otherwise he was sure Heather would have told him.

But of course, he thought and maneuvered around an open manhole, *the last person they'd want to know is the reporter who told a whole city he was going to find The Rose and reveal her identity.*

Duke rounded a corner and caught a last glimpse of Rockworth Plaza. No little guy in a black jacket with gold buttons was running after him. Duke stopped, placed his hands on his hips, and controlled his breathing. He glanced at his watch and noted ten o'clock. Either Heather was still in bed or she wasn't responding to his messages. Last week he would have accepted the bed scenario because he'd thought she was a rich girl who twittered away her days. But now he couldn't even picture her in bed. Sure, she'd slept late after her debutante party, but then she'd been up half the night. Who wouldn't sleep in under that circumstance?

A ribbon of frustration flurried through his gut and prompted Duke to send another text message. If this one didn't get a response, maybe their relationship was a lost cause.

※ ※ ※

The closer Debbie grew to the car, the more she struggled against her captor. "I'm not getting into that car!" she screamed and tried to kick the guy.

Good girl! Heather praised. She hunkered in front of the vehicle and dug the latex gloves from her pocket. If her plan worked, she'd need to shield her fingerprints.

"Get in here now!" Brenda Zapala hollered.

"I won't!" Debbie bellowed.

"If you don't..." the bald guy pulled a gun from his hip pocket and waved it in front of the girl.

Debbie curled her lips and spit in his face. "You aren't going to shoot me! I heard you talking last night. You have to keep me alive or you have nothing to bargain with."

The man grabbed a handful of hair and pulled. Her eyes wide, Debbie yelped.

"She's always been nothing but a spoiled-rotten smart aleck. I'll handle her," Brenda proclaimed.

Uttering a round of oaths, the man released the child and slapped her. She stumbled into the side of the vehicle.

Heather winced, gritted her teeth, yanked on the gloves, and prayed Brenda would come around the *front* of the car. Her prayers were answered. Crouched like a frog, Heather lunged up and shoved her fist into the magic spot that had taken down one of the Lubbock bad boys. Brenda's response couldn't have been more beautiful. She was slumping to the ground as Heather slung her against a building wall. Heather went for the bald man who was turning toward Brenda.

"Brenda!" he barked. "What—"

Heather showed him "what" with a hard kick to the side of his knee. Screaming, he doubled forward. Heather delivered another blow to his backside, and he sprawled to the base of the fire escape stairway. His gun clattered to the center of the street and spun to a stop.

"Debbie, get into the car!" Heather hollered. "I'm taking you to the police."

The weeping twelve-year-old didn't have to be told twice. By the time Heather scrambled across the passenger side and into the driver's seat, Debbie was not only in the backseat, she'd fastened her seat belt and closed her door. Heather shoved the car into reverse, slammed the driver's door shut, and crammed her foot on the accelerator. The vehicle lurched backward. Heather fishtailed into a parking lot, hit the brakes, and then shot out of the lot.

She progressed about fifty yards before she turned down a side road and glanced at her passenger. "You okay?" Heather asked and stopped for a red light.

Debbie wiped at her tears and nodded.

"Did they hurt you in any way?" Heather continued. The light changed and Heather drove forward.

"N–no. Just hit me a little."

Heather nodded. "Good. Hang on. This is going to get weird. But trust me, okay?"

"Okay," Debbie trembled out.

Heather was glad she came across as trustworthy because she had no idea what to do next. She'd gotten into this case far deeper than The Rose planned to go.

We were supposed to gather clues and pass them on, she fretted. *Not rescue victims.* But she couldn't let those people drive away with Debbie. No telling where they were taking her or what they'd do to her.

Her cell phone vibrated against her thigh, and Heather figured it was another message from Lorna or Brittan. She pulled to a stop at another red light. After a cautious glance in all directions, Heather removed the cell from her pocket and gazed at another text message from Duke.

Duke again! she thought. The subject line read, "Your secret."

The traffic flowed once more. Heather rolled through the intersection and pulled to a stop near a parking meter. She pressed the message and read, "Rose, your cover is blown. Eve Maloney lives at 212." Heather's eyes bugged. She rubbed her forehead as her mind spun with the implications. Duke had finally pieced everything together.

But maybe it's for the best, she thought as the perfect plan unfolded in her mind. First, Heather sent a quick text message to Lorna, and then she pressed Duke's speed dial number.

❋ ❋ ❋

As Lorna stepped into the ladies' room, her cell phone vibrated. She locked the door and flipped open the phone while eyeing the window that presented a view of the alley. As she and Brittan had assumed, the bathroom was at the back of the restaurant. She'd agreed to spy on the alley from the bathroom while Brittan kept her post at the table. That way if Heather needed backup they'd know it.

Before she approached the window, Lorna skimmed the text message from Heather, "Got Debbie Miller with me. Took down BZ and boyfriend in alley. Babysit them until police arrive, and then scram. Taking care of everything on this end. H"

Lorna gaped at the message and read it again. They'd agreed not to get directly involved in these cases—just gather clues and let the police do the dirty work. Now she was supposed to "babysit" a couple of kidnappers?

"Let's go for it!" Lorna challenged. She unlocked the door, jerked on the handle, and hustled back into the restaurant. She slowed when she passed Brittan and said, "Come on."

Brittan asked no questions. When they emerged into the sunshine, Lorna ducked her head, grabbed Brittan's arm, and leaned close. "Heather has Debbie Miller," she mumbled. "There are some, um, *leftovers* in the back alley she wants us to babysit until the police come."

"The kidnappers?" Brittan hissed.

Lorna nodded.

"Are we supposed to call the police?" Brittan asked. The two friends rounded the corner.

"No." Lorna shook her head. "Heather said she's taken care of everything."

They slowed as they neared the alley, finally stopping at the corner. Lorna peeked around the edge and spotted Brenda sprawled on the ground with her wig halfway covering her eyes. On the other side of the alley a bald guy lay in a fetal position, gripping his knee and groaning. A handgun lay six feet from him.

Brittan pulled her latex gloves from her pocket, slipped them on, and said, "I'll get the gun just to make sure they don't try anything."

"I don't think we have to worry about either of them going anywhere," Lorna drawled and fearlessly stepped forward.

THIRTY-FOUR

Duke was halfway to the Shay complex when his phone rang. He pulled it from his belt harness, glanced at the screen, and smiled. Flipping open the phone he said, "Gotcha!"

"Listen," Heather's voice was low, breathless, desperate, "you're right. We'll talk about it all later. First, I've got some...uh...information for you about the missing Miller girl."

Duke stopped. "Is that what you've been doing this morning?" he queried.

"Yes."

"Where are you?" Duke moved to the curb and scrutinized the street one direction and then the other.

"I'll give you the information if you promise me you won't print the contents of your last text message."

Duke gripped the back of his neck and tried to comprehend exactly what was going on. Heather sounded more like the spy he'd thought there was no way she could be.

"I know where the Miller girl is," she continued. "Do I tell you and let *you* take it to the police or do I just anonymously tip the police?"

"Tell me!" Duke blurted.

"Then promise me you won't...share any information you know. Got it?"

"Got it. Yes, I understand."

"Say it."

"What?" The whiz of the cars mingled with the buzzing in his overwrought mind.

"Say 'I promise.'"

"I promise," Duke said.

"Debbie Miller is with me," Heather revealed.

"With you!" Duke exclaimed and eyed the pedestrians who were now watching him.

"I rescued her," Heather explained.

He lowered his head and whispered, "Where are you, for cryin' out loud?"

"I'm parked at a meter near the corner of Dallas and Louisiana," Heather said. "We're in a blue Toyota. Just a second. I'll give you the license plate number." Duke waited through the sounds of a car door opening and closing and the muffled hum of the city. "It's KCB 90S," she said.

"KCB 90S," Duke repeated and committed the numbers to memory.

"Just a second. Let me get back into the car."

Duke heard the snap of a car door closing. "You need to call the police," she continued. "Also tell them the kidnappers are...*down*... in the alley behind the China Buffet near Sam Houston Park."

"You took them down?"

"I guess you could say that," Heather replied, a smile in her voice. "Look, you call the police. I'll sit here with Debbie until I hear their sirens. Then I'm disappearing. You tell them you received another tip from...well, you know who, and leave it at that. They don't have to know anymore."

"Yes, ma'am," Duke said. "Whatever you say, ma'am. You just call the shots. I'll get in line."

"Good!" Heather said over a chuckle. "Oh, and let's talk about the other business later, okay? Call me."

"I will, but it looks like I've got a story to write. Might be late tonight," Duke warned.

"Understandable," Heather responded. "Break a leg," she added before ending.

Duke gazed at his cell and knew beyond doubt that his dream woman was no longer a fantasy. *Not even a little bit!* He quickly searched his phone's address book for the police chief's number and made the call.

※ ※ ※

Heather waited with Debbie until she heard the first hint of a siren. Then she turned toward the girl and said, "The police are coming. I'm leaving now. I'm locking the doors. You'll be fine until they get here. It should only be a minute. Okay?"

Debbie nodded. "Okay." She leaned forward. "But you never told me your name."

Smiling, Heather said, "I am The Rose. I'd appreciate you not saying much about me. Now I've got to go. You are safe." She slipped out of the vehicle into the bustle of downtown Houston. Heather locked the car door just as she'd promised and, with the sirens growing louder by the second, she ran to the end of the street. Turning right, she slowed long enough to get her bearings. She picked up her pace once more and dashed to the next intersection. Within twelve minutes Heather was at the rental vehicle parked a block from the park.

Anxious to be gone, she called Brittan, who picked up on the first ring. "Where are you?" Heather asked.

"We're coming through the park," Brittan answered and sounded as breathless as Heather.

"Good. I'm at the car. *Hurry!* I don't have keys, and I'm sticking out like a billionaire in a pawnshop."

"Right. We're running," Brittan replied.

Soon Heather spotted her friends dashing along the sidewalk. All three debutantes piled into the sedan. Heather insisted on claiming the backseat, where she flopped like a beached whale. She shook as the adrenaline started to wane.

"Are you going to survive back there, Heather?" Lorna's face appeared near the driver's seat.

Heather shook her head. "Yep. I just can't believe we just did that. It's like a dream. In less than twenty-four hours I've attacked four criminals. It's enough to drive me to drink Diet Coke."

Lorna laughed. "You're really going downhill!"

"All in a morning's work, right?" Brittan quipped, and Lorna cranked the car.

"I'm shaking like a leaf too," Lorna admitted.

"I'm ready for a nap," Brittan drawled.

Giggling, Heather looked at her watch. "It's only ten-thirty!"

"But I've been wide awake since four." Brittan snapped her seat belt. "And I didn't go to sleep until after one."

"Two o'clock for me," Lorna admitted through a yawn. "Woke up at five."

"I didn't crash until about one-thirty," Heather reported. "But I slept until six." She sat up and clicked on her seat belt.

"So let's hear it! What happened?" Lorna asked.

Heather sighed. "Well, there I was in the alley and that creep came out with Debbie. Brenda left but came back quickly in a car. I couldn't let them roll off with her so I—"

"Beat them senseless," Brittan finished for her.

"Well, I didn't *kill* them," Heather said. "I did what I had to do. It was perfectly reasonable under the circumstances. And then I got into the car Brenda brought and drove Debbie to safety. I called Duke, and—"

"Duke?" Lorna and Brittan said in unison.

Heather covered her face with her hand. It was time to meet her fear head-on and come clean. She confessed everything and explained that Duke had promised not to leak a word.

Lorna cast a sympathetic glance over her shoulder while Brittan stared straight ahead and remained silent.

"I'll understand if you never speak to me again, Brittan," Heather said. "It was a thoughtless thing to take him into Eve Maloney's apartment, but at the time I didn't see how I could bail Lorna out any other way. What do *I* know about carpet shampooers?"

Brittan hesitantly nodded. "Sounds like Duke saved our hides twice. Once at Eve Maloney's place and then today." She removed her sunglasses, put on her regular glasses, and peered toward Heather. "What exactly would you have done if he hadn't sent you that text saying he'd figured out we were The Rose?"

"I have no idea," Heather admitted. "But I knew the second I saw the message that I could trade the location of Debbie Miller for his promise not to leak who we are. And I really do believe he'll keep his word."

"Let's hope so!" Lorna said.

"He will," Heather assured, "because he sent me a message before that one saying he was falling in love with me."

Brittan and Lorna shared a long glance.

"That's an odd way to tell a woman you're in love with her," Lorna commented.

"I know," Heather said. "But we're living an odd life. So why not?"

"And you believe him?" Brittan queried.

"Yes, I believe him!" Heather said through a smile. "You two are worse than my mother."

"It's because we love you, girlfriend," Brittan said with a broad grin. "And we're the ones who nursed you back to health last night when the same guy was backing off."

"I know. I know. But…" She dug her cell out of her pocket and scrolled to Duke's message. "Look. Here's the text message. Read it for yourself." She extended the phone to Brittan.

"Read it out loud," Lorna commanded.

"Last night miserable," Brittan read. "Falling in love with you. Can't stop it. Want to give us a try. Please call when you can. It's 9:10, Monday morning."

"Hmmm," Lorna said.

"Rose, your cover is blown. Eve Maloney lives at 212," Brittan continued.

"That was the next one he sent," Heather explained. "And that's when I called him. He called the police and the rest is history."

"All right," Brittan sighed. "Maybe he's okay."

"He's really wonderful," Heather said. "He just got hurt really young and has had a hard time getting over it."

"Well, I've been there too," Lorna confessed.

"How's Yo Mama handling all this?" Brittan asked.

"Yo Mama and I had a major...um...interaction before I went to Lubbock," Heather admitted. "I think she's realizing she's going to have to accept that I'm going to marry a man I love even if he's not who she wants me to. She's blaming it all on Grandpa Morris though. She says he ruined me."

"Would that we all could be ruined like you," Brittan mused.

"Maybe we should give Duke a chance," Lorna said. "But if he hurts you again he'll be chowing down on my tennis racket!"

All three friends laughed. "You're not half as mean as you sound," Heather teased.

"No, but she can drive a mean serve," Brittan said. "She smoked me last week, and I'm not *ever* going to play with her again. I don't know what possessed me to even try."

THIRTY-FIVE

Heather paced her room for a solid hour before she received a call from Duke. She paused near the French doors that led onto her balcony, covered her heart with her hand, and waited until she caught her breath enough to answer.

"Hello, beautiful," Duke crooned.

"Hi," Heather replied.

"Sorry it took me so long."

She gazed toward the western horizon where the sun left a trail of golden haze streaked with purple shadows. "It's okay," Heather replied. "I know you had a lot to do after..." Heather looked over her shoulder and decided not to mention the details. She was alone, but after her wild day she was feeling more cautious than usual. She didn't want to take any chance of a family employee overhearing. She'd come close enough today to blowing The Rose's cover.

"Yeah," Duke said, his voice thick with a grin. "Listen, I'm parking my truck outside your door. Wanna let me in?"

"Of course!" Heather exclaimed. "Why didn't you say so?"

"I just did."

"I'll be out there in two seconds," Heather said and disconnected the call.

By the time she opened the back door, Duke was walking toward the castle. Heather ran toward him, and Duke met her halfway, wrapping his arms around her. The kiss that followed put the predecessors to shame and left her breathless for more.

When Duke pulled away he said, "I've got so much to tell you." He rested his forehead on hers and then snuggled his nose against her hair.

Heather melted into the moment and couldn't collect one coherent thought. "I'm falling in love too," was all she could say.

Duke's lazy chuckle broke through the spell. He inched away and said, "Do you have any idea how much you've messed with my mind?"

"No." Heather shook her head.

"I kept having this nightmare that I was marrying you, but The Rose had become my dream woman. And there I was marrying you with her in the audience...or we were already married and she was calling me with all her charms. But I couldn't see her. And all the time—"

"I was The Rose," Heather whispered. Her claim echoed across the night's cool shadows.

"You were right under my nose but I couldn't see it," Duke admitted.

"I tried so hard to hide it from you. Lorna and Brittan and I have a pact," Heather explained.

"I know. I already figured that out." Duke's finger trailed down her cheek, and Heather tried to remember what she'd been about to say.

"My word is my word," she finally said. "It would have meant breaking a promise to them."

"I understand." Duke nodded.

"Remember that day I saw you outside City Hall and we went to lunch?"

Duke nodded.

"Remember running into a maintenance woman outside the men's room?"

His eyes widened. "That was you?"

"Yes. I'd just recorded Victor McIntosh's phone call," Heather explained. "Then I watched you pick the lock to the city manager's office."

"You *are* a spy, aren't you?" he teased.

"How do you know how to do that anyway?" Heather asked.

"My uncle is a locksmith. He taught me all sorts of handy skills when I was a teenager," Duke explained. He didn't give Heather time to respond before continuing, "So when you saw me outside City Hall that day—"

"I'd already seen you inside," she confessed.

He laughed. "I love it!" Then he shook his head. "And you brought down your own uncle?"

"Had to. Like I said, he was guilty and the law is the law. Besides all that, it felt good to vindicate Grandpa Morris."

"You're as tough as all get out," Duke averred. "And I love that too."

"Well, I've made my share of mistakes," Heather admitted. "And I knew the day I took you up to Eve Maloney's apartment I'd made a big one. I prayed you wouldn't piece it together, but when you did you wound up saving my hide."

"I didn't actually get it until I was in a meeting with Brittan's dad this morning."

"You met with Mr. Shay?" Heather asked.

"Yes." Duke pressed his fingertips against his chest. "I got to go into the holy of holies."

Heather snickered. "Why?"

"He's as excited about The Rose as the rest of Houston. Sales of the *Star* are at an all-time high. And he's fooled himself into believing I'm brilliant. He's even interested in reviewing one of my mystery novels."

"You *are* brilliant!" Heather breathed.

"Ah, I don't know," Duke hedged. "I'd have never written even one of those articles if The Rose hadn't visited me." He stroked her hair.

"But you did, and they were excellent." Heather spotted the first star of the night, blinking near the horizon like a wink from God.

"Anyway, Mr. Shay has family photos plastered all over the place. One of them is of you and Brittan and Lorna. When I saw the three of you together—"

"You knew," Heather finished.

"I knew I had to find out whose apartment Lorna was in that day. But I want you to know that I had already accepted that I was falling in love with you. I'd spent some serious time praying through my commitment issues. I wanted to call you this morning at one," he admitted, "but I waited until seven."

"I was awake at one," Heather explained. "I was praying that God would help me accept His will…no matter what it was. And I'm so glad it is you!" Heather squeezed him tight.

"I want something very clear," Duke continued, resting his cheek atop her head. "When I wanted to call this morning at one, it was to tell you that I was falling in love. I knew that, and I want you to know it was before I figured out you were The Rose. I don't want any doubts in your mind that I might be falling in love with you because you are the mysterious Rose. That's the reason I put the time in my text message."

"I have no doubts," Heather assured. She pulled away and gazed into brown eyes that were full of a heart drenched in love. "I can see it all over you."

"I told you on the beach that I'd like us to spend some time getting to know each other, to see if we might be compatible. Remember?"

Heather nodded.

"Well..." Duke pulled a tiny box out of his jacket, "I was wondering if you'd like to take that a step further."

Heather gasped as he opened the velvet box to reveal a magnificent ruby set in antique gold.

"It was my grandmother's ring," he explained. "Mom gave it to me over the weekend." He laughed. "Well, actually, she put it into my suitcase without my knowing it. There was a note and everything."

"So is your mother giving this to me?" Heather asked.

"Well, we'll say the family and I are," he replied. "Actually, even if she hadn't put this ring in my suitcase, I'd have gone out and bought something for you today." Duke gazed into her eyes before removing the ring from the box.

"I don't want to rush anything or make you feel pressured, but I want you to know I'm playing for keeps. Will you wear this?" he asked. "It will make us official." His voice trembled over every word. "I'm not pushing, but it would mean a lot to me if we were engaged."

"Me too!" Heather said. "Yes, yes, yes, yes, yes!"

Duke laughed and slipped the ring onto her finger. "It's not as fancy as other men could offer," Duke admitted. "I'm not in that league."

"You *are* my league, Duke Fieldman!" Heather breathed and laid a kiss on him that rattled the universe.

SERIAL SLEUTH STRIKES AGAIN

by *Duke Fieldman*

Known only as The Rose, Houston's own serial sleuth once again helps solve a major crime. But this time she got up close and personal with the victim. The recently kidnapped Debbie Miller encountered The Rose yesterday when she was rescued by the elusive Texas detective.

"I don't know who she is," Debbie said in a recent interview, "but she knows how to fight. My nanny and her boyfriend, Howie, were moving me from the restaurant her brother owns because the police had been heavy lately. Suddenly this woman comes out of nowhere and beats them up. Then she got into their car, told me to get in, and drove me several streets over and parked. She talked on the phone to somebody, but I was so upset I can't remember what was said.

"The next thing I knew I heard sirens, and the woman was getting out. When I asked her what her name was, she said she was The Rose."

When asked what The Rose looked like, Debbie states, "I can't really remember. It all happened so fast. She was wearing a hat, jogging clothes, and dark glasses. It was hard to tell what she really looked like, but I think she had red hair."

Three times now The Rose has left vital information in the offices of the *Houston Star*. The first packet came to the general manager, Solomon Gude. The other times the clues were delivered to this reporter. The Rose has helped solve a computer virus plot, a murder, a bank heist, and now a kidnapping.

This time The Rose was more direct but very careful and as elusive as the wind.

Stay alert, Houston! She could be your next-door neighbor. Who knows what she'll uncover next. Wherever she lives and whatever her plans, Houston is a better place because of our own serial sleuth.

About the Author

❋ ❋ ❋

Debra White Smith continues to impact and entertain readers with her life-changing books, including *Romancing Your Husband, Romancing Your Wife,* The Sisters Suspense series, The Austen series, and now The Debutantes series. She's an award-winning author, including such honors as Top-10 Reader Favorite, Gold Medallion finalist, and Retailer's Choice Award finalist. Debra has more than 50 books to her credit and over a million books in print.

The founder of Real Life Ministries, Debra recently launched Real Life Minute, which airs on radio stations nationwide. She also speaks passionately with insight and humor at ministry events across the nation. Debra has been featured on a variety of media, including *The 700 Club, At Home Life, Getting Together, Moody Broadcasting Network, Fox News, Viewpoint,* and *America's Family Coaches.* She holds an M.A. in English.

Debra lives in small-town America with her husband, two children, and a herd of cats.

To write Debra or contact her for speaking engagements, check out her website:

www.debrawhitesmith.com

or send mail to:

Real Life Ministries
Daniel W. Smith, Ministry Manager
PO Box 1482
Jacksonville, TX 75766

or call:

1-866-211-3400 (toll free)

More Great Books
by Debra White Smith

FICTION

The Austen Series

Amanda

Central Park

First Impressions

Northpointe Chalet

Possibilities

Reason & Romance

The Debutantes

Heather

Lorna (coming March 2008)

The Seven Sisters Series/
Sisters Suspense Series

Second Chances

The Awakening/Picture Perfect

A Shelter in the Storm

To Rome with Love

For Your Eyes Only

This Time Around

Let's Begin Again

Fiction/Parable

The Richest Person in the World (with Stan Toler)

NONFICTION

Romancing Your Husband

Romancing Your Wife

What Jane Austen Taught Me About Love and Romance

~ THE AUSTEN SERIES ~

AMANDA

Smart, funny, and generous, Amanda Priebe is a great friend to have...until the matchmaking bug bites. Deciding that her secretary, Haley, needs a beau, Amanda dreams up the perfect match—Pastor Mason Eldridge. Never mind that Haley is seeing Roger, a respectable dairy farmer. And it doesn't really matter that Mason might be attracted to someone else.

When it comes to her own heart, Amanda can't seem to make up her mind what she wants to do. The handsome and debonair Franklyn West is available...so is the ever-present Nate Knighton.

In this tangled web of best-laid plans, who will end up with whom? Will Haley find true love? Will Amanda realize what her heart's known all along?

A lively tale of plans gone awry, affection in unexpected places, and the ultimate power of faith and love.

CENTRAL PARK

Wrenched from her family, young Francine is terrified by her new life with her aunt and uncle in New York City. But their foster son, Ethan, comes to Francine's rescue. As the years pass, the bond between the two deepens...and they spend many hours enjoying the serenity of Central Park. When Ethan goes to Paris for a missions trip, Francine realizes affection has transformed into love. She dreams of the day Ethan will arrive home and share her love.

But when Ethan returns, he brings his new love, the beautiful Carrie Casper. And Carrie's playboy brother, Hugh, falls for Francine. Will Ethan realize the jewel he has in his friendship with Francine? Should Francine stay true to a love that will never be?

FIRST IMPRESSIONS

When Eddi Boswick is cast as Elizabeth, the female lead in a local production of *Pride and Prejudice*, she hesitates. Dave, the handsome young rancher cast as Darcy, seems arrogant and unpredictable. Accepting the challenge of playing opposite him, Eddi soon realizes that he is difficult to work with on and off the set.

But when a tornado springs out of nowhere, Dave protects Eddi...much to her chagrin. And he is shocked to discover an attraction for the feisty lawyer he can't deny. Sparks fly when Eddi misinterprets his interest and discovers the truth he's trying to hide.

Will Eddi's passionate faith, fierce independence, and quick wit keep Dave from discovering the secret to love...and the key to her heart?

⌒ THE AUSTEN SERIES ⌒

NORTHPOINTE CHALET

Texas native Kathy Moore loves her new home in Northpointe, Colorado. The 22-year-old's bookstore is thriving. And her social life is picking up. New friends Liza and her brother, Ron, an unrepentant heartbreaker, are constant visitors. It's her personal life that needs a dramatic twist—like the ones in the thrillers she devours.

Then one dark and stormy night, a kind stranger takes refuge in Kathy's store. When she learns he's Ben Tilman, one of the residents of the mysterious chalet overlooking Northpointe, Kathy is smitten. But Ben's reserved behavior suggests she's too young and flamboyant to be relationship material for him, an established pastor.

Suddenly, like in one of her suspense novels, an old man corners Kathy with warnings about the murderous Tilman patriarch—warnings she must investigate. Will Kathy's growing suspicions and topsy-turvy investigation put an end to her deepening relationship with the man of Northpointe Chalet?

POSSIBILITIES

"'A yardman?' Landon's thin eyebrows arched. 'You want to marry a yardman?' Her blue eyes couldn't have been wider...or more disdainful."

Practical, down-to-earth Allie is the daughter of Willis Elton, a wealthy, respected gentleman farmer. Although allowed to attend college and obtain a master's degree in horticulture, she is expected to marry well and take her place in society. But Allie has a problem. She's in love with the handsome Frederick Wently—the yardman.

Yielding to family pressure, she withdraws from the relationship. But as the years pass, her heart refuses to surrender. When Frederick turns up on the arm of a close family friend, Allie struggles with jealousy and heartbreak. What can she do to get him back? And should she even try?

An intriguing look at the twists and turns of love.

∼ THE AUSTEN SERIES ∼

REASON AND ROMANCE

Sense and sensibility collide when love comes calling for sisters Elaina and Anna Woods...

Ruled by reason, Elaina remains calm in every situation—even when she meets Ted Farris. Although attracted by his charming personality, she refuses to be swept away by love. Accused of never listening to her heart, Elaina finally gives in to her feelings. As her relationship with Ted develops into something magical, they seem destined to be together—except for one tiny detail. Will Lorna Starr keep them apart?

Anna longs for the day she'll meet her prince. When she's rescued by the handsome Willis Kenney, has her dream turned into reality? Inseparable from the start, neither of them worries about the past. Anna, refusing to listen to her sister's cautious voice of reason, lets her romantic heart run wild. Caught in an emotional whirlwind, she and Willis revel in the hope of two passionate hearts. Will their impulsive love endure despite the mistakes of yesterday?

Romance and reason merge in this captivating story about the joys and follies of infatuation and how faith in God reveals true love.

ROMANCING YOUR HUSBAND

Early days in a relationship are exhilarating, but they can't touch the thrilling love affair you can have now. Cutting through traditional misconceptions and exploring every facet of the Bible's message on marriage, *Romancing Your Husband* reveals how you can create a union others only dream about. From making Jesus an active part of your marriage to arranging fantastic romantic interludes, you'll discover how to—

- make romance a reality
- "knock your husband's socks off"
- become a lover-wife, not a mother-wife
- find freedom in forgiving
- cultivate a sacred romance with God.

Experience fulfillment through romancing your husband...and don't be surprised when he romances you back!

ROMANCING YOUR WIFE

by Debra White Smith and Daniel W. Smith

Do you want your husband to surprise you and put more romance in your relationship? *Romancing Your Wife* can help! Give this book to your hubby, and he'll discover ways to create an exciting, enthusiastic marriage.

Debra and her husband, Daniel, offer biblical wisdom and practical advice that when put into practice will help your husband mentally, emotionally, and physically improve his relationship with you. He'll discover tools to build a dynamite marriage, including how to—

- communicate his love more effectively
- make you feel cherished
- better understand your needs and wants
- create a unity of spirit and mind
- increase the passion in your marriage

From insights on little things that jazz up a marriage to more than 20 "Endearing Encounters," *Romancing Your Wife* sets the stage for love and romance.

THE RICHEST PERSON IN THE WORLD

Stan Toler and Debra White Smith

An intriguing key to success...

Keith Richardson needs something new. A successful stockbroker married to a beautiful wife, he has it all—or so it appears. But this morning he impulsively walks out of his Detroit office and catches the first plane to Seattle...heading to Mac's Place, a neighborhood coffee shop he frequented before he became such a success.

Laughter greeted Keith. The sweet smell of coffee wafted over him. "It's good to see you!" Joe exclaimed. Keith couldn't stop his grin. "I flew in for some real coffee." He settled onto his favorite bar stool. The fit was as good now as it had been three years ago. He relaxed and closed his eyes, savoring the moment.

Calling his distraught wife, Keith announces he needs time to think. Staying with Joe, Keith glimpses a lifestyle he longs for and discovers a scriptural truth he's never considered. Does he have the faith to embrace it? And what will Jenny think about this new direction? Discover a powerful principle you can implement for a more vibrant, satisfying, balanced life.